"What would you have me call you, then? 'Countess'? Or perhaps 'Lady Tess'?"

"No, no!" Tess protested hastily, wondering how he had found her out. She remembered the necklace hidden in her luggage.

"I think, sir," she said, "that I have unwittingly come into possession of something that belongs to you."

Sir Morgan's tawny eyes seemed suddenly to glitter like those gems.

"I believe you have," he agreed, gently brushing back the curls that had tumbled onto her forehead. "But I had not expected you to be aware of it, little one."

Fawcett Crest Books
by Maggie MacKeever:

A BANBURY TALE   23174-7   $1.50

LORD FAIRCHILD'S DAUGHTER   P2695   $1.25

A NOTORIOUS LADY   23491-6   $1.50

SWEET VIXEN   23902-0   $1.75

# SWEET VIXEN

Maggie MacKeever

FAWCETT CREST • NEW YORK

*SWEET VIXEN*

Published by Fawcett Crest Books, a unit of CBS Publications, the Consumer Publishing Division of CBS Inc.

ISBN: 0-449-23902-0

Printed in the United States of America

10  9  8  7  6  5  4  3  2  1

# Chapter 1

*"Marry the curate?"* gasped Tess, and dropped a par-boiled onion. "My dear Clio, you must be mad!"

Mistress Clio retrieved the onion from the stone-flagged kitchen floor and tossed it back to her sister before seating herself at the huge elm table. "You must admit," she said reasonably, "that he is extremely persistent. One can only conclude that you have encouraged him."

Tess bent over the huge coal-burning range, absently splashed cognac into a rich barley-sugar sauce, efficiently arranged the onions in a shallow pie dish, and poured the sauce over them. She eyed this culinary masterpiece, known to the household as Lady Tess's Buttered Onion Pie, added yet another dash of cognac, then popped it into the hot oven. Only then did she wipe her hands on the voluminous apron that protected her simple morning dress, which was so far from being fashionable that it was unadorned by so much as a piece of lace or a single flounce, and turn to regard her sister.

"You know very well," Tess replied, rather severely, "that I have no intention of marrying anyone. Let alone the curate! I cannot think why you should suggest such a thing."

This might seem an absurd remark for an attractive young woman of five-and-twenty to make, particularly when that young woman possessed a glorious abundance of hair so pale it appeared silver, perfectly sculpted features, a patrician nose, a graceful slender neck, and eyes of a pale blue-green like fine turquoise set off by dark lashes and flyaway brows that gave their owner a look of perpetual surprise; and it was rendered further absurd by the fact that Lady Tess, the Countess of Lansbury, was worth nearly a million pounds, all assets included, with an income of some £80,000 a year. Her sister, however, did not argue the point; indeed, that damsel saw no reason why she should.

"Good!" Clio grinned, rather mischievously. "Then there is nothing to keep you here."

Lady Tess frowned, as well she might, for the "here" to which her sister referred so unappreciatively was the ancestral home of the Earls of Lansbury, a gracious and ancient edifice with a rosy, gray-pilastered facade and surrounding parks where deer browsed in the shade of tall trees and peacocks strutted on the grass. "Where else should I wish to go?" she inquired. "I think you had better tell me, Clio, what maggot has got into your head!"

But Mistress Clio was a minx, and not disposed to reward this question with the straightforward answer that it deserved. "Poor Tess!" she said instead, in a commiserating manner. "You have been buried here on your estates for over a year. I fear it has made you very dull."

Lady Tess looked reproachful and pushed pale wisps of hair back from her brow. "Must I remind you of the reason for that seclusion? One does not go racketing about the countryside when one is in mourning." She did not add that, for herself, country life was ideal. Only once, as a schoolroom miss, had Tess been treated to a taste of city living, and that sojourn had hardly been felicitous.

"Yes, I know you think me unfeeling!" Clio pouted, quite enchantingly. "But all our combined laments will not bring Mama back." She lowered her gaze to the tabletop. "Besides, you know she always favored *you,* even though I was her own daughter, and she was only your stepmother! So did Papa, though that is quite understandable, since you were a constant reminder of his beloved first wife."

This graceless remark might bring down upon Mistress Clio's flighty head the unvoiced censure of the kitchen staff, all of whom—from the rotund cook, keeping a watchful eye on the pie bubbling so merrily in the oven, to the little ten-year-old kitchenmaid, polishing the countless copper cooking utensils that adorned the whitewashed walls—adored their countess; it might earn for her a vulgar utterance in French from the abigail who was engaged in concocting a batch of Roman Balsam from bitter almonds, barley flour, and honey, to be applied to the countess's sadly sun-browned complexion; but it brought the countess herself away from the stove and limping, with the aid of a cane, across the flagged floor. Lady Tess, thus engaged, was shown to be tall and slender of figure, a noblewoman from her untidy head to her dainty toes; and her halting progress was, to those who loved her, most painful to observe. The little kitchenmaid, who thought it a great tragedy that so kind a lady should be crippled, was forced to continually repress sniffles, lest the countess hear. Pity, as her servants well knew, sent the usually gentle Lady Tess into a terrible rage.

Fortunately, Tess had no notion of her various retainers' thoughts. She reached the table, seated herself awkwardly, and touched her sister's hand. "Our parents," she said carefully, for there was a great deal of truth in Clio's remarks, "only wished to make up to me what they felt I'd been denied! It was not a matter of loving one of us better than the other, I assure you. Nor did Papa revere the memory of my mother to the exclusion of yours. He had a very real affection for Mirian, as did I. In truth, she was the only mother I ever knew."

"He left *you* his fortune," Clio murmured, still refusing to meet her half-sister's eyes. "And he went to no end of trouble to ensure that you would inherit the title when he died."

There was little Tess could say to this, since it was undeniable that her father had arranged her succession through some complicated legal maneuver connected with the absence of male heirs. Nor did she care to further explain, within earshot of countless doting witnesses, that these acts of seeming favoritism were merely meant to compensate her for being lame. She might remain a spinster, Tess reflected, an ape-leader, and an antidote, but she possessed sufficient wealth to render the situation a great deal more palatable. "Oh, Clio!" she said helplessly. "You have Mirian's fortune and are far from penniless! If it is a title that you covet, child, then you may marry one."

Nor was there doubt of the truth of this. Mistress Clio was as dazzling a damsel as one might wish to see, with eyes of a sapphire shade, an enchanting little nose, slightly *retroussé*, dimples, and a mop of short and fashionable black curls. She had every intention of snaring a nobleman, she thought—but how was one to marry so advantageously when one had never been privileged to set eyes upon an eligible and titled gentleman? Through long, curling lashes Clio watched her half-sister's distressed face. She had gained the advantage; it only remained to make use of it.

"What is it?" asked Tess, so worried about Clio that she'd forgotten even her favorite pie. The cook, less dilatory, whisked it out of the oven in the nick of time and set it to cool on a windowsill. "What troubles you?"

Clio only briefly considered that she was behaving abominably. It was said of the Mildmay sisters that while Tess—who suffered the effects of a classical education, having been introduced by her papa to various branches of learning totally unsuited to a female—might be justifiably called a bluestocking, no great accolade in an age when brains as such were rather despised, Clio could be given credit for no brains at all. This was not only unkind, but untrue: Clio might excel at nothing more scholarly than piano-playing and needlepoint, but she was as scheming a minx as ever drew breath.

"Well?" demanded Tess.

"Cedric has made me an offer of marriage." Clio, a tremendous flirt, thus named the foremost, and the most raffish, of her innumerable admirers. "He has promised to take me to London, where I may go to balls and the theater."

"Cedric!" Lady Tess wore a face of perfect horror. "Good God, child, you cannot think of marrying him!"

"He'll take me to London," repeated Clio and turned her head properly sideways so that her audience, if any were so inclined, which they unanimously were not, might admire the fine lines of her profile. "I think I would fancy London, Tess."

Truly Ceddie would take himself to Town, thought Tess grimly, and speedily dissipate his bride's fortune in extravagances and gaming. Cedric, scion of a local squire, had gained little favor with the countess. "A wish to go to London," she observed sharply, "is hardly a reasonable basis for marriage! I beg you will reconsider."

Clio might have pointed out that Tess was hardly an authority on the matter, being rendered ineligible by a handicap for which even her great wealth could not atone; but, though selfish and thoughtless, Clio was not consciously cruel. She wrinkled her pretty little nose. "In truth, I do not like Ceddie all that well! But I should *dote* on London, I know it, Tess!"

It was obvious to the various auditors of this artless speech that Mistress Clio was again cutting one of her wheedles. It was also growing obvious to Lady Tess. "Think!" said she, somewhat craftily. "What if you should go to London as Cedric's bride and then—too late!—find your titled gentleman? How unhappy you would be! I think if you are to go to London, it must be without a husband in tow."

"Then I *may* go?" Clio's glance was sparkling. "You will let me? How *good* you are, Tess!'

This excessive exuberance caused the countess's dark brows to snap downward in a stern line. "Cut line, child!" she demanded. "And explain."

"You won't like it," Clio confessed bravely, "but truly, Tess, it is for the best, as you must see! The Dowager Duchess of Bellamy will have me with her, and will see to my coming-out, and I shall have my London season, and you need not worry about me."

"The Dowager Duchess of Bellamy," repeated Tess, looking quite ferocious, when her devious sister paused for breath. "How came you into contact with the Duchess of Bellamy?"

Clio had the grace to blush, an enchanting act which she performed at will. "I wrote to her." She eyed the countess's irate countenance. "Why should I not, after all? She is a connection of mine! It is not seemly that the duchess should not even know that I exist."

It was with no small effort that Tess contained her growing wrath. No use to rip up at Clio, who despite her earlier complaints had been from the cradle spoiled and fawned upon, and who as a result was entirely too accustomed to having her own way in everything. "Did you not consider," she ventured merely, "that your mother must have had some reason for never informing us of her connection with the grand Bellamys? Have you not thought it odd that Mirian never spoke of her past or of her family? Or that she refused to go to London when she had relatives there?"

Clio shrugged. *"You*'re the one with a nose for mystery. I see none! The duchess is all graciousness, I vow." She dropped a sadly crumpled letter on the tabletop. "As you may see."

Reluctantly, Tess picked up the missive and perused its contents. The Dowager Duchess of Bellamy, seemingly a woman of few words, had truly invited Clio to London with a view of formally presenting her to Society. It was an invitation that caused Tess's thoughts to whirl. Unfair, of course, to deny Clio the opportunity—yet Tess could not but fear that her sister's love of excitement would carry her almost unconsciously into the company of the idle and frivolous, if not the truly depraved. Nor could one be sure that this unknown duchess would be of sufficient strength and enterprise to ensure that a madcap damsel conducted herself with a decorum and propriety suitable to her rank and tender years. She put down the letter. "You wish to go."

"I do." Clio rose and smoothed her elegant sprigged muslin skirts. "And I shall! If *you* will not accompany me, dear Tess, I'm sure Ceddie will!" With this Parthian shot, she skipped from the room.

Mildmay Manor was not an establishment in which strict lines of social demarcation were observed, and the Countess of Lansbury was not a lady to demand obsequiousness from her servants. No sooner had Mistress Clio made her blithe departure than the cook abandoned the *pièce de résistance* that she was perfecting for that day's dinner, a lighthouse made of rout-cakes standing in the middle of a tempestuous sea made of trifle, with a distressed mariner in colored sugar clinging to a rock of meringues *à la crème*; the abigail deserted the paste that she intended to apply to her mistress's sun-tanned complexion, by force if need be; and the little kitchenmaid left off polishing the copper and inched, wide-eyed, closer to the huge elm table where her superiors gave every evidence of engaging in a council of war.

Tess looked at the various concerned faces that were turned toward her, and sighed. "Abominable chit!" she said ruefully. "It is no more than one should expect from her, I suppose."

The abigail gave vent to an expressive snort. "An *enfant gâté*, that one, a spoiled child!" She pursed her lips. "You must not be blaming yourself, *ma cocotte*."

Lady Tess also frowned, not at the abigail's temerity in addressing her as a "little chick," but at the notion that she was blameless in the matter of her half-sister's shortcomings. "I should have paid more attention to what was going on," she protested. "Had I not had my nose forever buried in a book, I would surely have seen that Clio was growing shockingly hot-at-hand." The abigail opened her mouth and received a severe glance. "Don't argue, Daffy! That I am at least partially at fault for Clio's waywardness is as plain as the nose on my face."

Delphine regarded that charming appendage, which was adorned by a dab of flour. Even the countess's detractors —and these were not inconsiderable, due to her ladyship's tendency to discuss with authority not only Napoleon's deprecations against the English and the economic ramifications of his Continental blockade, but also the progress of the war in the Peninsula and the repercussions of the newly passed Regency Bill—had to admit that she had a beautiful, refined appearance and a deceptively demure manner. Delphine barely repressed another rude expulsion of breath. Lady Tess might claim an awesome amount of book learning, but she didn't know the first thing about dealing with a determined miss like Clio.

"I fear," said the countess gloomily, "that my sister possesses a strong streak of the Mildmay stubbornness."

At this prodigious understatement, Delphine did snort, but the untimely sound went unheard, the cook having chosen that moment to thwack down on the table a cup of tea so strong that a cat could trot on it, laced with cream and barley sugar and a liberal, if surreptitious, dosage of cognac. "She'd create a regular sensation," announced that worthy, squeezing her ample bulk into a chair, "if she was to have her debut. 'Tis a proper shame Lady Mirian —no disrespect intended, my lady—didn't see to her come-out."

"True," sighed Tess, who had never even briefly entertained a longing for a come-out of her own. "I often wondered why she did not, for Clio is of an age, and can only conclude that Mirian did not wish to resume relations with the Bellamys. Apparently she did not even care to visit London for fear of encountering one of them! And now Clio is determined to be taken to the Duchess of Bellamy's bosom. What a devilish state of affairs!"

"*Voyons!*" interrupted Delphine, who had a strong aversion to conversations that merely belabored the obvious. "You might as well bow gracefully to defeat. That one will go to London, with or without your consent—and with or without your escort! Me, I suspect that she would prefer it to be without, lest you put a damper on her style."

"Daffy!" Lady Tess was clearly horrified. "It would be disastrous if Clio were to go alone to London and be suddenly thrown into the whirl of fashionable life. She hasn't the least notion of how to go on."

"Then you'll have to tell her, won't you?" suggested Cook. "And see that she doesn't take up with a fortune hunter, or worse! Drink your tea, my lady. And wipe your face, if you please!" It was Cook's private opinion that Lady Tess was wasted in this bucolic setting. For all the mistress's lameness, she was far from an invalid. Sure and wasn't the Countess of Lansbury the finest horsewoman this countryside had ever seen?

Lady Tess swiped ineffectively at the offending flour with her apron, then laughed. "How absurd you all are—for I must assume you are hinting at the same thing, Daffy! If truth be told, I have little more notion than Clio of how to go on in Society."

"No," agreed Delphine, then added, with all the assurance of one whose parents had been so high in the domestic hierarchy that they had gone willingly with their aristocratic master to the guillotine, "but *I* do. There's nothing for it, *ma cocotte*, but that Mistress Clio shall have her trip to London, and we shall accompany her. Else you will have the little wretch running away."

Since London was equated in Tess's mind with the accident that had left her lame, it is little wonder that she greeted her abigail's announcement with less than enthusiasm. "You have a damnable habit, Daffy, of hitting the nail on the head. I suppose I must allow Clio her debut." The countess propped her elbows on the table and dropped her chin into her hands. "I will admit to *you,* my friends, that the prospect fills me with dread!"

It was a prospect, judging from her sour expression, that inspired the abigail with little more enthusiasm. Not so the little kitchenmaid, whose somewhat hazy notions of the metropolis included such disparate elements as jewel-encrusted aristocrats and pumpkin-shaped coaches and circus elephants. "London! What larks!" she breathed.

# Chapter 2

*Bellamy House was a typical London town house,* rising five stories high into the soot-clouded air, an edifice of gray brick enlivened by crimson window-arches and roofs. Steep, dark staircases led from the gloomy basement kitchens into the cramped and crowded servants' quarters on the uppermost floor.

Not only the attics were crowded. Into the front drawing-room were crammed long and narrow gilt-framed looking glasses of baroque style; a couple of sofas, curved and carved in flower designs; several smaller ones, vaguely Empire in shape; armchairs and side chairs to match, constructed of rosewood and upholstered in dark red; and numerous additional chairs and tables of indistinctive character. An Aubusson carpet with superlative roses lay on the floor. From brass poles with enormous china flowers at the ends descended heavy velvet drapes and curtains of Nottingham lace. Presiding over this impressive chamber was the Dowager Duchess of Bellamy, a white-haired old woman with a malevolent countenance and a beaklike nose that had once been referred to by the irreverent Beau Brummell as "the Bellamy curse." This feature branded irrefutably the duchess's offspring, all of whom attended her, and all of whom looked to some degree uncomfortable.

The dowager duchess grinned. "How *nice* of you," she said with heavy sarcasm, "to attend me so promptly!

'Twill be to your edification, I vow, for I've news of a singularly wonderful nature to impart."

There was little reaction to this promise, which sounded very much like a definite threat to those acquainted with the duchess's little ways. Sapphira, her spirits rendered ebullient by a double dose of opium, surveyed her family. Disappointing, the bunch of them! With a fine sense of drama, she settled back into her Bath chair to wait.

The dowager duchess was not long required to hold her tongue. "Well?" demanded Drusilla, second of her children, a lovely brown-haired woman with a bitter voice. "What is this news? Witness us tremble with breathless anticipation!"

Sapphira awarded this temerity with a look of sharp dislike. "You continue to drink far more than is good for you," she remarked, "and to gamble wildly. Any losses you may sustain, my girl, are your own! You needn't think I'll come to your rescue."

"I don't!" muttered Drusilla, and shifted in her chair. Bellamy House was by rights the residence of the present duke, Giles Wynne; but the Duke of Bellamy had, since the death of his wife in childbirth several years previous, evidenced more interest in political affairs than in domestic arrangments. It was a situation that little recommended itself to the duke's sisters, both of whom would have given much to get out from their mother's domineering thumb. Alas for the hopes of Drusilla and Lucille! Giles, immune to interfamily warfare, seemed perfectly content to let his mother rule the roost. Not, thought Drusilla sourly, that his objections would have any effect! Confrontation with the dowager duchess was remarkably like collision with a stone wall.

"We are," announced Sapphira, adjudging the moment ripe, "shortly to welcome a visitor." Having secured a unanimous attention, she settled herself more comfortably in the invalid chair. The dowager duchess was a martyr to rheumatism, a fact which those of gentle sensibilities thought to explain her legendary ill-temper. Sapphira's family labored under no such delusion. The dowager

15

duchess was, bluntly, a vituperative tyrant, prone to nasty whims and eccentricities, and her favorite pastime was to set her long-suffering children chasing their own tails.

"A visitor?" whispered Lucille, eldest of the Bellamy progeny, a pale and faded lady whose chief characteristic was an overwhelming desire to antagonize no one, particularly her vicious parent. "Who, *Maman*? Shall I order a room prepared?"

Sapphira awarded this daughter no more opprobrium that she had the other. "No," she replied, with disheartening glee. "I've already seen to it. The chit shall have Mirian's chambers."

This pronouncement caused the sisters to exchange a glance and brought even the duke from his reverie, which dealt, predictably, with matters of government and finance and the controversial Corn Laws. "Mirian's rooms?" he queried, as Drusilla asked suspiciously, "*What* chit?"

"Told you I'd arouse your interest!" grunted Sapphira, gnarled fingers clenched around the arms of her chair.

"And you have," agreed Giles calmly, from his stance by the fireplace. He was a man of five-and-thirty, of medium height and excellent physique, and only Brummell was so unappreciative of his friend's aristocratic demeanor as to term him a "mighty icicle." "Having done so, *Maman*, do you think you might elucidate?"

Sapphira gazed, with a doting expression, upon her son. Giles was a handsome man, his air of distinction only enhanced by The Nose, with his father's brown hair and her own dark eyes and their combined stamp of breeding and elegance. Some might call him haughty, but his mother disagreed. It was only proper that the sixth Duke of Bellamy should be aware of his consequence. She nodded. "As you say. The chit is Mirian's daughter, and I have engaged myself to bring her out."

The reactions to this blunt statement were no less than she wished. Though Lucille said nothing, her hands fluttered in distress; Drusilla swore inelegantly; Lucille's husband, Constant, wore a look both calculating and chagrined. Only Giles maintained his customary air of boredom. "Interesting," he murmured. "Do you mean to tell us why, or are we to be kept in perfect ignorance as to what is going on?"

Sapphira shrugged, then clenched her teeth against the pain. "I'd a fondness for Mirian," she retorted. "I've a notion to see this girl of hers."

That the dowager duchess should nourish a warmth for anyone seemed, at the least, impossible; but Drusilla and Lucille both recalled that Sapphira had once been fonder of the thankless Mirian than of themselves. "A season!" protested Lucille unwisely. "Have you thought, *Maman*, of the trouble, the expense?"

"Bother the expense!" retorted the dowager duchess, further startling her audience, for she was a notorious nipfarthing. She shot her daughters a spiteful glance. "The chit will be no trouble to *me*. You'll attend to the thing, Lucille; Drusilla will play chaperone. The role of duenna may curtail some of her wild habits and extravagance."

Drusilla, who prided herself on making a dashing appearance, a feat which she accomplished at the cost of being forever dunned by unpaid dressmakers and milliners, looked as if she'd swallowed a bitter pill. Lucille, contemplating the numerous details attendant upon a young lady's entrance into Society, had recourse to her vinaigrette.

"It occurs to me," remarked the duke, pulling on his gloves, "that no one has inquired after Mirian. Has she explained why she left us so abruptly, *Maman*? I trust she is in good health?"

"Were Mirian in good health," snapped Sapphira, "I doubt the chit would be coming *here!* I regret to inform you, my son, that Mirian is dead." The duke received a hawklike stare. "Or perhaps you already knew?"

"I?" Giles raised a brow. "How could I?"

The dowager duchess ignored this not-unreasonable inquiry. "The girl appears to know little about Mirian's connection to us, and only learned of it after her mother's death. Some papers, I believe. It seems Miss Clio cares little about the past. Doubtless the chit is something of an opportunist."

"As Mirian was!" Drusilla was unable to longer contain

her indignation. "Mark my words, this girl will turn out to be no better than her mother was."

"You seem to be very nearly in convulsions," observed Sapphira unkindly. "Try some of your sister's patent remedies—heaven knows she has enough to set up as a pharmacist! I wish the two of you might try and learn some self-control."

"It is odd," ventured Constant, with some vague hope of restoring the peace, "that anyone should fail to divulge a connection with so old and venerable a line. This Mirian was raised by you, Duchess? A distant relative, I apprehend?"

Sapphira grimaced at her son-in-law, a stout and pompous individual with thinning hair and unfortunate pretentions to dandyism. "You apprehend very little, Constant!" she responded rudely. "Mirian was my orphaned niece. It is all as distinctly in my recollection as if it happened yesterday." She rose stiffly from her chair. "Enough of this nattering! My patience is exhausted. I swear I wouldn't give a ha'penny for the lot of you. Lucille, see me to my room!"

It was not in Lucille's nature to argue with her overbearing parent. Too, she welcomed the opportunity to escape to her own chamber, there to ruminate over this distressing development and fortify herself with Dover's Powders, Cerelaum, and Morrison's Pills. With an inscrutable glance at her siblings, she silently offered Sapphira her arm. With an equal lack of comment, the others watched their progress.

"I have plans for the chit," announced Sapphira abruptly from the doorway. The dowager duchess was not one to deny herself the last word. "And I'll brook no interference! I might remind you all that *I* hold the purse strings." On this ominous note, she exited.

Constant, at least, needed no reminder that he owed Sapphira the very bread he ate. Gloomily, he stared after his mother-in-law, then turned his head to meet the duke's knowing gaze. Well Giles could afford to be amused! thought Constant resentfully. Having a fortune of his own, Giles wasn't constrained to dance to Sapphira's tune. The rest of them were not so blessed. Sometimes Constant wondered, uncharitably, if Giles tolerated the presence of his quarrelsome family merely for the diversion that it afforded him. It must be acknowledged that this suspicion was extremely perceptive: the duke had more than once remarked to the most intimate of his cronies that the efforts of various of his relatives to ingratiate themselves with Sapphira made better watching than a farce.

"I, too, will take myself off," said the duke, eyes as merry as if he had access to his brother-in-law's thoughts, "having an engagement at White's with a large cold bottle and a small hot bird. You two will find much to discuss, I'm sure."

Constant glowered impotently as Giles strode unconcerned from the room. He had little love for the elegant duke, envying his title and his impeccable taste and the bottomless pocketbook that had procured for him that exquisite cravat, the superbly fitting long-tailed coat of blue cloth and breeches of fashionable yellow, those highly polished top boots. He further envied the duke's success with the fair sex. Though Giles had, since his young wife's death, been immune to the lures cast out by marriageable ladies, and though he was both fastidious and discerning, he was by no means a monk.

"Insufferable!" exploded Drusilla, angrily pacing the floor. "Constant, do shut the door!"

This was, in line with his thoughts, a most promising omen. Constant sped to do her bidding, then regarded Drusilla hopefully. Gad, but she was a handsome figure of a woman in that fetching gown of white muslin with its crimson tunic trimmed with pearl beads on golden disks; and none too selfish with her favors, if rumor was correct. He eyed her splendid bosom, heaving with agitation, and sat down rather abruptly on a rickety little chair, its back all spindles and balls, its seat fashioned of gilded cane. It was not the first time that Constant had been made aware that he had married the wrong sister. Drusilla's vivacious manner and rather amoral outlook were far better suited to a man of his tastes than Lucille's vague indecisions and conciliating ways.

"I fear," said Drusilla, who was well aware of her brother-in-law's sentiments regarding herself and viewed them with little surprise and even less gratification, "that Sapphira is displaying symptoms of eccentricity verging on madness! To bring that chit *here!* My mother is a positive bedlamite."

So much for romance, reflected Constant sourly. "What d'you mean? Think you to put her in an asylum?"

"If only I could!" Drusilla wore so evil an expression that Constant decided himself fortunate that she was uninterested in dalliance. "Giles would never stand for it, curse him. We may only circumvent her as best we may."

At these grim words, Constant felt an onset of one of his liverish depressions. His corsets creaked as he squirmed on the hard chair. "Why?" he inquired, hopeful that a logical attitude might spare him the worst of Drusilla's rage. A pity, but this lush creature could conduct herself with all the vulgar ill-temper of a common fishwife. "What can the chit signify? I'm sure you will find some way to avoid playing chaperone."

Drusilla turned on him, lip curled in disdain. "As if that were all! What a ninnyhammer you are, Constant. Must I remind you of my mother's habit of forever changing her will? If we don't look to our interests, we will find ourselves in the basket and that chit named as Sapphira's heir!"

Constant goggled. This was a contingency he had not previously appreciated. "Surely not!" The protest lacked conviction. "Giles would not tolerate such a thing."

"Why should Giles care?" sneered Drusilla, hands on her ample hips. "With his many titles and his wealth? No, Constant, it is up to *us* to circumvent the danger. Lucille will be of no help; Sapphira has only to glance in my sister's direction to frighten her into submission. We may rely only on ourselves."

Constant was stricken dumb by this intelligence. So spendthrift that he had quickly wasted his wife's portion as well as his own, Constant lived in perpetual terror that Sapphira might do as she had so often threatened and turn him off without even a farthing. It was much too dreadful to contemplate. "She means the chit for Giles, of course," continued Drusilla. "That, too, will not serve! Should matters arrange themselves as she wishes, Sapphira will be so pleased that she is likely to leave her fortune to them, and Giles certainly has no need of it."

"But Giles doesn't wish to marry again!" protested Constant, all at sea. "I've heard him say so. Why should he? He already has an heir."

"Pah!" exclaimed Drusilla scornfully. "Think you Giles can hold out against my mother? He is far too concerned with his own comfort to long withstand her will."

"Perhaps," offered Constant, "he might wish to share Sapphira's fortune with us?"

This suggestion did not appreciably increase Drusilla's estimation of her brother-in-law's intelligence. "Sapskull!" said she. "Would you, were the situation reversed? If only I had been granted a conspirator with some claim to wit! I, at least, wasn't born yesterday."

Unabashed by this ridicule, Constant waggled a wise finger. "I see what it is! You're afraid the chit will cut you out! Oh, famous! But Sapphira will not let the girl near your Wicked Baronet, for all she thinks him a charming rogue. He is listed by many matrons as dangerous; young girls are warned against him."

"I'm not worried about *that*," snapped Drusilla, with something less than truth. The gentleman thus named was incorrigibly fond of the ladies and nurtured an apparent belief that none would naysay him for long. It was a conclusion not without basis in fact: any number of frail creatures had accompanied that charming rake on the downward path to perdition without so much as a backward glance.

"Maybe you *should* be," snickered Constant, rubbing damp palms on his plump thighs. "You've been dangling after him for years, and with very little effect." It occurred to him that, if this Miss Clio proved handsome, he might embark upon his own game. What bliss, to see Drusilla receive a set-down! Perhaps Sapphira's *protégée* even possessed a fortune of her own. Constant's small eyes gleamed.

Drusilla contemplated an ugly porcelain vase and

thought wistfully of the satisfaction she would derive from breaking it over her brother-in-law's head. But aggravating as he was, she needed Constant's assistance. "This accomplishes nothing," she grumbled, "We must make our plans before the girl arrives. Pay attention! I think I've hit upon a scheme."

# Chapter 3

*"A well-brought-up young lady,"* decreed Delphine, taking advantage of the captive audience fettered within the confines of Lady Tess's elegant traveling coach, "is never allowed to be alone with a man, even for a half-hour in the drawing-room. No young girl goes anywhere unattended. At balls, she sits beside her chaperone until asked to dance; after each dance she is returned to her chaperone's care. To dance more than three times with one man is considered forward." She paused to regard Clio, who was looking sulky as a bear. "Attend me, *poupée!* Innocence is highly valued by the *ton.* No man wishes to marry a girl with a bold eye. And don't sit with your ankles crossed!"

Clio pulled a rebellious face, but obeyed. She looked lovely in a carriage dress of white poplin with a deep blond flounce and a blue levantine pelisse edged with floss silk; and that she chafed already at the restrictions that were being placed on her, her sister knew all too well. But if Lady Tess was having second thoughts about this London venture, which promised to be at the least exhausting and at the worst—if Clio took it in her head to fly in the face of convention, which was not at all unlikely—disastrous, she kept those misgivings to herself.

"It sounds so very *dull!*" pouted Clio, and Tess concentrated mightily on her book—*Itinéraire de Paris à Jerusalem* by Chateaubriand—lest she become embroiled in the fray. In a world where a squint was damning, a limp could only be fatal; Tess had turned to books in compensation for what in reality she would be denied, and her reading had been both panoramic and unorthodox. The countess had thus gleaned a worldliness that was startling in conjunction with her circumscribed existence, but she knew better than to offer to share that knowledge with her sister. Mistress Clio was hardly likely to take advice from a confirmed, if well-meaning, spinster.

Delphine labored under no such handicap. "Imbecile!" said she, but kindly. "However, girls aren't expected to know much, merely to amuse. You will do well enough." She frowned severely as Clio gave vent to rage. "No, no, *poupée*! You must cultivate a low silvery tone and never, even in stress or anger, allow that tone to rise. Else you will be thought ill-bred."

Clio was not so easily cowed. She fussed needlessly with her exquisitely frivolous bonnet. "I should have married Ceddie!"

Tess closed her book—it was growing dark and she had not seen to read for some time—and barely repressed a sigh. "Enough for now, I think, Daffy." The countess appreciated her abigail's motives, which were equal parts concern for Clio's future and long-deserved revenge, but this constant bickering was wearing on her nerves. "It's growing dark; I fear we must seek shelter."

Delphine noted with alarm that her lady's piquant face was looking rather drawn. Cursing herself for an unthinking fool, the abigail quickly made Tess's wishes known to the coachman. The Lansbury berlin might be the most modern of carriages, a well-sprung vehicle which was also nicely fitted out, its pale blue interior boasting beading along the roof as well as braid and silk fringe, its doors fitted with hanging pockets and trimmed on either side with a padding covered in taffeta and morocco leather, and emblazoned on its exterior the Lansbury coat of arms; but due to her crippled leg, the countess was not a good traveler, and such a protracted journey could only bring her discomfort.

"Poor Tess!" said Clio, and patted her had. She might resent her sister's wealth and title, she might nourish a slight contempt for one whom fate had decreed would never have a beau, but she also loved Tess dearly, when she thought about it, which was seldom. "Has all this bouncing around caused you discomfort? I knew how it would be! Daffy should have let you accompany us on horseback."

Delphine, at a wry glance from her mistress, withheld comment. Pleased by her small triumph, and totally unaware of the scandalized consternation that would have ensued had the Countess of Lansbury arrived at Bellamy House with as little pomp as the rawest underbred countrywoman, Clio sank back on the lushly upholstered seat, her spirits so miraculously revived that she did not even protest again that this journey to London was proceeding at a snail's pace.

It was not so much Tess's leg that troubled her as her aching head, and that was due not so much to the jolting of the carriage as to confined quarters and enforced inactivity. Lady Tess refused to be restricted by her handicap, and enjoyed a life of no little physical activity. It scarcely mattered on her own estates if she was noted to walk with less than grace; the servants were long used to their lady's ungainly gait. With sinking heart, Tess realized it would be far different in London. There her limp would make her the cynosure of all eyes. Oh, if Clio had not made it necessary that she go!

Clio's thoughts also centered on the metropolis, as did Delphine's. It seemed to Mistress Clio that the reality of a London season was going to fall far short of the anticipation thereof, due entirely to Daffy's eagle eye. Perhaps she truly should have married Ceddie, even though she didn't like him very well—but the die was cast, and she must make the best of it. Nibbling on her lower lip, Clio mulled over the various ways in which she might lull her watchdogs into a false sense of security. The thing would be difficult but not, for a young lady of Clio's vast resourcefulness, impossible.

Delphine was not thinking of Clio at all, but of her mistress. The countess's pale complexion was not due to Daffy's Roman Balsam, or even to her infallible Cosmetic

Lotion which consisted of horseradish and cold soured milk, but to nervous strain. Delphine had a fair notion of how Tess would hate to be gawked at and whispered about, and her heart, which was extremely tender beneath that rather prickly exterior, fair bled for her young mistress. The ladies breathed a collective sigh of relief when the carriage drew at last into the courtyard of a coaching-inn. No sooner had it rolled to a stop than Daffy, scorning aid from coachman or steps, was out the carriage door and yanking energetically at the bell-pull which would summon the innkeeper to them. Clio, without a thought for her sister, was hard on the abigail's heels.

Lady Tess moved in a more leisurely manner, waiting for her coachman to assist her to alight, looking around with frank interest at her surroundings. The great cobbled courtyard was scored deep by coaches' iron-shod wheels; the gabled inn itself, which was sadly derelict, was built in an Elizabethan manner, its weather boarding interspersed with square-cut bay windows. An overhanging upper floor of half-timbering was inset with plaster panels and lit by a variety of diamond-paned windows. A pity, she thought, as the coachman guided her over the rough stones, that the structure had been allowed to fall into such disrepair. In its heyday, the inn must have been charming. Now it bordered on the macabre.

"Thank you, John!" she said, and awarded her coachman the sweet smile that caused her servants to unanimously believe her the kindest of mistresses. "You may take the horses around to the stables, and then have yourself a nice mug of ale." The coachman bowed respectfully and took himself away.

The interior of the old inn, with its heroic-sized oak beams, might have interested Tess as greatly as the exterior, had she not been so fatigued. Odd that there was no one to greet her, she mused, as she proceeded with some difficulty over the ancient, uneven flagstones. Tess had only a hazy notion of how business was conducted in such places, but it didn't seem exactly efficient for guests to be left to find their own way about.

But the countess was not long alone, for the narrow

hallway led her into the taproom. Tess strongly suspected that she had no business there, but her thoughts were quickly distracted by the scene therein. The room was filled with rough-looking men—local visitors, Tess supposed, come in for a tank of ale and a chat over the taproom fire, which was blazing merrily in a huge granite fireplace at least eight feet long and two feet deep, supported on two shorter columns of similar girth. None of these worthies appeared particularly pleased by the intrusion of females into their domain, though any number eyed Clio with appreciative interest. That graceless damsel, Tess noted wryly, was looking exceedingly demure and hovering uncommonly close to Delphine's voluminous skirts. Daffy herself, undaunted by such overpowering odds, was engaged in loud altercation with the ungenial landlord.

"Ain't nothing I can do about it," stated that hirsute individual, then spat with remarkable accuracy into an empty can halfway across the room. "We're full up. You'll have to go elsewhere."

*"Vraiment?"* Delphine drew herself up in a manner that caused several of the men to shift their attention from Clio. Delphine was a fine figure of a woman, particularly when in a temper, as she was now. *"Tout même*, you will provide for us three bedchambers, one for my mistress, the Countess of Lansbury, one for her young sister, and one for myself. Bestir yourself, my man! My lady is wearied of traveling and would rest."

That the landlord meant to take exception to this highhanded manner was obvious, but the words died unborn in his throat as Lady Tess stepped into the taproom. Not only did all eyes turn to her, there they remained.

Tess grimly supposed that she must be a curiosity unviewed by such provincials except in a traveling freakshow. Accustomed to considering herself in such a light, the countess possessed no idea of how she appeared to these rough men. Though she did not know it, Lady Tess outshone mere beauty and cast even her sister into the shade. The clouds of fair hair that tumbled to her waist, unfettered by bonnet or pins, the old black pelisse that enhanced her slender fairness, gave her a fairy-tale appearance that was only strengthened by her characteristic look of faint surprise, as if she had stepped unwittingly into another world.

Clio was not at all pleased at this reaction to her sister, who was too shy to tease and sparkle and thus unworthy to hold men so spellbound, and quickly hurried to her side. "Tess!" she exclaimed with fine, if unaccustomed, solicitude. "The most terrible thing! The landlord says there is no room."

Lady Tess was as guilty as any other of pampering Mistress Clio, but at this moment she was too exhausted to concern herself with that maiden's pretty ploys. "So I heard, child," she said absently, and shook off her sister's hand. Clio, her charming act of sisterly concern thus brought to naught, looked outraged. Tess did not see, being concerned with navigating the uneven floor. It was an act of the utmost bravery, conducted under the weight of countless curious eyes.

"Sir," said she, halting at last before the landlord, "I understand that you have no room for us. But perhaps a private parlor, and some food? When my horses have rested, and we have refreshed ourselves, we will proceed on our journey."

"Nonsense!" came a voice behind her. Startled, Tess spun around so quickly that she would have lost her balance if not for the strong hand that supported her arm, and gazed up into a pair of smiling amber eyes that were strangely familiar. "Sir Morgan Rhodes at your service, Countess!" he remarked, maintaining possession of her arm. Tess was speechless. "I fear mine host has misled you. It is not that he lacks rooms, but that he fears his accomodations are far inadequate for a lady of quality." The tawny eyes moved to the landlord. "Isn't that so, Jem?"

The man shuffled uneasily. "As you say, Sir Morgan," he muttered. "It ain't fitting that Quality should stay here. There's no one to wait on them, for one thing."

"It is up to my lady, surely," suggested Sir Morgan, in a mild voice that held more than a hint of steel, "to decide what is proper. I daresay her woman can see to her needs."

"How *kind* you are, sir!" cried Clio, skittering gracefully across the room to hover by Tess. "My sister, as you can see, is not strong. If we were forced to continue our journey tonight, she would be all pulled about."

This intervention gained for Clio no more than Sir Morgan's idle glance, which flickered over her with as little interest as if she were a piece of furniture, before returning to Tess's face, an act which earned for him Delphine's wholehearted approval. "Lady Tess?" the abigail inquired briskly. "Do you choose to stay?"

"Yes." Tess was rendered by Sir Morgan's glance unaccountably shy. "You will see to the luggage, Delphine?"

*"I,"* muttered Clio sullenly, "wish to be shown to my room. At once!" Tess was roused to worry by that tone, which betokened an imminent tantrum, but Sir Morgan once more intervened.

"Follow me, ladies," he suggested, with an enchanting crooked smile. Now that he no longer stood so close, Tess had ample opportunity to observe her rescuer. Sir Morgan Rhodes was a man of perhaps forty, swarthy-complected, with raven-black hair, clad carelessly in expertly cut buckskin breeches, riding boots, and pale cloth coat. He was tall and muscular, with the air of an outdoors man; his features were aquiline and saved from harshness only by the humor in his odd-colored eyes. Such details did not paint a true picture, Tess thought. There was a charm about the man that was no less effective for being indescribable. She followed him into the hallway and gazed with dismay at a steep, dark staircase.

"Poor Tess!" cried Clio, with a malice that was not entirely excused by piqued vanity. "I fear you will never be able to climb the stairs. Shall I call Daffy? Perhaps between us—"

"No!" Considering her sister with something closely akin to dislike, Tess grasped her cane. "I shall manage quite well, thank you."

"Suit yourself, then." With a rather immodest display of pretty petticoats and neat ankles, Clio ran up the stairs.

But this was a challenge that Tess was not to face. "That chit," remarked Sir Morgan, "needs turning over someone's knee." Without further ado he swept Tess off her feet and into his arms and proceeded up the staircase. "Shall I offer you my assistance? It would render me no small gratification to administer the brat some salutary discipline."

"She is a trifle spoiled," admitted Tess, stricken bewildered and breathless by his audacity. It seemed only natural that she should secure her precarious perch by grasping his board shoulders. "She is also very young. My sister means no harm, I assure you! And now, sir," for they had gained the upper hallway, "you may set me down!"

"I might," agreed Sir Morgan, treating her again to that devastating smile. "And then I might have the privilege of watching you march down the hallway. You do it well, of course, but why bother when there is no need?" Tess glowered furiously at him, but to no avail. "The rear bedchamber, I suppose," he added, after a cursory glance along the hallway. "Your graceless sister will have appropriated for herself the front room, it being altogether larger and more commodious." Tess was summarily borne to a small chamber at the back of the house which contained little more than a narrow chest of drawers and a chintz-hung bed, where she was deposited carefully. "There!" Sir Morgan's amber eyes were alight with amusement as he divested her of the shabby pelisse. "See how I exert myself to make you comfortable?"

"You are all kindness!' retorted Tess and reached resolutely for her cane. "Tell me, sir, are you always so insufferably overbearing?"

"I am," admitted Sir Morgan cheerfully, and deftly twitched the cane from her grasp before busying himself with a bellows at the grate. "And you are uncommonly lovely, Lady Tess!"

In such a situation, Mistress Clio would have fluttered her long lashes, blushed over and over again, and uttered faint and patently insincere protests. Lady Tess, a stranger to the art of flirtation, merely stared at this bold gentleman and broke into her deep, husky laughter. "Compliments amuse you?" inquired Sir Morgan, quirking a brow.

"Oh, no!" gasped Tess. "I mean, yes! You see, I have never before made the acquaintance of a rake."

"So I am no better than one of the wicked?" Having successfully accomplished his mission, Sir Morgan abandoned the fireplace to prop a heedless boot on her bed. "Having never before been exposed to such, how would you know?"

"It is obvious!" Tess propped herself up on one elbow, her shyness forgotten in the pleasure of the exchange. "I have read a great deal, and you have about you an air of profligacy akin to that of the French aristocracy before the Revolution. I daresay you fell into licentious ways when very young and are now entirely preoccupied with sin."

Sir Morgan's lips twitched, for she sounded quite delighted with her discovery. "Are you not frightened," he inquired, "to find yourself alone with a libertine?"

Tess's look of surprise grew more pronounced. "Good God, no! Why should I be? A man of the world is hardly like to waste time on a poor creature like myself. No wonder Clio was so miffed! Your casual air of indifference would be irresistible to her." Her glance held a trace of worry. "You understand that for myself such things do not signify."

"Of course they do not," Sir Morgan conceded politely. "What happened to your leg?"

The countess was quite morbidly sensitive about that appendage, and Sir Morgan's impudent query caused her to scowl. "A carriage accident when I was but a girl," she replied coolly. "It need not concern you, sir."

"No?" So far was Sir Morgan from being snubbed that he leaned forward to take her ankle in his hand. "I think it concerns *you* overly, little one! I suppose it aches abominably?"

"No," said Tess faintly, amazed not only by his temerity but by his gentleness. She tried once more to track down that elusive memory, but could not pinpoint the resemblance that was so naggingly familiar and at the same time so vague.

"It is entirely your own fault," Sir Morgan remarked,

relinquishing the ankle, "for straining it in superhuman feats that no one expects of you. Never mind, I know just the thing to make you comfortable." He turned to the door.

"I will not," announced Tess gruffly, "be coddled, sir!"

Sir Morgan paused at the threshold, brows raised. "You misunderstand. I have not the least intention of coddling you."

It was some time later when Delphine puffed up the steep staircase, having at last bullied the unamiable landlord into providing additional accommodation for the coachman, the postilions, and the groom; it was later still when Clio had grown reconciled to the fact that, due to the advent of yet another overnight guest, she must share with the abigail her room. These matters satisfactorily arranged, Delphine proceeded down the hallway to check on her mistress. She paused aghast on the threshold, for before her was a truly bacchanalian scene. Lady Tess lay on her bed, skirts up to her knees, while Sir Morgan massaged her lame leg with what smelled strongly like horse liniment. Nor did the countess appear in the least disturbed by the impropriety of the situation, a fact perhaps accounted for by the bottle of Old Constantia that she and Sir Morgan had shared between them. Indeed, so far was Tess from shamed awareness that she was discussing with great enthusiasm the new regent's retention of his father's advisors.

"It is perfectly reasonable," commented Sir Morgan, very much at ease. "Prinny had made up his mind to dismiss the Tory government as soon as he was installed as regent, but the queen advised him that such a move was certain to retard his father's recovery. Or so our regent claims. Myself, I suspect Prinny is more afraid of rousing his father's wrath."

"A fine regent!" Tess drained her glass. "I do not know what that concoction is, and it definitely smells vile, but it is nigh miraculous. I vow I could dance a jig!"

Delphine deemed it time to make her presence known, lest her addlepated mistress attempt that very thing. "Humph!" she ejaculated disapprovingly.

"So you've chosen to make an appearance at last," remarked Sir Morgan, obviously no stranger to compromising situations. He winked at Tess. "I will take my leave of you; doubtless your woman wishes to read you a terrible scold. And I will leave the liniment since it has done you so much good."

"Thank you," murmured Tess, a wary eye on the frigid Delphine. "I am indebted to you also for your company."

Delphine waited for Sir Morgan to depart, then firmly closed the door before turning on her mistress a wrathful countenance. Tess forestalled the lecture by simply holding up a hand. "Dear Daffy," she murmured, "you are very cross! I assure you I have conducted myself with perfect prudence—and really Sir Morgan's lotion did me a world of good! It was very pretty in him to offer it to me. Now, would you help me into my nightdress?"

It was not the liniment but Sir Morgan himself, thought Delphine sourly, that had brought that flush to Tess's cheeks and that sparkle to her eye, and a most damnable event it was. *Tres seduisant*, that one, an artist in the matter of feminine seduction, but of course the countess would not realize. Tess appeared sleepy, and Delphine reluctantly held her tongue.

In point of fact, slumber was elusive that night, and Lady Tess passed much time wistfully contemplating the carefree life of dissipation that a splendid sinner like Sir Morgan must lead. Consequently, she was very much alert when the door to her chamber swung open. Stealthily she gripped her cane. The intruder had little chance to escape from such a weapon, and little hope of evading it in a chamber so small. Though Tess's leg might be weak, her arms were correspondingly strong. She waited only for the man to draw nearer to her bed, then brought down the cane with considerable force over his unwary head. He fell with a heavy thud.

It was one of the men from the taproom, candlelight revealed, and the force of the blow had shattered her cane. With some vague idea that she might have killed him, Tess bent over the inert body. No, he still breathed. But how the devil was she to go for help without the aid of her cane? In any event, it was unnecessary to do so. Fully dressed, Sir Morgan stepped into the room. Tess, unaware that she looked quite charming *en déshabillé,* thought it queer that he gazed, with a thoughtful expression, not at the unconscious man but at her.

"An intruder," explained Tess unnecessarily, and sank back down on her bed. "I fear I may have injured him."

Sir Morgan glanced around the small chamber. "Was anything disturbed?"

"I think not." Tess frowned at her opened portmanteau, which Delphine seemed to have packed with unusual carelessness. "He hardly had time. I heard him enter, you see."

"Could you not sleep, little one?" Sir Morgan seemed unaccountably amused. "I suppose I must rouse Jem and dispose of this brigand."

"Do you think he meant to rob me?" Tess queried. "Poor man! He is probably very poor, with a large family to feed."

"He is more likely," retorted Sir Morgan wryly, "a smuggler or a highwayman. This place is notorious for such and possesses for their convenience five entrances and exits, passages within the walls, and cupboards with false backs. You may note tomorrow that a gibbet stands outside. More than one villain has dangled there."

"Fascinating!" commented Tess, wide-eyed. "Highwaymen!" shrieked Clio from the doorway, and turned a becoming ashen shade. She swooned but, since after a cursory glance Sir Morgan ignored her altogether, it was into Delphine's arms.

In no time, it seemed, the rest of the inn was aroused and crowding into Tess's small room. Arms wrapped around her knees, the countess watched the proceedings with great interest, noting that the landlord's shocked protests lacked sincerity. In no time the intruder, still unconscious, was dragged away.

"I'll take care of this," said Sir Morgan, and grasped the broken cane. Heedless of Delphine's basilisk stare, he touched brown fingers to Tess's cheek. "Try and sleep now! I'll guarantee you no more disturbances this night."

"You have been put to a great deal of inconvenience for my sake!" Quite unself-conscious, Tess smiled at him. "I am extremely sorry for it."

Again she received that crooked grin. "You need not be," he replied, golden eyes alight, "though you have caused me a great deal more inconvenience than you know." With this cryptic utterance, he strode from the room.

"Well!" gasped Clio, making a remarkable recovery. "What boundless effrontery! I wonder if he is a fortune hunter, Tess? He certainly lost no time in attempting to cajole you!"

*"Voyons!"* spat Delphine, but the countess only laughed. "Don't be silly, child!" she replied. "Sir Morgan can nourish no warm feelings—proper or otherwise—for someone like myself. He was only being kind."

Delphine doubted strongly that Sir Morgan was so chivalrous, but acceded to her mistress's plaintive request for solitude. With a forceful hand, Daffy propelled Clio from the room. "All the same, my lady," she pronounced severely from the doorway, "it's glad I am that on the morrow we will see the last of him."

Tess drew the bedclothes up to her chin. "Yes, I suppose we shall," she murmured, with only the slightest of frowns.

# Chapter 4

*Tess was not to be granted* even that last glimpse of Sir Morgan; she slept late on the following morning and thus did not witness his departure from the inn, a fact which vastly pleased her abigail. Delphine's relief, alas, was but short-lived. Sir Morgan had not forgotten the countess; he had left behind her mended cane and a note that for all its brevity had been enough a *billet-doux* to make Tess blush and laugh aloud. Delphine would have greatly liked to peruse that missive. Somewhat unwisely, she made her wish known.

"Oh?" Lady Tess could, when the occasion warranted, be extremely intimidating. "Am I a child, Daffy, that you would read my private correspondence? You will confine your chaperonage to my sister, if you please! I wish to hear no more of the matter." Having emphatically squelched her abigail, she returned to her book. It was mere subterfuge—the coach's jolting made reading very difficult—but Clio and Delphine, neither of whom possessed a fondness for the written word, were equally deceived.

Mistress Clio glanced sideways at her sister, then down at her own clasped hands. She knew she had behaved badly, and was sorry for it; and she had every intention of apologizing to Tess, though not in front of the censorious Delphine. Clio's self-centered behavior was due more to immaturity than to any basic character defect. She would grow into an unexceptional young woman providing no one, goaded beyond endurance by her capriciousness, murdered her first.

In one matter, though they would have been startled to know it, Clio and Delphine were in perfect accord, and that matter concerned none other than Sir Morgan. The greatest blackguard alive, thought Delphine, quite forgetting her initial favorable impression of the man. Both *diabolique* and *débauché*, a true libertine, as evidenced by his conduct regarding Lady Tess! No matter to *him* that by his behavior he might have sullied her reputation beyond all mending! Were it known that the countess had been closeted with a gentleman in her bedchamber for well over an hour, she would be ruined.

The abigail sighed heavily, but even that did not earn for her Tess's forgiving glance. Delphine had not meant to question her mistress's conduct, but to put her on guard against a born intriguer of the boudoir sort, and the attempt had failed. What now? she wondered, not a little alarmed. She saw that she would be required not only to keep a watchful eye on Clio, but on her mistress. The world would never believe that Tess flouted the conventions only through sublime innocence.

In this, Delphine grievously misjudged her mistress. Tess might be totally unaware of her own beauty, but she was far from ignorant of the rigid rules that governed conduct between well-born ladies and gentlemen. Simply, Tess did not think of herself as one to whom those rules applied. The game of hearts was not meant for such as her; if she felt a faint regret at her exclusion from the lists, it was understandable, and little signified. She had liked Sir Morgan very much, had appreciated his blunt manner and his thoughtfulness, had enjoyed talking with a man whose mind was as agile and well-informed as her own; but he had not touched her heart. Were they to meet again, Tess felt that she might call him friend, and with that she was content. She recalled his irreverent note and grinned, an act which her companions mistakenly attributed to the words of Chateaubriand.

Mistress Clio was also pondering her sister's innocence to such extent that she ignored the passing countryside. It was little wonder that Tess had no little understanding of the ways of men, for she had had only one suitor, the unworldly curate, and consequently no practical experience. Clio suddenly wondered—she was by no means the fool her behavior implied—if that omission was due to a lack of inclination on the part of the gentlemen, or because Lord and Lady Lansbury had surrounded Tess with a wall of solicitude that no gentleman could penetrate. Struck by this unique thought, Clio frowned.

Aware that she had given both her companions cause for consternation, Tess leaned forward to touch her sister's arm. "Look!" she said, and gestured toward the window. "While you have been woolgathering, we have arrived in Town."

Relieved by this indication that she was to be forgiven so easily, Clio cast her sister a grateful glance. She gazed obediently outside, but accorded little attention to the incessant stream of elegant carriages, the well-mounted horsemen, the countless pedestrians. Mistress Clio was not accustomed to devoting her private reflections to other than herself, and found it a difficult exercise.

It was not benevolence that caused the countess to treat her young sister with such kindness—Tess was too well used to Clio's fits and starts to take offense—but a strong suspicion that the girl had sustained a blow to her pride. Clio was not used to such offhand treatment as Sir Morgan had administered; young men had flocked around her ever since she had left the schoolroom and she could not be expected to find in a rake's conduct a most salutary moral. Tess did and was grateful to him for it. Sir Morgan might admittedly be a man of little principle, but he was not so depraved as to offer a young girl false coin.

In this manner they passed the journey, which was not without its small excitements and alarums, each wrapped in her own thoughts: Delphine in grim recollection of the squalid little debauch she'd interrupted in so timely a manner the evening before; Tess in amused recollection of the debauchee's outrageous behavior and even more outrageous remarks; Clio in frenzied contemplation of how she might warn her elder sister that a lame lady no longer in her first youth was easy prey for a reckless and profligate man who was demonstrably more at home in the fleshpots than in the drawing-room. Despite what her mentors might think, Clio was only slightly miffed that her artful lures had earned her cavalier treatment from Sir Morgan. It was not in her nature to bypass an opportunity to flirt with a handsome gentleman, particularly one whom she instinctively knew to be a connoisseur; but in truth she didn't care a button for him.

As disparate as their thoughts were the ladies' impressions of the town. Clio saw only richly dressed gentlefolk and fashionable shops and bastions of the nobility which she hoped to breach; Delphine gazed astounded on the street-sellers who dispensed steamed baked potatoes from brightly painted cans, ginger beer from mahogany fountains with gleaming brass handles, treacle rock and hot meat pies and peppermint sticks. It was Tess who saw the ramshackle tenements and stinking alleyways, the ragged filthy people, the poverty that lurked forever on the edges of London's magnificence.

"Look," she said, "in the distance. That complex is the Tower, the most venerable pile in London. The oldest building there is the White Tower, built by Bishop Gundulf under orders from William the Conquerer in 1089." This information earned neither comment nor praise. Tess lapsed again into silence, and at length the carriage halted in front of the Bellamy town house in Berkeley Square.

"Tess!" hissed Clio, as they descended from the coach. Her unusual contrition was prompted by a conviction that Tess was suffering Cupid's sting, an arrow in the breast that had left a festering wound. "I must speak! I have behaved abominably to you, and I beg you will forgive me for it."

"Bosh!" replied Tess. That this brusqueness was due to a painful twisting of her lame ankle, she did not explain. "I am hardly like to condemn you for the heartlessness of your conduct, child!" With that she turned away, leaning heavily on the mended cane.

Clio's mouth opened and closed wordlessly. Laboring under a strong sense of ill-usage, she followed her sister to the double front doors. Delphine, who had proceeded them, lifted one of the heavy knockers, fashioned like lions, and let it fall. They were admitted into an entryway, bright with Indian red tiles set in purely classical patterns, and left there to cool their heels.

"Clio!" said the countess, a trifle acerbically, "you *did* inform the Duchess of Bellamy of our intended arrival?"

"Of course." Clio gazed at the splendor of her surroundings with delight. Then her jaw fell. "Tess! I quite forgot to inform her that you were coming, too!"

What Lady Tess might have replied remains unknown; the entryway was invaded at that moment by a small boy, an impish-looking child of perhaps ten years with a most impressive nose, and a huge dog, obviously of dubious parentage, a positive mountain of multicolored hair and uncoordinated parts.

"You must be my cousin!" announced the lad and with grubby fingers clutched Clio's arm. She regarded him with fascinated horror. "I'm Viscount Wyncliffe. *You* may call me Evelyn!"

Tess, who had a fondness for precocious little boys, might have interrupted at that point since Clio looked to be on her verge of histrionics, had not the dog, sensing an animal lover, chosen to make known his approval of her. Tess was fragile of build and he was not; in the energy of his greeting, he knocked her to the floor.

"Nidget!" cried Evelyn, and rushed across the hallway to tug ineffectually at the beast, which was joyously saluting Tess's face. "I am dreadfully sorry, ma'am! Nidget has no manners but I am teaching him. He must like you very much to behave so! I hope you aren't hurt?"

"I don't know," gasped Tess. The dog's massive front paws were planted firmly on her ribs. "Do you think you might induce the monster to get off me?"

"I think so," replied Evelyn cautiously, pulling on one large canine ear, and consequently buffeted mightily by a frantically wagging tail.

"What the deuce is this?" inquired a calm masculine voice. "Evelyn, if you do not remove that confounded dog immediately, I will have him destroyed." While Evelyn might have realized the emptiness of this dire threat, Nidget did not. Cowed, he slunk away.

With a deep breath of relief, Tess struggled to her knees. A hand was placed beneath her elbow. "Allow me to assist you," offered the helpful gentleman, and Tess looked up into a pleasant, if somewhat detached, face. It was easy to guess that this was Evelyn's father; they shared not only The Nose but the same dark eyes.

"Thank you." She availed herself of his support.

"I hope that wretched dog has not injured you?" he inquired, in tones of the most polite, and with a look of total unconcern.

"No." Tess was chagrined, not by his patent disinterest, but that she must ask his further aid. "If I might have my cane?"

This simple request procured for her the gentleman's immediate attention. He glanced at her as if seeing her for the first time, then looked about him for the desired article. It lay some way across the tiled floor, and beside it a small book. Though such menial errands were clearly not what he was accustomed to, he fetched them both, and returned them to Tess with a raised brow. "Chateaubriand?" he murmured. "Heavy reading for a young lady, surely?"

Tess rewarded this absurdity with a level gaze from her clear blue-green eyes. "Poppycock!" said she.

Lucille hovered in the doorway. It had been a day so distressing, as were most of Lucille's days, that she devoutly wished herself in a nunnery. "*Maman* is waiting," she ventured timidly.

"Then by all means we must hasten to her. She is in a devilish temper as it is." Giles turned cordially to Clio. "You must be my young cousin. May I say how pleased I am to make your acquaintance, and apologize for this dreadful *contretemps*?"

"Pray say no more!" replied Clio, who had been hard put to remain silent while her sister monopolized the attention of yet another personable man. "It does not signify."

"Please," whispered Lucille, twisting her hands. Clio

41

dimpled as Giles offered his arm, and they followed the faded woman down the hallway, trailed by Tess, who was flanked by Evelyn and Nidget, both of whom had apparently constituted themselves her devout admirers. Bringing up the rear of this small cavalcade was Delphine who, though perfectly aware that she should by rights remove herself to the nether regions, had no intention of leaving the disposition of her charges to happenstance. It was glaringly obvious to the abigail that this was an abominably ill-run household.

Sapphira positively dominated the drawing-room, seated as she was in her invalid chair with a gold turban on her head and a hideous cashmere shawl wrapped around her shoulders, her daughters and son-in-law grouped subserviently around her, and a glass of negus—sherry and hot water sweetened with lump sugar and flavored with grated nutmeg and lemon juice—in one gnarled hand. Clio took one look at this rather malevolent apparition and gulped audibly. Tess repressed a smile.

"Come here, girl!" snapped Sapphira. "Let's have a look at you." Flushing under the combined scrutiny of so many eyes, Clio obeyed. She appeared quite charming in her flounced white cambric gown and her green sarsenet pelisse, and the white gauze bonnet so lavishly adorned with tea roses and foliage; and she looked so unusually subdued that Drusilla immediately decided that her Wicked Baronet would never award *this* damsel a second glance, having precious little interest in the infantry.

"Extravagant and undisciplined!" announced Sapphira, who, though of caustic nature, possessed remarkable acumen. "You have a look of your mother, young woman! I doubt not that if you're not keenly watched, you too will involve yourself in various scandals and escapades." Clio's unhappy face reflected only too accurately her reaction to these words. The dowager duchess chortled and her sharp eyes moved to Tess, who was standing near the doorway, one arm around Evelyn, who was leaning blissfully against her good side, and Nidget at her feet. "Who's that creature?" she snapped. "Some sort of a companion, I suppose? I can't see why you had to bring *her* along."

There was perhaps some basis for the duchess's misapprehension: due to the fact that Clio's letters were self-centered masterpieces of omissions and poor grammar, Sapphira had no knowledge of the Countess of Lansbury; and Tess, who still wore her old black pelisse, and who had in her encounter with Nidget lost all her hairpins so that her pale curls were as usual in wild disarray, certainly lacked the least appearance of a gentlewoman. There was, however, no excuse at all for Tess's subsequent behavior, for she merely sketched an awkward little curtsy and made no attempt to set matters right. "My name is Tess," she said, with a humility that made Delphine wish to box her ears. "I told Clio she would have little need of my company here, but the dear creature would not hear of me remaining behind." Clio, astounded to hear herself spoken of in such doting terms, bit back a giggle. It was growing obvious that her sister was set off on a lark, and while Clio had never known such a thing to happen before, she thought it would be great fun. "She has been," added Tess, making it impossible for either her sister or her abigail to render explanations without making her appear demented, "in my care since she was born, you see."

Had Sapphira been sufficiently interested in Clio's companion to consider this statement, she might have thought it odd indeed that an infant should have been placed under the supervision of a child who could not at the time have been more than seven years old; but Sapphira was not accustomed to wasting thought on paid servitors. "Find them," she said, with a dismissive gesture to Lucille, "rooms in the servants' quarters. I would speak privately with Clio."

Delphine had tolerated a great deal in the past few days, but she would not stand for this. *"Ma foi!"* she cried, drawing herself up to her full five feet. "It is *mal à propos*. My—" She caught Lady Tess's gimlet glance and quickly changed her words. "Mademoiselle Tess is not accustomed to being treated as a servant. Mademoiselle Clio will insist that she be given a proper room of her own."

"Hoity-toity!" snapped Sapphira but Clio dared not follow Delphine's lead lest she encounter, not for the first time, an energetically wielded hairbrush. "It is true," she interposed. "Tess is accustomed only to the best. I would not have her subjected to any hardship."

"Hardship!" snorted the dowager duchess. Lucille turned ashen. "Think you I keep my servants in chains? You do your people no favor by pampering them, girl! While in *my* house, your women will be treated as befits their station!"

"Eh?" Delphine's plump cheeks were flushed. "Then there is nothing for it than we must leave immediately." She almost hoped the evil old Tartar would take her up on the threat. Far better, thought Delphine, that she and Lady Tess return immediately to the country, where the countess would be safe from both gazetted rakes and foul-tempered dowagers. Now that she had met the dowager duchess, Delphine had no doubt that Clio was in capable hands.

Sapphira might well have granted Delphine's wish, as indicated by the rancor writ large on her mottled face; but Giles, who had been watching with some interest the manner in which Tess, while this storm raged about her, engaged in a whispered conversation with Evelyn, and who furthermore possessed a perfectly good grasp of the science of mathematics, chose to speak. "You must not do that," he interjected smoothly. "My mother was laboring under a misapprehension. Of course you must all be properly housed! What would Clio do without her companion and her abigail?"

His kindly intervention earned for the duke not a single grateful word. Clio, realizing belatedly that she would go on very handsomely without the protection of her two most diligent well-wishers, was crestfallen; Delphine, understanding that she was to act as lady's maid to that abominable minx, looked sour. Tess awarded the Duke of Bellamy a glance that indicated not only her awareness of every word of the conversation but the diversion it had afforded; and Sapphira exploded with rage. "You dare defy *me*?" she screeched, parrotlike. Fearing an onslaught of the vapors, Lucille grabbed for her smelling salts; and Constant tried to hide his bulk in a window recess. Drusilla exhibited no reaction at all, being caught up in unhappy thoughts of the pretty birds of paradise who vied continually for the attentions of her favorite profligate.

"Defy you?" repeated Giles, as if it were a novel idea. "It is after all my house, *Maman*."

"Lucille!" The dowager duchess cast her eldest daughter a meaningful look. "See these people to their rooms!"

"Do not trouble yourself, Lucille; I shall see that our guests are comfortable." Giles bowed elegantly to Tess. "This is your first trip to London? Perhaps you will allow Evelyn and me to introduce you to the city."

"Do say yes!" cried that young man, and danced around them in circles, the dog barking at his heels. "And Nidget, too, for there are a great many things he has not yet seen." He tugged at Tess's sleeve. "You will not mind if Nidget comes along? I promise that he is very sorry for knocking you down, and will not do so again."

Tess gazed down upon the dog who indeed looked quite penitent, tongue lolling, black eyes raised to her mournfully, and who furthermore threatened to trip her with every ill-considered bound. Then she looked at Evelyn, regarding her hopefully. "Then he is forgiven." She smiled. "Nidget must come along."

The Countess of Lansbury might be in excellent spirits, having met two delightful gentlemen in the space of two short days, but her abigail was less ebullient. Sadly, Delphine considered the implications of the scene she'd just witnessed; and even more sadly she listened to her mistress's lively, and very knowledgeable, remarks concerning Chateaubriand. Delphine knew, as Tess so obviously did not, that paid companions read not French literature but romantic novels or tomes to improve the mind; she was perfectly aware that the duke's partisanship was nigh unprecedented and for purposes unthinkable; and she further realized that his defense of her had made for Tess a formidable enemy. The abigail's misgivings worsened as the duke showed Tess into what had to be the choicest guest chamber, which had certainly been reserved for Clio. The countess gave voice to her enchanting laughter. Delphine frowned so terribly that her eyebrows met her nose.

# Chapter 5

*Mistress Clio, despite a sleepless night* passed in contemplation of the ceiling—hearts and darts set in longitudinal compartments—of her candlelit bedchamber, was in tearing spirits. Whistling in a most unladylike and tuneless manner through her teeth, she performed her ablutions at a washstand covered with gilt arabesques, with a marble basin inlaid with silver fish, then moved to inspect herself at the painted and gilt dressing table with a mosaic top. Quite nice she looked, she thought, in her round gown of lawn with its long sash. The dowager duchess would find no cause for criticism.

Gaily, Clio tripped out into the hallway and made her way to the breakfast room. The Duchess of Bellamy had, on first meeting, been overwhelmingly formidable, but Clio was not of a temperament that long sustained awe. Furthermore, Clio had evolved during those long sleepless hours a Plan.

Rather to her surprise, for it was still an early hour, several of her newly discovered relatives were already in the breakfast room, a chamber in which there was a great deal of rococo gilt furniture and yellow damask. Clio suspected that the room might be rather vulgar in its opulence, but no hint of this showed on her charming little face as she made a pretty curtsy to Sapphira, seated near the head of the table. The dowager examined her from head to foot, and did not seem displeased. "Good morning!" cried Clio enthusiastically. "Oh, isn't it a *lovely* day?"

Various members of the family might be rendered slightly nauseous by such ingenuousness, but Sapphira thought it fitting. "Come here, girl," she said, with such marked approval that Constant and Drusilla exchanged a pregnant glance. Lucille merely applied herself with determination to her eggs. "Sit there, across from me."

Clio cast a wicked little smile at the footman who held her chair. He blushed. She seated herself, content. An hour that gained Clio no masculine appreciation was like a day without sunlight.

"Hah!" Sapphira gulped a dish of chocolate. "So you wish to enter Society, miss? You'll find it very tedious! Dinners and balls are given by the older generation to entertain royalty and statesmen and politicians. Young people are merely allowed to attend."

"It doesn't sound dull to me," Clio replied serenely. She'd already taken this old woman's measure: Sapphira thrived on conflict. "Balls and concerts, routs and promenades! It will be beyond anything."

"Humph!" Sapphira was disappointed; she had expected the girl to be entirely crushed by her vague threat. "Prodigiously like your mother—not but what I consider my daughters were entirely to blame for *that* kickup! I had not expected Mirian to behave so abominably! A pretty to-do there was over it—but I shall say no more." She paused expectantly but Clio placidly bit into a biscuit.

Mistress Clio was not being deliberately provocative; hers was a one-track mind, devoted usually to herself, and now engaged in schemes concerning her half-sister. It was not to be expected that she should also take upon herself the solving of the puzzle of why her mother had become alienated from the Bellamys. "I suppose," barked Sapphira, "that your father knew the whole? I would like to hear the tale! Mirian behaved in the most disgraceful manner—though I suppose she would not admit it!"

"Papa!" Clio paused in honest confusion, the biscuit

suspended in midair. "Knew what, ma'am? I vow I'm all at sea. What would Mama not admit?"

"A country bumpkin, no doubt," deduced Sapphira, with gleeful malice, "with no conversation and less curiosity. He'd think himself blessed to marry so far above his station and forbear to ask questions lest the answers prove unpalatable."

"You mistake the matter, *Maman*!" Giles appeared, elegant in a single-breasted cloth coat, checked waistcoat, striped nankeen trousers, and pristine cravat; and took his place at the head of the table between Sapphira and his young cousin. "Clio's father, as she apparently failed to inform you, was the Earl of Lansbury. A scholarly gentleman, I'm told, and a bit of a recluse." He studied Clio. "She also failed to inform you that her journey here was enlivened by an encounter with highwaymen."

"How," demanded Clio, briefly forgetting her missish guise, "did you know of *that?* We agreed to say nothing of it, since no harm was done."

Giles accepted a cup of coffee and leisurely sipped the steaming liquid. "It is my habit," he explained, "to indulge in an early morning ride. I saw your carriage—it is most elegant, *Maman*; our Clio travels in style—and engaged in conversation with your coachman. A most informative man! It was he who told me of the attempted robbery."

Clio was in a quandary; what else had the coachman said? She was full of admiration for the talent of Tess in this daring attempt to bamboozle the dowager duchess, which freakishness the countess explained as an attempt to avoid being herself presented in Society, where she would feel like a fish out of water; but Clio could also see that the deception was proving very difficult. Nor, if the truth be told, did Tess's self-effacement please her sister, who had very different ends in mind.

Giles was speaking again; apparently the coachman had not given them away. "Imagine!" he said, helping himself to a slice of ham. "They were set upon, ambushed in broad daylight! That they escaped unscathed was due only to the pistols carried by Clio's footmen, the skill of her coachman, and the excellence of her horseflesh. Miraculous! I trust you appreciate your people, cousin."

"Oh, I do!" Clio replied fervently. She could only assume that Tess had somehow gotten word to the servants. Had Clio but known it, the coachman deserved more than praise, having had scant sleep the night before performing his superhuman feat, due to Sir Morgan's request that he guard his mistress's bedroom door.

"Shocking!" agreed Constant. His jowls wobbled as he shook his head. "I have often lamented the condition of the roads. But you are in looks today, Miss Clio! We must be grateful that so dreadful an experience did not overset your nerves. It would be usual, I believe, in most young girls."

"*I*," pointed out Clio, with commendable honesty, "am not like most young girls." Oddly, she thought she heard Giles stifle a laugh.

Sapphira was speaking, and in stern tones. "It is considered rude," she decreed, "for a young woman not to affect an air of being a little carried away by the gentleman she is conversing with! You will do well to remember that, if to get a husband is your aim."

Clio looked at Constant, with his stout and flabby figure and, as she had already learned, damp hands, and almost rebelled. "Surely," murmured Giles, "we need not consider such things within the bosom of the family." Clio cast him a grateful glance, which he appeared not to see. "Need Clio concern herself with snaring a husband so soon? She can be no more than seventeen."

"Eighteen!" protested Clio, stung.

"Quite old enough," agreed Sapphira, in such good spirits that Drusilla poked a sharp elbow into Constant's ribs. "She'll put up her hair and lace herself into her corsets and we'll present her at a large dinner party followed by a ball. And then," she smiled malevolently, "we shall see!"

"A pity," said Giles, but did not explain the remark. Instead, he turned to Clio. "You have seen your companion this morning? I trust she has taken no harm from yesterday's unhappy encounter with my son's beastly dog?"

"I have," Clio lied cheerfully; she had deliberately

avoided an encounter with her sister until her plans were more firmly laid. "You must not worry about Tess, though it is good of you to concern yourself. My, uh, companion is a great deal stronger than she appears."

"Dowdy-looking female!" snarled Sapphira. "We'll get precious little use from her."

"I should hope," objected Clio, so sternly that she startled even herself, unaccustomed as she was to taking up the cudgels in her sister's defense, "that you would not try to do so! Tess must not be thought insufficiently elevated in rank to be admitted into the highest company. She is better born than I am myself." Belatedly, she paused; one could hardly explain that the countess claimed maternal connections with foreign royalty. "It is not a happy tale; we do not speak of it."

"Then, perhaps, she would enjoy sharing your come-out." Giles was bland as custard. "Society offers vast amusements."

That the duke had an ulterior motive in making this astonishing proposal, and that Tess would be angry as a wet hen, Clio did not even momentarily doubt; but it fitted in excellently with her own schemes. "A splendid notion!" she cried, and clapped her hands. "I wonder that I did not think of it myself. I should be so much more comfortable with my dear Tess at my side." This was not entirely true, but Tess was bound to be so dazzled and discomfited that she paid her sister little heed. One must make sacrifices, Clio thought virtuously, for the common good.

"Mad, the pair of you!" announced Sapphira, regaining use of her tongue. "To foist that frowzy-looking creature off onto Society? I never heard of such a thing!"

"You have now, *Maman*." Giles was totally unconcerned with his mother's wrath. "I, for one, find your objections ludicrous. Indeed," and he smiled enigmatically, "I think I can guarantee that Clio's companion will enjoy a tolerable success."

"She limps!" snapped Sapphira, who had taken a violent dislike to Tess the moment that her son had shown interest in her. "Lud, but the wench will make a pretty object of ridicule—and doubtless bring shame down on all of us. I tell you, I won't hear of it."

It wasn't often that Drusilla was presented with an opportunity to thwart her irascible parent and she took immediate advantage of it, never dreaming that it was an action she would speedily regret. "A tempest in a teapot!" she yawned. "The girl can't expect to get a husband, but I expect she might enjoy herself. She needs only the proper clothes to appear presentable, and I'm sure it will be no additional bother for me to take her around." The offer was not prompted by generosity; were Tess present to chaperone Clio, Drusilla would be free to follow her own pursuits, namely one Wicked Baronet.

"Then it's settled," said Giles. "Tell me, Clio, are you, like your companion, an admirer of Chateaubriand?"

"Gracious, no!" Clio giggled. "Tess is the bookish one."

"By all that's holy!" Sapphira grimaced terribly. "What must my son needs do but take up a crippled bluestocking!" She glared. "Are you sure you aren't one yourself, miss? It's my contention that a girl who's taught more than French and dancing is automatically a bore!"

Lest her mother animadvert further on the subject and in the process undo what had been accomplished, Drusilla engaged upon a worldly, frivolous, gossiping kind of conversation to which no one paid the slightest heed. Lucille kept a cautious eye on the dowager, who was crumbling her toast and staring ferociously into space; Constant glumly regarded his plate, wondering if his brother-in-law's queer conduct was occasioned by an admiration for Clio or Tess, or sheer cussedness; and Giles, typically, mused upon the warehouses of the East India Company and the West India Company, where valuable goods were spoiling and rotting as a result of the Continental blockade.

Clio, paying little heed to the talk that flowed around her, was extremely pleased with herself. There was an odd exhilaration attendant upon arranging someone else's life, and Clio had discovered in herself a remarkable aptitude for that very thing. Tess would thank her, in time.

52

She stole a glance at Giles. He had a consciousness of his superior standing, of course, was most exemplary in politeness and manner, and preserved an air of fine indifference over almost everything; and would serve her purposes admirably. Who would have thought Tess would turn out to have such appeal for the gentlemen? Certainly not Tess herself! Clio smirked. Tess would like the notion of being a duchess very well, once she got used to it. How could she not? Clio would have liked it very well herself, and thought it positively noble that she should give up to her sister this particularly handsome specimen.

"Lord Lansbury!" said Sapphira, so abruptly that Clio almost dropped her cup. "Rich as Croesus, as I recall. You might have told us that you were a great heiress, girl!"

Clio was fast developing an ability to keep her head in a crisis. She held her tongue and dropped her gaze to the tabletop. *"Maman!"* reproved Giles, while Constant wondered if this information might prove to his advantage, and Drusilla's eyes narrowed consideringly. Even Lucille, who was no less dependent on her mother's pocketbook and her mother's goodwill than the others, pricked up her ears. "You are embarrassing Clio."

Sapphira was not displeased that Giles should concern himself with the girl's sensibilities, and even less displeased that she'd chosen a fortune for her son. "You're off to Westminster again? I suppose I should be grateful you don't go instead to some low dive of a cellar to bet some £1,000 on the number of sewer rats a terrier can kill in an hour!" Lucille gasped, Drusilla looked unhappy, but Giles only smiled. The dowager turned her dark eyes on Clio. "My son's prominent place in Society and his close friendship with the royal family have caused him to be labeled a mouthpiece of the fashionable world. He is more talked of, more envied—and in some quarters, more disliked!—than any other member of the *ton*. Yet what must he do but work for the betterment of commoners, not that they appreciate it! 'Tis a wretched waste of time."

"I am sure," murmured Clio, thinking that Tess would

approve, "that his efforts are commendable." For herself, she would prefer a man of leisure whose morning routine concerned nothing more weighty than a stroll to the caricature shops or to Tattersall's.

"Bah!" observed Sapphira. "Giles, you will forgo your efforts at reform for at least this day and show your cousin the town."

"I am loath to disappoint you," Giles replied, with patent insincerity, "but I have already made plans. Perhaps some other time."

"I, too, have an engagement," announced Drusilla, as she rose. She was fashionably attired in a white muslin gown with elbow sleeves, lovely pearl buttons, and an open center front over a slip. Clio studied the yellow slippers and Paisley shawl with amber tones that completed the ensemble and thought enviously that Drusilla looked fine as fivepence.

"Meeting the Wicked Baronet, are you?" inquired Sapphira, with malice. "Amazing how he can drink till all hours of the night, then rise at dawn to embark upon another debauch! I wish you joy of the encounter—not that it will do you any good!"

Expressionless, Drusilla crossed the room. She was not to escape so easily. "My daughter," remarked Sapphira to the room at large, "has fallen into licentious ways. I fear she has strong passions and indulges them with great latitude—for which that rogue is doubtless to blame! Where does he take you today, Drusilla? Another excursion to the East End? To hobnob with the riffraff in the sordid lodging houses of Whitechapel, the teeming slums of Spitalfields?"

"Nonsense, *Maman!*" retorted Drusilla, in a voice that shook perceptibly. Sapphira's omniscience was to her family a source of constant wonder and equal discomfort. "I am only meeting Morgan in the park." Quickly, she fled.

"Morgan!" gasped Clio, before she thought. *"Here?"*

"What's this?" Sapphira pounced. "Don't tell me you know the rascal!"

"Perhaps," admitted Clio cautiously, aware that Giles

looked intolerably amused. "If the man of whom you speak is Sir Morgan Rhodes."

"You will not continue the acquaintance." Sapphira was obviously displeased. "He is audacious, insouciant, impetuous, and a womanizer of no small degree. Even were you a marvel of discretion, which I don't for a moment expect you are, that rogue's attentions would ruin you."

"But *Maman*," protested Lucille, "you allow Drusilla to associate with him! I have always found Morgan to be most kind."

"Nincompoop!" retorted her fond mother. "It is a good thing that I do not require you to think for me." She scowled at Clio. "A lady's reputation resides not in what she does, but in what she is considered to have done—and there is very little, believe me, that Drusilla is not credited with! However, she behaves herself properly in public; and though Drusilla's friendship with Morgan has gained her fame as a dashing widow, no doors have yet been closed in her face. I suppose it is partially because people recall that she was once betrothed to him and broke it off to wed that gay rattlepate who died so inconsiderately and left her penniless. She is thought immune."

"I only met Sir Morgan once," offered Clio, severely shaken. "He stayed, as we did, at an inn in Hertfordshire."

"Oh?" Sapphira, thus intent, looked rather like a vulture. "Odd that he should put up at an inn when his home is in that area. Explain *that*, girl!"

"I cannot," replied poor Clio. "We had very little conversation—he will not even remember me." But he would remember Tess, she thought, and wondered how she might prevent their meeting again. It struck her belatedly that Sir Morgan might very well give them away. It was no great deception, of course, but Sapphira was bound to be furious.

"Little matter if he does!" decreed the dowager duchess, after considerable thought. "I repeat, you will have nothing to do with him, though you will see him often enough in this house. Morgan has not only the dubious distinction of being Drusilla's chosen quarry, he is a friend of Giles."

Worse and worse, thought Clio. The duke appeared lost in thoughts of his own. "I have," she said sincerely, "no desire to further the acquaintance. Just who *is* Sir Morgan?" Even the untutored Clio knew that forewarned was forearmed.

"The Wicked Baronet?" Sapphira grinned. "He truly is magnificent. Morgan not only lives in the grand style, he possesses it. He has excellent taste in food and wine, patronizes only the best tailors, rides only the best hunters, admires only the loveliest women, and mixes with only the best company." The smile faded. "He is not for the likes of you, miss! That rascal's heart has never been touched by anyone. His taste is for highflyers; he's never been known to cast so much as a glance at a green girl. And you may be thankful that it's so!"

But he'd glanced more than once at Tess, Clio thought unhappily. In fact, he'd made a dead set at the countess! Clio was distressed beyond measure. She might magnanimously wish for her sister a fair portion of domestic bliss, and somewhat less magnanimously wish for herself freedom from the restraints imposed by Tess and Delphine, but she in no way desired that her sister's heart should be broken by a careless rakehell. Tess might not realize that Sir Morgan held a strong fascination for her, but Clio knew well the symptoms, having first encountered them herself at the tender age of twelve. "Oh, dear," she murmured weakly. This arrangement of her sister's life was going to be more difficult than she'd initially perceived. One thing was certain: Tess must be kept as long as possible unaware of Sir Morgan's unfortunate proximity.

"You must not believe all my mother says," offered Giles, with an air of helpfulness and a great deal of secret mischief. "Morgan is not so black as she paints him. Were she to be entirely honest, *Maman* would admit that Morgan is a great favorite with her."

"With *me*, yes," the dowager duchess repeated meaningfully. "But I'm not an inexperienced young girl. Heed my words, miss! You'll award Sir Morgan no more attention than courtesy demands."

They obviously both thought her already half-smitten, and Clio could hardly explain that it was her elder sister who was so lacking in sense. "Yes, ma'am," she replied meekly. If this wasn't the most odious development! There was nothing for it but that Tess must wed the duke with all possible speed.

# Chapter 6

*Blissfully ignorant of her sister's schemes,* Tess was enjoying a delightful afternoon. The Duke of Bellamy was the most considerate of companions, whisking her off on a tour of the Palace of Westminster, escorting her through the ancient building known as the Court of Requests, where the House of Lords met, and pointing out a tapestry representing the Spanish Armada, gift of the States of Holland to Queen Elizabeth; showing her the Great Hall which Richard II had covered with a magnificent molded and carved double hammer-beam roof; guiding her through St. Stephen's Chapel, in which the Norman kings had made their *devoirs*, and the celebrated Painted Chamber in which Edward the Confessor had died; and then whisking her off to Gunther's, the celebrated pastry cook in Berkeley Square, for an apricot tart. If Tess had any complaint to make of the proceedings, it was that Clio had inexplicably refused to accompany them. Nor, though Tess did not consider it, had young Evelyn and the faithful Nidget been privileged to join the expedition.

"The French privateers," continued the masterfully devious Duke of Bellamy, "have captured a staggering number of British cruisers and merchantmen. The devils seem to know the English coasts and routes of trade, the tactics of British cruisers, even the times of arrival and departure of our convoys. We lost over six hundred ships last year alone! Those plaguy privateers have grown so bold that they take their prizes in plain view of farmers on our shores—a humiliating spectacle, I assure you."

Tess frowned and controlled her nervous mare with practiced ease. A newcomer to intrigue, and unaware of the extremely enlightening conversation that had passed between the Duke of Bellamy and her coachman, the countess only thought it a happy coincidence that the duke should have chosen to go on horseback. "I believe," she responded, "that as a result of Napoleon's devices, the national economy is in a shocking state. Mills and factories have had to close down, the cost of bread has risen to near famine point, the export of British manufactures and colonial produce has fallen by nearly a third. It seems that only Wellington thwarts the Neighboring Monster's schemes." Shyly, she smiled. "Do you know, at times I almost admire the Corsican? Look at the havoc he has wrought!"

If Giles thought it odd that a lowly and impoverished gentlewoman-companion should be so well-informed, or handle a horse with such skill, or converse with one so exalted in station as himself with such lack of self-consciousness, he gave no sign. Instead, he made a polite reply, and while she was still wrapped in thought, guided her into the leafy glades of Hyde Park. "And how," he asked smoothly, as she glanced in puzzlement at the countless well-dressed ladies and gentlemen who congregated there, "do you find our city? I trust that, in my home, you have been made comfortable."

"Very." Tess, aware that the duke had for some quixotic reason of his own exerted himself greatly in her behalf, awarded him a quizzical glance. "I would like to ask you a question, if I may, though you will think it verges on impertinence."

"Ask away," Giles said cheerfully, his thoughts well-hidden. Had Tess been a mind reader, she would have been very much amazed. "What do you wish to know?"

Tess looked at him again, wondering how she might tactfully proceed. There was no doubt that the Duke of Bellamy was a very personable man, flawless in both ap-

59

pearance and manner; there was equally little doubt that he could, if he chose, be formidable indeed. Again she wondered just why he was exerting himself to please her. "It concerns Mirian," she replied hesitantly. "Clio's mother. You must know we were told nothing of her association with your family, or of the years she spent in your house."

The duke said nothing, merely waited patiently. Tess, who had spent a profitable half-hour quizzing his jovial housekeeper, grew uncomfortable. "I know," she added, even more hesitantly, "that you and Mirian were close friends. Can't you tell me something of her youth, and what caused the estrangement?"

"You have been gossiping with the servants." The duke's voice was devoid of either censure or wrath, and as effective as a slap in the face. "Perhaps you would do better to address your inquiries to them. I daresay you have already learned that my cousin and I were unofficially betrothed. As to why Mirian fled from my house, I cannot say. She did not see fit to inform me."

That tone had cowed many a peer; Tess only looked thoughtful. "Oh," said she. "It must have been devilish unpleasant for you, poor boy! You were both very young."

The duke might be deuced high in the instep, but he also possessed a lively sense of the ridiculous, and it amused him greatly to be thus consoled. "You are an odd female!" he remarked bluntly. "An enigma, in fact. Why should you concern yourself with Mirian? Clio does not appear to harbor any particular interest in her mother's past."

Tess was not so uncharitable as to comment that Clio harbored scant interest in anything but herself, particularly to a gentleman who might make that volatile miss an ideal husband. "Clio," she murmured, "is not of an inquiring nature. I was devoted to Mirian."

"Ah, yes." The duke was at his most bland. "I was forgetting that you, as Clio's companion, must have answered to Mirian. She was kind to you, I suppose, and you were grateful; it was always her way. You cannot judge by *that*, you know! I believe that even the most vicious of criminals have been kind to dogs."

Stung, Tess opened her mouth to protest, then closed it on the words. There was little explanation she could make without revealing the truth of her relationship with Mirian, and the depth of her deception. For the first time, Tess wondered if this masquerade hadn't been a trifle ill-advised. It was not only Clio who had inherited the Lansbury impulsiveness; Tess had conceived a notion and acted on it without regarding the consequences. She had meant simply to hover in the background, to impose restraint if necessary, while Clio enjoyed her debut; now came the growing suspicion that the deception had been less than wise.

Tess was not destined to long remain in the background. Not only had Clio already taken steps in her sister's behalf; the duke, while Tess was thus preoccupied, had maneuvered her smack into the midst of the fashionable throng. Hyde Park at this hour was the gathering place of beauty and wealth; before Tess was aware of what was happening, she had been introduced to Lord Petersham, famous for the Cossack trousers and double-breasted coat named after him, and known for his expertise in all matters of fine teas and snuff; the Duchesses of Rutland and Argyll, among the most celebrated beauties of the day; the Ladies Cowper and Jersey, who after a whispered consultation promised vouchers for Almack's; the eccentric Earl of Morton on his long-tailed gray. It is not to be imagined that these people, in smiling upon the Duke of Bellamy's companion, were merely being kind: Lady Tess, on horseback, was in her element and so far forgot her loathsome limp that she positively glowed. In the riding field she felt no need to efface herself, to dress in a drab and unfashionable manner that drew no attention; and consequently wore a habit of deep blue, simply and superbly cut, black half boots and York tan gloves, and a small beaver riding hat from beneath which escaped countless silver blond curls. Unaware of the duke's Machiavellian tendencies, and equally unaware that a woman of her supposed station

61

would be totally overcome by mingling with such exalted personages, the countess laughed and spoke quite naturally with all and sundry, not even turning a hair when presented to the exquisite Beau Brummel, absolute *arbiter elegantarium* of fashionable society, who lingered so long in animated conversation that eyebrows rose and tongues wagged mightily about the Beautiful Unknown.

"How Clio would have enjoyed this!" she breathed to Giles, who was clearly in a good humor. "What a great pity that she did not accompany us. It was for her, you know, that you should have procured those vouchers to Almack's! It would hardly be the thing for *me* to attend."

"I had nothing to do with it." The duke threaded his way among elegant carriages. "It might amuse you to view the stratagems undertaken by hopeful mamas with daughters in the Marriage Mart. You are honored, you know! I doubt few mere companions have set foot within those exclusive walls." He turned his head to observe her, rather narrowly. "My sisters will see that Clio receives her voucher, never fear. You need not concern yourself."

Little did he know, thought Tess, and hoped that Clio would find among the town's young bucks a *parti* who might inspire in her a fondness that lasted longer than a week. With luck, the *parti* might also be eligible! Recalling Clio's past conquests, however, Tess had little faith in this. It was too much to ask, she supposed, that Clio should fall in love with a gentleman as thoughtful, and as eminently eligible, as her current escort. "Have you always," he inquired, thus adding to his growing list of virtues a considerable acumen, "concerned yourself so with the girl?"

"If only I had!" replied Tess absently. "Clio needs a firm hand." She recalled herself. "Naturally, it is not my place to criticize!"

"Naturally." The duke was wry. "Do not distress yourself. It is obvious that Clio has been allowed to run wild."

Fortunately for Lady Tess, who was finding in herself little apitude for deceit, a diversion presented itself at that moment in the form of Mr. Romeo Coates, who drove a kettledrum-shaped carriage drawn by white horses. Taking exception to the closely passing wheels, the countess's mare reared up, thus presenting Tess with an admirable opportunity to further display her expertise. She did so, keeping her seat without effort, and calming the nervous horse with a single word.

"Your handling of the reins," remarked the duke, "is admirable."

"Honey and I are old friends." Tess stroked the dappled neck. "She's been with me since she was a foal; I had the breaking of her myself."

The Duke of Bellamy was enjoying himself to such an unusual extent that further comment concerning his companion was elicited from those spectators who knew all too well the rarity of his smile. "How kind of Clio," he murmured, "to let you bring the mare to town. But then, Clio would not wish you to be bored while she engages herself with fashionable frivolities."

"How perceptive." Tess wore a faint and becoming flush. "Dear Clio has always been *most* considerate."

That Clio showed little evidence of extending this laudable thoughtfulness to others, Giles did not mention; instead, he whisked his somewhat discomfited companion off to meet no less than the prince regent, a ludicrously fat gentleman with a florid complexion. Prinny, a connoisseur of lovely women, professed himself charmed.

"Your Grace!" protested Tess, whose cheeks were now quite rosy. "For what purpose are you presenting me to all these people? I cannot think they will thank you for bringing to their attention your cousin's companion."

"Ah!" replied the duke, and blandly guided her down Rotten Row. "Clio has already told me that your birth is better than her own." He quirked a brow. "Some mystery, I apprehend."

Tess nodded stiffly, her thoughts awhirl. If it were not impossible, she would suspect that Giles knew the truth of her charade, and was amusing himself at her expense. But how *could* he know? Tess was totally unacquainted with Society, her reclusive father having included among his scholarly acquaintance very few peers; and Tess's servants had been warned to make no mention of their mistress. It was most perplexing. She listened with only half an ear as the duke expounded upon the history of Hyde Park, informing her that in the days of William and Mary it had been a rutted haven for highwaymen; then pointing out Hariette Wilson, queen of the Fashionably Impure, an auburn-haired woman seated in a carriage lined with pale blue satin, surrounded by a crowd of horsemen. Tess was further bewildered by the duke's attentiveness, and could not imagine its significance. An event was shortly to take place that would drive these various considerations temporarily from her mind.

Ahead of them was a smart cabriolet, a light open conveyance perched upon two great wheels and upholstered in crimson. In it sat a lady, attended by a powdered footman in gorgeous livery and a bewigged coachman in a three-cornered hat and French gloves. By her side, on a beautiful black horse, was a swarthy gentleman. Tess gasped, then bit her lower lip.

"You've seen Drusilla," observed Giles. "Come, let us greet her! I will introduce you to her friend. You will find Morgan amusing. He is something of a rogue, and eschews the marriageable young girls paraded before him in favor of philandering—but it hardly matters if Morgan is both wildly extravagant and excessively bold, since he was born to wealth of the most enormous."

"Oh, no!" Tess was as pale as if she expected at any moment to receive her deathblow. "I could not."

"No?" Giles cast her a dark-eyed glance which held traces of mingled speculation and mischief. "I had not thought you a coward! You must not hold it against Morgan that he is, as the French have it, in constant need of a bed. There, I have embarrassed you! It is your own fault, for making a man feel so comfortable that he may say anything."

"Don't regard it." Tess resolutely ignored her hot cheeks. "In truth, I have a bit of a headache—doubtless a touch of the sun! I beg you will postpone this particular introduction to another day."

"Nonsense!" Giles urged her forward. "I promise you will like Morgan very well."

It was obvious that the duke had mistaken her reluctance for maidenly modesty. Short of creating a scene, Tess had no choice but to allow her mare to trot easily at his side. What to do? she wondered. Too much to hope that Sir Morgan would not give her away.

Observing their approach, the gentleman rode to meet them. "So!" he said, as they came abreast. "I had not hoped to encounter you again so soon, little one."

The countess was rendered speechless, but Giles stepped neatly into the breach. "You are already acquainted with my cousin's companion, Morgan?" He did not look especially surprised. "It merely confirms my long-held opinion that the world is prodigious small. You will excuse me, I hope? I must speak with my sister."

"I believe," remarked Sir Morgan, as Giles moved down the path, "that I scent a mystery. Are you less than you appear, little Countess, or more?"

For the first time she looked directly at him, but saw only her reflection in those golden eyes. "I can imagine," she said, "what you must think! And I thank you for not giving me away."

"Why should I?" inquired Sir Morgan. "No great sin, surely, to pass yourself off as a lady at a country inn. You are a deep one, are you not? Now I learn that you are not the Countess of Lansbury, but simply Tess; and that the rag-mannered Clio is not your sister, but your mistress." He shook his head. "You might be in the practice of daily dissimulation, so cleverly did you take me in."

Had the countess not been in such great affliction, she might have noted various inconsistencies in this attitude; but Tess, rapidly coming to think herself a plaything of fortune, was almost overwhelmed by Sir Morgan's worldly manner, his air of authority, and his splendid presence, and was feeling incoherent indeed. "You've found me out," she confessed weakly. "It was a great temptation, you understand. And Delphine was sure it would secure for us rooms at the inn."

"Very astute," approved Sir Morgan, with his wicked smile. "You must not fear I will betray you! In truth, I have always wished to meet an adventuress."

"Oh?" inquired Tess, who was recovering her wits. "Do you mean that you have not? Well then, Sir Morgan, I am delighted that I may oblige you."

"You may oblige me even further, in time." Careless of convention, he reached out and gently tugged an errant curl. "I make you fair warning that I intend to pursue our acquaintance, little one."

Lady Tess, with her vast inexperience, had no way of interpreting the look that he bestowed upon her, and returned it with her frank gaze. "Why should you warn me?" She laughed. "I should like very well to pursue our friendship, and you have promised that you mean me no harm."

Sir Morgan's harsh features were more than a little rueful. "So I have," he replied, and released her. "What a talent you have for delivering me set-downs, Tess!" The countess, as was her habit, looked surprised.

Though Tess might not understand the quality of Sir Morgan's regard, others were less naive. Drusilla, for one, knew that the gentleman for whom she cherished a decided partiality was gazing upon another woman with the expression of a hunter who has sighted fresh prey. "I make you my compliments!" she snarled at her brother, who was watching the encounter with a deceptive air of boredom. "It is just like you, Giles, to try and throw a spanner in the works."

"I?" The duke was all offended innocence. "Dear Drusilla, I haven't the slightest notion of what you mean." He glanced again at Sir Morgan. "Wonderful, isn't it, how he speaks to her with all the familiarity of an old acquaintance? The Wicked Baronet certainly has a way with the ladies! You had best look to your interests, sister, or you will find yourself out-jockeyed."

Though Drusilla was hard pressed to preserve her composure, she knew better than to rip up at Giles, who was known within the bosom of his loving family as a "damned knowing one" and, alternately, a "cursed cold fish." She fixed Tess, whom she would hardly have recognized in such fashionable attire, with a fulminating eye. So Giles thought his sister would be out-jockeyed? The duke would for once be proven wrong. Drusilla contemplated various means by which her unexpected rival might be disqualified from the race.

# Chapter 7

*"I tell you,"* grumbled Tess, "it doesn't signify!" Irately she regarded her companions. "If you persist in this idiocy, I shall be quite out of patience with the pair of you." Clio and Delphine exchanged a glance, for once in perfect accord.

The bedchamber allotted to Lady Tess by the Most Noble the Duke of Bellamy was exceptionally grand, containing not only a great double bed with a very high, straight back decorated in a somewhat sinister manner with rows of spindles, Gothic finials, vertical channeling, and carvings of birds, vines, flowers, and cornucopias; but also a commodious bureau, a tall marble-topped chiffonier, and a lofty double-doored wardrobe with a cornice that nearly reached the ceiling, all carved to match. The room was far grander than Clio's own quarters; but Clio, due to the distressing tenor of the conversation, neither noticed nor cared.

"I wish you would consider!" she insisted plaintively. "If you persist in this association with Sir Morgan, you will find your name being bandied about in the most odious way."

"You have no need to trouble yourself." The countess was sprawled inelegantly on the bed, her lame ankle propped on a mountain of pillows. Sir Morgan's liniment having been but recently applied, the room stank like a horse barn. "Since no one here *knows* my name, 'twould be no great catastrophe."

This unreasonable and extremely bird-witted attitude brought down further censure. "Oh, *la vache!*" swore Delphine, who was busy at an armoire constructed of walnut, with carved panels outlined in gold leaf. "Are you dedicated to being your own executioner, *ma cocotte?* Think of Clio, if you cannot think of yourself! You are thought to be a distant relative. Any scandal that touches you will also involve her, and there is an end to a grand marriage."

Tess propped herself up on an elbow and studied her sister who, seated on a lovely little chair on which were painted flowers in oil, inlaid with mother-of-pearl, and upholstered in white satin, was unusually glum. "Clio!" she exclaimed. "Have you been fretting yourself to flinders because you fear Sir Morgan will lead me into a scrape? He will not, I promise you."

If that rogue were to lead Tess anywhere, thought Clio unhappily, it would be up the garden path, and that possibility did not seem at all unlikely in view of the way he was reputedly throwing the hatchet at her. "He is a rough diamond," she said carefully. "A man with little regard for anything, and certainly not for propriety."

Tess's look of perpetual surprise grew into sheer astonishment. "Propriety?" she repeated, in tones of shock. "Good God, Clio!"

There was, perhaps, some cause for the countess's amazement. Mistress Clio's past career was so far uncharacterized by any notable regard for the conventions that she had barely been prevented on any number of occasions, most notable among them an episode concerning a handsome young under-gardener, from dragging the honorable Mildmay name straight through the mud. Clio did not consider this; her purpose, which did not promise to be easily achieved, was to prevent her sister from fixing her affections on a noted profligate. Clio was no stranger to the ways of gentlemen. Sir Morgan obviously meant, for some incomprehensible reason, to make Tess the object of a flirtation; he had already, though Tess might not realize it, taken her fancy to an alarming degree. "I could never look at him without a shudder," Clio added, somewhat unfairly. "You know that this acquaintance is not at all the thing, else you would have told me of the meeting, and not have left me to hear of it third-hand."

"Ah, that rankles, does it?" Tess smiled. "Forgive me, child! I did not know you wished to be my confidante." Idly, she ran her fingers through her masses of fair hair. "You are making mountains out of molehills, the pair of you! I assure you Sir Morgan nurtures for me no evil design." She glanced at Clio, who looked thoroughly unconvinced. "Think, child! If Sir Morgan cherishes romantic notions, it is doubtless for demure immorality in silk and fine linen, and *not* for a fubsy-faced old maid who is not at all in his style, being plain, highbrow, and awkward! I would not have you set your face so strongly against the man when he has been nothing but kind."

This fine logic did not achieve its desired effect but, if anything, the opposite. Clio looked at the countess and truly noticed her for the first time, not as Tess saw herself, a born spinster further condemned to that unenviable state by an insuperable handicap, but as Sir Morgan must see her, an exceptionally ethereal young woman with an unusual and appealing unworldliness.

"He is not the paragon you seem to think him!" Clio cried. "Not only is the man known for his eternal wenching, he is drawn to gaming and low life, and is no stranger to the night houses of Leicester Square and Charing Cross, the slums of the East End, the opium dens of the docks!"

"Gambling," Tess replied patiently, "is the national vice. How is it *you* are familiar with such wretched places?"

"I'm not!" Clio glowered. "But I do have ears, and I heard Sapphira complain that Sir Morgan has taken Drusilla to such places. Tess, can't you see that he is not a gentleman?"

"Have I claimed he is?" Tess looked quizzical. "You have no need to trouble yourself, Clio. I suppose it was from Drusilla that you learned I had encountered him again?"

Seeing no need to enlighten her sister as to the precise nature of that overheard conversation, during which Drusilla confided venomously to Constant that she wished nothing more than to be presented with Tess's head on a platter, Clio nodded gloomily. Little had she thought her sister's happiness would prove so difficult to arrange, or that Tess would prove so hot-at-hand. Clio had nurtured high hopes of the outcome of her sister's outing with the Duke of Bellamy; it was obvious to her knowledgeable eye that Giles was already half-smitten with Tess; and what must occur but that during it Tess should encounter Sir Morgan again! The Fates were against her, Clio thought. She had come to London to live a life of fashion and leisure, and to be entertained by the highest in the land; and it was imperative that she get Tess settled speedily so that she might get on with it.

"All men," announced Delphine abruptly, turning away from the armoire, "are constantly in search of prey. You must take a footman with you in the future, *ma cocotte!* It is imperative that you protect your reputation."

"*My* reputation?" Tess dissolved into helpless laughter, and Delphine scowled. "You are infected by Clio's sudden missishness, Daffy! Never have I been so diverted! But this is fustian, and I wish to hear no more. Let us speak of other things."

Fustian? thought Clio, but did not quibble lest Tess take one of her rare, but nonetheless alarming, distempered freaks. She wondered if Sir Morgan, among his other sins, might be a fortune hunter, seeing in Tess a rare opportunity to feather his nest. If so, he was hardly likely to listen to reason—Clio had already considered, as a last-ditch attempt to remove Tess from his clutches, appealing to Sir Morgan's better nature, providing he had one—and even less likely, thus petitioned, to whistle a fortune down the wind. The alternative, were Sir Morgan *not* on the lookout for a rich heiress, was even worse: he would play fast and loose with Tess, shattering her hopes in a diabolical manner that would leave her both broken-hearted and disgraced. Or, thought Clio, perhaps it was true that Sir Morgan believed Tess a mere adventuress, in which case he need not concern himself at all with her good name. She nibbled on the inside of her cheek. If only there were some way out of this coil!

Tess, who had grown weary with these various unflattering estimations of Sir Morgan's character and who, if truth be known, was not only unmoved by his attentions but eminently heart-whole, deftly changed the subject with an inquiry about Clio's shopping expedition, undertaken the day before in Lucille's company. It was not to be expected that Clio, who after all was long accustomed to be more than a little self-centered, should forgo this opportunity to wax enthusiastic about the new items of attire that she had bought, and the dizzying wonders that she'd seen. "It was beyond anything!" she concluded, clapping her hands. "Just think, Tess, everything is to be delivered in only a few days, for Sapphira has arranged that the ball will be this Friday. She sent out the invitations ages ago. It will be the first rout of the season, and the grandest, if Lucille is to be believed." She glanced at Delphine, who nodded. "You are also to attend," Clio added cautiously.

"*I?*" Tess, who had paid this enthusiastic diatribe little attention, looked horrified. "Nonsense, child."

"No, it's not!" Clio was mutinous. "Sapphira has agreed." That this concession had been made under great duress, and achieved only with Giles's support, she did not explain. "Do not argue, Tess! If you do not make an appearance, neither shall I, and no one shall make me for I will lock myself in my room!"

Tess, who had no notion of Clio's plans on her behalf, and who furthermore had never known that damsel to forgo any pleasure, was clearly bewildered. "Clio!" she protested weakly.

Clio had no intention of failing to appear at her own ball, which would not only bring her to the attention of polite society but which she intended to utilize to such good effect that she would become instantly the rage of the park, the ballroom, and the opera; but she knew the usefulness of her threat. She stuck out her lower lip and glowered terribly.

"But, Clio!" repeated Tess, no stranger to that mulish expression, which usually betokened a tantrum of awesome degree. "I have nothing to wear. And I would be extremely uncomfortable."

Mistress Clio had no interest whatsoever in her sister's

comfort or the lack thereof. "Yes, you do!" she cried triumphantly, grinning at Delphine. "You have any number of new things, including a ball dress! I ordered them yesterday."

"How could you?" Tess was visited by an unpleasant conviction that the reins of her life had been taken out of her hands.

"Easily!" crowed Clio. "Delphine gave me the measurements, and she will make whatever alterations are necessary. Nor need you worry that I will make you look a quiz, for even you have had to admit that I have excellent taste." No more drab grays and browns, she thought complacently. Clio was finding in herself a remarkable talent for management, and her thoughtfulness was in no way canceled out by the fact that she embarked upon the task of clothing her sister in the same frame of mind as she might the dressing of a favorite doll. "There! I have removed your last objection. You have no choice but to attend."

"I see." Tess was regarding her abigail with a look of one betrayed. "Very well, I will make you a bargain: I will attend this wretched ball, but on one condition. In the matter of Sir Morgan, you will say no more to me."

Clio considered this, and agreed. It was no great price to pay, since her words had thus far had little appreciable effect. She hoped Giles would be so overwhelmed by Tess's appearance in formal dress that he would be swept right off his feet, and that would be an end to the matter. The duke would be more than adequate competition for a rakish baronet. If not—and Clio frowned—there was but one other course left open, and that was the fixing of Sir Morgan's interest on herself. It was not at all what she wanted, but Clio supposed she might derive some little satisfaction from playing so deep a game.

"I've looked for you everywhere!" cried Evelyn, bursting without ceremony into the room. He looked unusually neat in a frilled shirt and nankeens, and even Nidget, at his heels, had been haphazardly groomed. "The horses have been waiting this age and if we do not hurry, Papa will be cross." Then he saw Tess, lying on the bed, enduring Nidget's violatile greeting. "Don't you mean to come along, Aunt Tess? I promise you Astley's is more fun than anything!"

"Aunt Tess," interrupted Clio, delighted that at least Evelyn had already succumbed to Tess's charm, "is not feeling particularly well. You shall come and tell her all about it when we return."

With this Evelyn had to be content. Clio smoothed her cottage vest of green sarsenet laced across the bosom and worn over a promenade dress of cambric muslin with wagoner's sleeves, made a final adjustment to her green velvet bonnet trimmed with white satin and coq feathers, and with her improbable escort sailed from the room.

"She's in good looks," remarked Tess, swinging her feet to the floor. "I make no doubt the Duke of Bellamy will be impressed."

If the servants' tittle-tattle was to be believed, the present duke was unlikely to be impressed by anything less than a highflyer of incomparable beauty, but Delphine did not explain that unpalatable fact to her mistress. Nor did she explain Clio's motives—for between that volatile miss and the disapproving abigail had evolved a tacit conspiracy—which were not to dazzle Giles but to lay the groundwork for a future *sortie*. *"Tiens!"* she said. "We will return to the subject of Sir Morgan, if you please!"

"But I do *not* please!" Tess yawned and reached for her cane. "I am growing positively sick of the man's name. Poor thing! To be the object of such constant calumny."

Delphine was not so easily deceived. "That one is bound for perdition. Take care you do not accompany him, *cherie!*"

"I would not like to accuse you of impertinence, Daffy." Tess's voice was firm. "You will speak not another word to me on this matter. Now leave me! I wish to be alone." Delphine exited, muttering darkly.

The countess breathed a deep sigh of relief, then crossed the room to a carved rosewood dressing table cradled between deeply in-flaring cabriole legs. She did not pause to inspect herself in the elegant mirror between the cabinets, illuminated at night by six candles growing out of flower baskets, as Clio would automatically have done, but rummaged in a drawer. When she withdrew her hand, diamonds sparkled on her palm.

Clutching this bounty, Tess limped back to the bed, then spread the gems out on the counterpane, there not to regard them with pride or greed, but with speculation. Nor did she place them around her neck and preen, as a vainer woman would have done.

It was not that Tess disliked such baubles as this necklace—she possessed several such pieces, of no lesser worth—but this particular item had never resided in the jewel case that Delphine guarded so zealously. The countess had never set eyes on this necklace before the previous night, when she had found it inexplicably resting among the items of intimate apparel packed in her portmanteau.

"The intruder at the inn," she murmured thoughtfully, and poked the necklace with an inquisitive finger. As is the way with such cold stones, it made no response. "Doubtless *he* was responsible! The highwaymen accosted us in an attempt to recover it."

It was a reasonable explanation, so far as it went; none other than that intruder had gained access to her portmanteau. But why? Perhaps she was meant to innocently transport the necklace to London, there to be reclaimed; but if so, why the confrontation with highwaymen? Perhaps—and she poked the gems again—there was not one party involved, but two, and both determined on possession of the necklace. It was probably stolen; there was little question but that someone was desperate to reclaim it, and would try again.

A more prudent lady would have immediately turned over the necklace to Bow Street, there to be dealt with by those stalwart representatives of the law; Tess didn't even consider so poor-spirited an action. It was speedily coming clear to the countess that her life—having hitherto consisted of such tame pursuits as walking before breakfast, picking flowers, riding, reading, sketching, and playing the harpsichord—had lacked a certain excitement; and that it had changed drastically, and for the better, in the past few days. It was also clear to her that Sir Morgan was in some way connected with the necklace. Had he stolen it, she mused, and fearing discovery arranged for an accomplice to hide it in her luggage? If so, he'd had no need to arrange for that futile attempt at highway robbery. Had he but asked, Tess would have cheerfully returned the necklace to him. It was not her place to interrogate or condemn.

But why, she wondered, making her slow way to the window, should Sir Morgan have stolen the gems in the first place? Were his affairs in such a sad case? Or perhaps he had not stolen them at all, and they had come into his possession by some unexceptionable means, and he was behaving in such a circuitous manner to protect someone else. It was all most puzzling, and marvelously intriguing. Tess didn't know when anything had so exercised her mind.

She stared unseeing into the gardens below. It was the necklace, naturally, that prompted Morgan's interest in her, but she could hardly explain *that* to Clio and Delphine! Their objections seemed ridiculous to Tess, who saw no reason to hold the man's reputation against him. Of course he was a rake; how could he be otherwise when his charm was so great that few women would find themselves indifferent to it? In truth, Tess was far from disliking him herself, though her approval had been earned by his easy manner and his superb horsemanship, and not by his expertise in affairs of the heart. It was not that she doubted that expertise; indeed, she knew instinctively that Sir Morgan bowled over feminine hearts like tenpins; but it was an arena from which, due to her limp, she was permanently disbarred. Tess wondered why this fact, which she had accepted all her life, should suddenly make her melancholy.

No matter! She returned to her bed, picked up the jewels, and locked them safely away. Sir Morgan had entrusted her with the necklace, for whatever reasons, and she would keep it for him until he requested its return. The countess was not of a temperament to envision bogymen lurking behind each bush, and not of a cast of mind to condemn her fellow man; she no more considered that possession of stolen jewels placed her in a very ticklish situation than she berated Sir Morgan for involving her in an undertaking that was dangerous. In fact, Tess's overall view of this abominable fix was that here was adventure more exciting than any she'd ever dreamed.

# Chapter 8

*Sir Morgan,* had he been privileged to know of it, might have been highly diverted by the fact that he was playing havoc with the thoughts of three highly disparate females; but that gentleman, accustomed from the cradle to making mincemeat of ladylike scruples, wasted little time in contemplating his conquests, particularly not when engaged at Gentleman Jackson's Bond Street boxing saloon, where he displayed himself to such good advantage that several young bucks were stricken with severe cases of hero worship and determined on the spot to emulate him. A regular out-and-outer was Sir Morgan, up to all the rigs, with a very handy bunch of fives; and if his reputation in other matters was a trifle unsavory, it was not to be regarded in so notable a Corinthian.

It was not Sir Morgan's reputation that concerned Drusilla, but his conduct toward herself, which had been a great deal more circumspect than she cared to admit. At first Drusilla had tried to convince herself that such restraint sprang from the high regard in which he held her, but she was speedily forced to admit that this air-dreaming was unworthy of even her young nephew. Morgan might allow her to accompany him on explorations of the worst parts of town; he might gratify her by appearing at her side at routs and balls when no more exotic entertainment was at hand; but he never by so much as a word or gesture indicated that his emotions were seriously involved. Drusilla was being driven frantic by such elusiveness; and her temper was further exacerbated by the marked approval that he displayed toward Tess. Since the countess could hardly enlighten the world regarding the nature of that interest—to wit, one valuable diamond necklace—Drusilla planned and schemed.

As did Mistress Clio, halfway across the town, and with such fervor that she was oblivious of the signal honor accorded her in being transported in the duke's phaeton highflyer with its towering wheels and yellow wings, a vehicle that was hardly designed to hold two adults, a child, and a large dog, but which Evelyn apostrophized as being bang-up to the nines. Clio was also blind to the various fascinations of London as expounded upon by that lad, including traveling fairs with mountebanks and bearded women and wirewalkers, Punch-and-Judy entertainments, dancing bears, and circus menageries. So preoccupied was Clio that she didn't even spare a glance for one of London's splendid mail coaches, painted maroon and black with scarlet wheels, the royal coat of arms emblazoned on its doors.

They arrived at last at Astley's Royal Amphitheater, in Lambeth's Westminster Bridge Road. Though the exterior was unimposing, being fashioned of ships' masts and spars with a canvas ceiling stretched on fir poles and lashed together with ropes, Clio was informed by the duke that Astley's—which had been founded in the previous century as a riding school and the first Royal Circus—had been twice burned down and rebuilt only a few years past as the handsomest pleasure haunt in London. Evelyn promised that the sights to be seen within were little short of miraculous. Nidget wagged his tail enthusiastically.

"Astley's," added the duke, after assuring the burly individual who appeared to be in charge that Nidget was docile and well-behaved and could be trusted to neither bark nor slip his leash, "is noted for entertainments based on horsemanship and superb equestrian feats." Clio looked puzzled. "Trick riding," he explained, exhibiting neither dismay at her ignorance nor any hint of the boredom that constantly plagued him.

"How nice." Clio wondered how to introduce the various matters that concerned her. Had Mistress Clio been one to pass time in contemplation of the masculine admiration which came her way, she might have found it odd —as would many of the duke's acquaintances—that so top-lofty a gentleman should engage himself for several hours in such mundane pursuits and with such lowly company. However, she did not question it, and looked around her with curiosity.

The interior of the amphitheater was truly splendid, especially when viewed from their vantage seat, and lit by a huge chandelier containing fifty patent lamps. Clio stared at the ring of sawdust, separated from the orchestra on a very large stage and framed by a proscenium arch as high as the gallery above the three tiers of boxes; then turned to glance at Evelyn, chattering in his excitement like a magpie. "It is a pity," she said, abruptly taking the plunge, "that my, uh, companion could not accompany us. Tess likes horses more than almost anything."

"She is certainly an accomplished rider," replied Giles smoothly, after warning Evelyn to keep firm hold of his misbegotten hound. "For which I'm sure you deserve no little credit. You are very good to your companion, cousin! I hope she is grateful for it."

"I am?" inquired Clio, mystified.

"Come, come, cousin! You needn't be modest with *me*, although I'm sure it does you credit." There was a disturbing twinkle in the duke's dark eye. "Few females in your friend's position would have the opportunity to gain such expertise. Her duties must be very light."

"Oh, *that*!" Clio laughed rather hollowly. This deception was proving horridly difficult to maintain. "Tess is no mere servant, Your Grace! She has been like an elder sister to me."

"I repeat, it does you credit. There are many who would find such a creature—I refer to her disability, of course!—painful to look upon."

Clio frowned. This attitude was not only uncharitable, it did not bode well for her plans. "Pooh!" she said. "*I* do not regard it, and I am surprised that you should! Tess is the most excellent of companions—and, anyway, it is vulgar to be always looking joyful and full of glee and to be tearing about like a madcap."

"True," agreed Giles, chastised.

"I do not think," added Clio, skillfully laying siege, "that anyone could consider Tess vulgar! It would be most unfortunate if *you* were to hold her in such poor esteem, when she thinks so highly of you."

"She does?" The duke raised his brows.

"She does." Blithely, Clio perjured herself. "Tess and I are close friends, you know, and she confided to me that she greatly enjoys your company."

"Oh?" Clio was encouraged by the duke's startled expression. "Then I am flattered."

"And so should you be!" It occurred to Clio that so proud a gentleman was hardly likely to consider allying himself with a woman of Tess's supposed situation in life. "I will tell you, though I should not, that Tess is a great deal more than she seems."

"Ah!" Giles looked suitably intrigued. "The mystery of her birth, I apprehend?"

"Exactly!" Clio was pleased with his intelligence. "You understand that I can say nothing now—circumstances prohibit my speaking—but I hope to soon make the entire matter clear. And *then* Tess may take her rightful place in Society!" Carried away with her own inventiveness, Clio sighed. "Poor Tess! To be denied her true station for so long."

"One might almost," the duke offered obligingly, "call it a tragedy."

"Definitely a tragedy! You have no idea." Clio lowered her voice. "I trust you to say nothing of this, but when that happy day dawns, my dear Tess will not be considered ineligible for marriage with any lord in the land."

"Marriage?" Giles looked positively fascinated. "She is on the lookout for a husband, then?"

Clio laughed merrily. "What woman isn't?" she parried, speaking for herself. "It must be very depressing to find oneself on the shelf." She leaned closer. "It is not only Tess's birth that renders her eminently eligible! It must remain our secret, but my companion is not without means."

Giles might have asked why such a paragon should so efface herself but, being of a Mephistophelean disposition and finding in Mistress Clio's utterances greater artistry than in the spectacles being enacted in the sawdust ring, he refrained. "Cousin," he remarked, with the utmost sincerity, "you astonish me! I would like to hear more of this companion of yours."

"Alas," mourned Clio, her imaginative powers exhausted, "I can say no more! In truth, I have already told you far too much! I beg you will not reveal to Tess your awareness of her situation." Upon receiving his assurance that his lips were sealed, she allowed herself a sad little smile. "I shall miss her sadly. Tess is the perfect companion, always understanding perfectly what one means to say and entering into one's sentiments, always willing to listen to one's troubles and offer sound advice—the ideal person with whom to share one's life, in short!"

Whereas Tess would have been startled half out of her wits by this paean, Giles only smiled. "She is also," he added, "an extremely beautiful woman."

"I suppose she is," agreed Clio doubtfully. It was decidedly promising that the duke should think so, but she could hardly be expected to view her sister in that light, being accustomed from her childhood to thinking herself the Beauty of the family. "She's not in the common way, at any rate."

"She's so far from it," Giles said wryly, "that she has caught my friend Morgan's eye, and that is no small accomplishment, cousin—as could be attested by any number of women who have been trying unsuccessfully to do so for years."

Clio regarded him with dismay. "What of Drusilla? I thought she and Sir Morgan were as good as betrothed."

"Drusilla would like to think so." Those of his cronies who would have been startled to see the Duke of Bellamy in such surroundings would have been further stunned by the knowledge that he was thoroughly enjoying himself. "They are already long married off by rumor, but the truth is that Morgan is highly unlikely to marry anyone. He is entirely too set in bachelor ways."

Clio refrained from informing the duke that Sir Morgan's habits were more those of the most depraved libertine than of a harmless bachelor, and strove valiantly to disguise the fact that his offhand statement had made the blood run cold in her veins. "Morgan," continued the duke, setting the seal on her distress, "professes that it is not in his nature to think of the future, which he leaves to take care of itself. He worries as little about his responsibilities as he counts his possessions and his wealth."

"Wealth," repeated Clio, seizing upon the opportunity to learn more of the man. "I suppose Sir Morgan must be plump in the pocket or he would not gamble to such an extent." Giles looked inquiring. "Your mother has said that he is a fearless plunger, willing to gamble on anything from the turn of a card to a race between flies crawling up a wall."

"My dear cousin," retorted Giles drily, "rid yourself of the notion that those who play at the board of green cloth are invariably well-heeled! More often they are not. If a man's ambition is to break the bank it is a great advantage to him if he's richer than the bank, for no one dares play double or quits with a gamester who can afford to go on losing till he wins; but it is not invariably the case."

"Morgan," offered Evelyn, rapt upon the sawdust ring, where a clever monkey performed on horseback, "is a regular Trojan!"

"So he is, you impertinent puppy!" agreed Giles, and turned his attention to the performance. It was not the monkey who caught his lordship's errant eye, but a lovely bespangled lady who accomplished stunning feats with a broadsword.

"Sir Morgan?" Clio prompted subtly. "So his pockets are to let?"

"I did not say that." The Duke of Bellamy's gaze returned to her, she thought reluctantly. "Morgan plays hard and plunges deep, but he contrives to be beforehand with the world. For all he wastes the ready, I doubt he is in difficulties. I cannot say if his estates are encumbered, but he's certainly not at *point non plus*." He looked stern. "Are you developing a *tendre* for Morgan, cousin? It is a piece of impudence on my part, but I should advise you to hold my friend at arm's length."

"You misunderstand!" Clio blushed, quite mortified at this assumption that she held warm feelings for a man who she thought never ought to have been allowed to glimpse the light of day. "The first occasion when I met him at the inn was a very curious one, but I was not at all taken with his manner! Sir Morgan's behavior is that of a man who has neither good nature, honesty, nor common sense."

"I see," murmured Giles, with patent disbelief. Clio reminded herself sternly that it was his opinion of Tess that signified, not of herself. "Tell me, cousin," she said hastily, "are you also a gamester, like your friend?"

"I?" The duke smiled, a charming exercise. "I am hardly a gamester, as you call it, although I belong to several clubs where gambling is the members' main occupation. It is an amusing pastime."

"It seems very odd to me," ventured Clio.

"My dear," replied the duke, at his most aloof, "it is a man's world."

Yes, thought Clio, and the Duke of Bellamy was so proud as to despise the opinion of that world altogether as regarded himself. Yet he was also the highest of sticklers, and would tolerate no unconventional behavior in anyone else. Clio thought of her sister and experienced a severe qualm as to the wisdom of the course she had embarked upon, for even Tess's most devoted friends could not deny that the countess was prone to eccentricities. Clio truly believed she had so far played her cards excellently with her handsome cousin. If only Tess could be trusted not to completely bungle the thing!

It was true that Clio had caught the duke's interest with her Canterbury Tales, but Giles was not one to long dwell upon patent taradiddles. No sooner had Clio ceased speaking than his thoughts flew immediately to the problems that plagued England, the countless unemployed, the starvation level of wages and soaring rates of taxation, the riots and machine-smashings that had broken out in industrial regions. Since Evelyn was equally preoccupied, rapt upon a stunning display of equestrian showmanship, it was not surprising that Nidget should have found it easy to slip away.

His absence did not go long unnoted, being as he made his way straight for the sawdust ring, there to wreak happy havoc among the performers, barking ferociously at the monkeys, snapping enthusiastically at the horses' heels, causing the bespangled lady to narrowly miss a grievous mishap with her broadsword. "Nidget!" cried Evelyn. His voice was lost in the pandemonium. "The deuce!" uttered the duke, gloomily.

It was some time before peace could be restored, Nidget so greatly enjoying this new pastime that he was only with great difficulty restrained; and an even longer time before the duke, via the distribution of great largesse, had soothed the ruffled tempers of those disparate individuals who clamored for the mongrel's blood. "Nidget only meant to be helpful!" explained Evelyn as the small party was somewhat ungraciously escorted outside. "He thought the horses were running loose and he was herding them!"

"Ah!" retorted the duke, with unruffled *sang-froid.* "Why didn't *I* think of that? It explains all! Next you will tell me that the beast should be praised instead of condemned!" Hopefully, Nidget groveled at his feet.

"Well, he should!" In crowing spirits, Evelyn grinned. "It was very brave of him."

"Young cawker!" Giles bestowed upon the dog a severe look. "All the same, you and that abominable cur will go home in a hired hack, Evelyn! And it will go the worse for you if I so much as set eyes on that mongrel again today."

Evelyn accepted this sign of severe disfavor with no lessening of spirit; to ride alone in a job-carriage was no small treat. "Yes, sir!" said he.

Having satisfactorily procured a hack, and having instructed the driver to take Evelyn, no matter what that young man might request, straight to Berkeley Square, the duke assisted Clio into his phaeton. "My son," he apologized, "is something of an imp, and that dog is a curst nuisance. I trust you will forgive them for the unpleasant interruption of our outing."

Clio might have informed her cousin that Tess had a

great fondness for rag-mannered mongrels and mischievous boys; she might have told him that she herself had no great appreciation of equestrian displays; but she did neither of these things. Mistress Clio was an ardent admirer of the opposite sex, and flirting was as natural to her as breathing. "I would not have you distress yourself, your grace!" she replied, with a coquettish glance that was as effective as it was absent-minded. "I have enjoyed myself vastly. As for Evelyn and his dog, they are high-spirited perhaps, but delightful all the same."

"It is you who are delightful," responded Giles, with a look that sent Clio's senses pleasantly reeling. "It was a happy day when you appeared at Bellamy House." Clio stared. "I had not known that I was bored," he explained kindly, "until my tedium was enlivened by a dazzling young woman who is as enchanting as she is incorrigible."

"You refer to Tess, of course," said Clio cautiously.

"No, cousin!" retorted the duke, a distinct warmth in his eye. "I refer to you."

"Palaverer!" Clio's merry laughter did not quite disguise a certain violence of feeling. "I don't know why you should think you must flatter me."

"I *don't* think it," the duke replied cordially. Clio saw instantly how it would be: she was the most unfortunate of beings, destined to perish in her own intrigues.

# Chapter 9

*Lady Tess could not have said* why she continued with her masquerade, now that Clio promised to catapult her into the social whirl that she had wished to avoid. It was not because she feared to be courted for her wealth; Tess had no expectation of being courted at all. Nor was it because the polite world, which might heap upon a limping serving-wench ridicule and scorn, would observe a countess thus afflicted with pity, a thing above all others that Tess abhorred. The most likely explanation, as Tess's own mother would have immediately observed, had she not been twenty years dead and consequently incapable of communicating her wisdom, was that the Countess of Lansbury had taken the bit between her teeth and was bent on kicking up a lark for no more worthy motive than sheer perversity.

Tess's inquisitiveness had led her to tour Bellamy House, a structure which she immediately condemned as the worst of its kind, with painted paneling and gilded fireplaces and countless stairways which, since the kitchens were in the basement and the house contained additional stories for eating, sleeping, and entertaining, the servants continually and laboriously climbed. Nonetheless, despite all the damnable steps, Tess had found her way into the kitchens and was now enthroned in a huge armchair that was reserved for the staff's leisure moments.

The expedition had not been without its burlesque incidents, including a confrontation with Sapphira, who had expounded at some length upon her son's passion for quality in everything and then, lest her meaning be mistaken, had added that the duke's kindness was not to be misconstrued as anything warmer than sympathy for a female who limped, a warning that Tess had accepted so cheerfully that the dowager duchess recognized her instantly as a Paphian girl set on ensnaring Giles and had erupted into terrible rage, wishing Tess to the devil and ordering her to her room. As if that were not terrible enough, Tess next encountered Constant, who quickly made it clear that he would enjoy a rather heavy-handed flirtation with her behind his wife's back. It was with great relief that Tess escaped to the nether regions where, if she was not precisely greeted with open arms, the household servants being too well accustomed to the dowager's vicious temper to welcome any interruption of their established routine, she at least felt at home.

"So you can tell me no more about Mirian," mused Tess. "It seems singularly odd that she should never have mentioned Sapphira—or, indeed, any member of the household!"

"By the Holy I cannot." Mrs. Bibby, a plump and comfortable matron with brown eyes and gray hair, sank into the armchair on the other side of the fireplace, from which vantage point she could keep a wary eye on the cook who was engaged in the creation of a blancmange. "She had a restlessness upon her, did Miss Mirian, from the time she was a slip of a colleen, but arragh! 'Twas not I who'd be thinkin' she'd steal off into the gloamin' in such a huggermugger style, never to be seen or heard of again. Turned us topsy-turvy, she did and all. But I never believed for a minute she'd eloped with a gentleman."

"Was there one?" asked Tess, intrigued. "A particular gentleman?"

"Ach!" clucked Mrs. Bibby, "Of course there was. Like bees to a honey pot they flocked, from the day she left the nursery. Ye'd not be knowin', but Lady Clio has a great look of our Miss Mirian at that age."

Tess gazed unseeing about the kitchen, a dark and cheerless place containing deal tables and a dresser, chairs on which the servants took their meals, a huge range filled with ovens and broilers which must, she thought, consume enormous quantities of coal. In the big wooden sink were batteries of iron and copper saucepans, frying pans, skillets, skimmers, and sieves of varied fineness; arranged on the counter were fancy molds for puddings, jellies, and aspic dishes, preserving pans, bread tins, and milk bowls.

Almost as numerous as these utensils—which, alas, did not guarantee the quality of the meals served at Bellamy House, the cook being both nervous and inexperienced—was the kitchen staff. All of them, from the maid who was baiting odd-looking curved-sided tins with brown sugar to, she hoped, entrap the huge black beetles she'd found thick around the fireplace that morning, to the housemaid who was rubbing the stove with scouring paper, to the cook herself, were blatantly listening. "You forgot the ground almonds," Tess commented idly, and the cook started, then stared at her blancmange. Cream, lemon peel and cinnamon, sugar and isinglass—she flushed. The intruder was right. "What do you garnish it with?"

At this unheard-of interference, the cook flushed beet-red. "Stewed pears or quinces, m'lady."

"Excellent," Tess approved. "Currant jelly, or jam or marmalade are also very good." Unaware that she had demonstrated a rare ability to deal with servants, the countess returned her attention to the housekeeper. "Do you know, Mrs. Bibby, I've thought of something odd. Someone *must* have known of Mirian's whereabouts; certainly her man of business did. Mirian had her own funds; there had to be some correspondence when they were initially transferred. Would he have kept it from the family?"

Mrs. Bibby knew nothing of such matters, holding that mysterious institution known as "the Exchange" in a deep reverence shared only with the Almighty; but she did know human nature. If this inquisitive woman was a penniless dependent Mrs. Bibby was prepared to eat her favorite hat, a lavish concoction consisting of a great deal of purple satin, frilled and ruched, topped by ostrich feathers of a virulent pink. "Sure and my mind's away entirely!" she exclaimed. "The old duke—his lordship's father, that is—was alive then, miss! He'd have known, if anyone; he'd a great liking for the colleen." She sighed reminiscently. "A great man, a dear man he was."

Tess did not pursue this topic, though she suspected that relations between Giles's father and Mrs. Bibby had been a great deal warmer than the association between a duke and his housekeeper should be. Little wonder, she reflected, recalling Sapphira's wicked tongue. "We shall probably never know." Grasping the cane, she rose awkwardly. "A pity, but there it is."

Mrs. Bibby was not immune to the sight of Tess struggling with her cane. "Dinna fash yourself, hinnie! There's one other person as might know, and that's Miss Mirian's closest friend, Celest. A regular slyboots *she* was, and meant for no good end. It's sorry I am, m'lady, but I cannot tell you more than that."

"Not even Celest's last name?" Tess was engaged in valiant combat with the coconut matting that covered the kitchen floor.

"Nay." Mrs. Bibby was no fool; this queer miss was more accustomed to issuing orders than to obeying them and, furthermore, a great deal more interested in the long-departed Mirian than made sense. She grimaced. It was not without the practice of considerable guile that Mrs. Bibby had so long held her high position in Bellamy House; much as she liked Tess, she liked her comforts more. A shame the girl had brought her questions into the kitchen, but there it was: the dowager duchess would have to be told.

Tess, mounting the steep stairs with grim determination, had no presentiment that she would be in need of good wishes, and soon. She was thinking of Clio, who seemed simultaneously blue-deviled and jubilant. Tess would have been startled to learn that the capricious Clio had discovered a great partiality for a particular gentleman; and positively stunned to discover that she herself was in a position to blight her sister's romance. The countess puzzled briefly over Clio's conduct, then dismissed it. Her young sister forever wavered between being in the boughs and in the dumps. Tess achieved the top of the stairs, and idly made her way along the hallway.

She did not mean to move with particular stealth, but the thick rug muffled the sounds of her halting footsteps and her cane; she certainly did not intend to eavesdrop, but the door to the front drawing-room stood slightly ajar and voices issued from within.

"More fool you!" growled Drusilla savagely. "That girl is fast worming her way into Sapphira's good graces. You know what must be done."

These intrigue-fraught remarks would have sounded a death-knell for the scruples of a far more conventional lady than Tess. She moved to the wall and stood staring, she hoped with apparent appreciation, at a masterful rendition of a gentleman in sixteenth-century attire. A Bellamy ancestor, she thought, regarding his nose. What the devil did Drusilla mean to do about Clio, and why?

"Myself," muttered Constant, seated again in the spindly little chair, "I think it's a damned hum."

With an oath Drusilla flung aside *The Lady's Magazine,* having derived little enlightenment from an article entitled "High Life and Fashionable Chit Chat." Like an agitated tigress, she stalked up and down the room.

"My patience is exhausted!" she snarled. "Are you so blind you cannot see what stares you in the face? It must be so, since you continue to live far beyond your income."

"I suppose *you* don't!" retorted Constant, following her handsome figure as best he could with his eyes, the high points of his shirt collar making it impossible to turn his head, and recalling rather unhappily the vast sums of money that he owed Messrs. Howard and Grubbs, moneylenders much patronized by the fashionable world. "You're just annoyed because Sapphira has said you must play goosebody."

Drusilla battled a strong urge to lay violent hands on her blockish brother-in-law. "My mother," she remarked, suppressing her blood-thirst only through heroic effort, "doted on Mirian. I suppose had Mirian not run away she might have figured in Sapphira's will—but, try as she might, Sapphira was never able to trace her one step."

Constant, prey to an unwelcome notion, let his mouth drop open.

"Precisely!" said Drusilla. "You are a vain, silly fellow, Constant, but you understand well enough once things are explained. Now Mirian's daughter has turned up, with her oddities of manner and *sauvageries* that are so strongly reminiscent of her mother, and with her silly little head turned by the exaggerated praises that have been bestowed on her. I do not intend that history should repeat itself! Should Clio, too, settle on Giles, she willl have made a *most* unfortunate choice."

Tess, in the hallway, frowned at Drusilla's tone, which was absolutely ominous. Did Clio, by her presence, somehow present a threat to the other members of the family? Or was it Clio herself who was threatened and, if so, by whom? Drusilla? Giles?

"So we must move to prevent it," concluded Constant ponderously. "But how? There's the rub."

"I've told you how." Drusilla resumed her impatient pacing.

"Yes," agreed Constant, "and I don't like it above half!" Drusilla's fidgeting made him uneasy, suggesting as it did violence barely held in leash. "There must be another way."

"I flatter myself," snapped Drusilla, "that I'm a trifle less empty in the cockloft than *you*! Don't try to outthink me, Constant, it is beyond you." She smiled unpleasantly. "I fear my dear cousin Clio's nervous agitations are destined to grow to serious heights."

Constant was not eager to give the reins over to Drusilla, whose tendency to rush her fences was likely to send them both tumbling head over heels. "There's always Sir Morgan," he ventured hopefully.

"Morgan?" demanded Drusilla, with more than a touch of irritation. "What has Morgan to do with this?"

"He could have everything to do with it." Constant leered. "I'm sure the Wicked Baronet would be happy to do you a favor."

Drusilla, having the advantage of long acquaintance with the gentleman in question, was more inclined to the view that Morgan obliged no one but himself. "*What* favor?"

"Why, to take Clio off our hands! If Sir Morgan were to make the girl the object of a flirtation, Giles wouldn't stand a chance."

Drusilla considered this bizarre notion, and found it abhorrent. "Rot!" she replied. "You forget that Morgan has a penchant for clever women. Clio would bore him unutterably within an hour."

"It might still be worth a try," Constant persevered. He had a great admiration for Morgan, as a result of that gentleman's legendary escapades. "He seems to like the other wench well enough, by your own account."

"Morgan is amusing himself." With admirable nonchalance, Drusilla shrugged. "Tess has a superior understanding, or so he claims, and he would revel in the speculative glances cast in his direction while he conversed with her. I suspect, too, that she is rather fast; Morgan would not waste time where he was not sure of eventual conquest."

"You are mighty unconcerned." Constant was not so short of wit that he did not suspect that Drusilla was severely disturbed. "It seems to me that your cavalier has taken a fancy to the wench."

"Nonsense!" Drusilla raised her brows. "I believe I know Morgan better than you do. He may be totally lacking in principle, but he possesses a strong sense of propriety. He may lead the girl on, even to the point of prompting her to toss her hat over the windmill for him; but once she has shown herself not immune, and in the process given rise to a great deal of scandal-broth, he will abruptly lose interest. Clio's companion will be left to wear the willow for him, and I'm sure it will be no more than she deserves."

"And you don't care a button for it!" jeered Constant, stricken with admiration for her cold-bloodedness.

"I hope," replied Drusilla stiffly, "that I am not entirely heartless! I remonstrated with Morgan after that first occasion in the park, for this Tess is not the sort of female to sustain the crushing blow that Morgan will inevitably deal her; but he merely laughed and seemed not in the least affected by the event." She lifted her hands and gracefully let them fall. "I do not see that I should be expected to do more."

"Certainly not." Constant recalled the brusque manner in which Tess had dealt with his kindly advances, a manner not at all in keeping with her lowly position in the world, and thought it would do her a great deal of good to be brought down a couple of pegs. "All the same, I find it in myself to pity the wench."

The wench, in the hallway, had swung around to gaze with mingled anger and horror at the doorway. With her back thus presented to the stairs, she did not remark the arrival of a caller, and consequently started so dreadfully that she dropped her cane when the visitor at last spoke in her ear.

"Eavesdroppers," murmured Sir Morgan, catching her by the shoulders, "cannot expect to hear good of themselves, little one! A superlative amount of nonsense can in this manner come to one's ears."

"Oh?" Tess leaned against the wall as he stooped to retrieve her cane. "I was merely admiring this painting. And I do not see why you persist in calling me 'little' when I am far from small!"

Sir Morgan did not question the fact that an unremarkable painting should bring such heat to her cheeks or so angry a sparkle to her eye. "You *are* tall for a woman," he conceded, with only the slightest of smiles. "What would you have me call you, then? 'Countess'? Or, perhaps, 'Lady Tess'?"

"No, no!" Tess protested hastily. Sir Morgan was regarding her with an amused understanding that made her wish to slap his face. It was quite marvelous, in view of the various pieces of information she had gleaned during the past hour, that she should recall the necklace hidden in her portmanteau, but remember it she did. Perhaps, she mused, it was the light in the hallway that made Sir Morgan's tawny eyes seem suddenly to glitter like those gems.

"I think, sir," she said gruffly, "that I have unwittingly come into possession of something that belongs to you."

"I believe you have," agreed Sir Morgan. With a quizzical expression, and a great deal of impropriety, he gently brushed back the curls that had tumbled onto her forehead. "But I had not expected you to be aware of it, little one."

# Chapter 10

*The Dowager Duchess of Bellamy's elegant barouche* wound its way through the busy crowds that thronged the streets of London's fashionable West End. It passed by tall houses that overhung the streets, shops with gleaming plate-glass windows filled with silverware and engravings, books and paints and fine glass; and stopped at last in Piccadilly, at the entrance to Bond Street, where houses and shops faced each other across a narrow carriage-way.

"You may pick us up in Oxford Street," said Lucille to her coachman, as a footman assisted her to alight. Clio and Tess followed in a mutual silence that, had she known them better, would have stricken Lucille as queer. She did not, however, yet realize that Mistress Clio was a chatterbox, or that Tess's sad habit was to talk aloud to herself, and consequently considered them both prettily behaved. They were also, she thought, subjecting themselves to a critical eye, as they were unexceptionably attired. Clio looked smart as paint in a pink and white striped percale half-dress with a flowered embroidered border and white ruchings, with green knots of ribbon on the mameluke sleeves and gored skirt, and a bonnet to match. Tess, too, looked very nice in a figured muslin gown worn with blue kid shoes, a bonnet of white thread-net trimmed with lace, kid gloves and reticule, all of which had been procured for her by Clio. If only she didn't limp, concluded Lucille, the girl might do very well.

It was not Lucille's habit to question the obvious, and

thus she did not join the rest of her family in puzzling over why Clio should be so determined to push her companion forward. Nor was Lucille, for all she knew the intricacies of fashion to a nicety, accustomed to applying those precepts to herself. What little money there was for such frivolities was spent in Constant's efforts to peacock it over his acquaintances. Lucille did not mind her husband's spendthrift ways any more than she minded that he appeared a figure of ridicule. She had married him on impulse, in hope of escaping the house in Berkeley Square to embark upon a life of her own; it had not served, and Constant had proved a lamentable failure as a provider. For the fact that her husband's fishlike eye often strayed to other women, and for the existence of the plump and middle-aged widow who served his more unmentionable needs, Lucille was grateful. Truth be told, she disliked Constant very much.

"My cousin has told me about Bond Street," offered Clio, with little hope that her sister would take up the gambit. The entire household knew that Sir Morgan had encountered Tess in the hallway of Bellamy House, and had been discovered by Drusilla and Constant in an improper attitude. "This, and St. James's Street, are the province of the gentlemen. No woman who values her reputation is seen here in the afternoon."

"By your cousin, I assume you mean Giles?" Tess asked innocently. The gentlemen, she reflected, certainly possessed a knack for having things their own way.

"Yes." Clio glanced at the countess. "Tess, he is the *nicest* man! And he has a high regard for you."

"Has he?" Tess asked absently. She was thinking not of the estimable Duke of Bellamy, but of his reprehensible friend. Morgan, on discovery, had merely laughed and released her, going to join Drusilla and Constant in the drawing-room while Tess fled. A hairsbreadth escape! she thought wryly. Whatever else the Wicked Baronet might be, he was not easily discomfited.

"Oh, yes!" gushed Clio. They strolled along Bond Street, past a music shop and a picture gallery and a silversmith, pausing while Lucille made several purchases from Mr. Savory, the apothecary. "He has told me so."

"How nice." Tess gazed at the smart hotels, Long's at the corner of Clifford Street, and Steven's on the corner opposite, both with saddle horses and tilburies outside. Lady Tess liked the duke well enough, but she had certain more pressing matters on her mind.

"I *do* wish you'd listen to me!" wailed Clio, so intent on her own pursuits that she failed to notice the approving glances cast her by several Bond Street beaux. "And I wish you wouldn't constantly refuse to go along with us! I don't like these outings half so well when you won't come."

This bizarre remark earned Tess's full attention; in the past Clio had many times complained that the countess was forever at her heels like a guard dog. "Oh?" said Tess, with commendable restraint. "It is *your* season, child, not mine! I am thought to be your companion, if you recall."

"Whose doing was that?" snapped Clio. "I wish you would reconsider, Tess, and own up to the sham." Much easier then, she thought, to make Giles see the countess's worth.

"Never!" Tess retorted immediately, unconsciously thrusting a spoke into her sister's wheel. "It is you who should consider, Clio! Sapphira would be so furious at being taken in that she would doubtless close her door to us, and then where would we be?"

"We could take a house of our own," Clio insisted stubbornly, "and *you* could bring me out."

"No, my dear, I couldn't," Tess interrupted firmly, before this notion could take hold. "For one thing, I doubt there are any decent houses left for hire—mothers bringing their daughters to London for a season will be already established, you know! Even more important, I am not known here, and could not procure you the *entrée* into society."

Clio sighed and toyed with her sunshade. Abominably difficult, these efforts on behalf of someone else! She wondered why she had ever undertaken such a thing, which was resulting in little more than cutting up her peace. Once set on a course, however, Clio was not one to admit defeat. "Wouldn't it be nice," she persisted, with a devious wistfulness, "to live all the time in a grand establishment like Bellamy House, with servants to wait on one hand and foot, and to move in the first ranks of society?" Tess, whose country estates were far from shabby-genteel, looked startled. "The duke's wife must do so," Clio added craftily. "She must command every elegance, and no small consequence."

"True," agreed Tess, wondering if her hoydenish young sister suddenly wished to attain respectability.

"Giles would make a good husband, I think," Clio ventured. "And he must be very rich. His wife must be very fortunate, don't you agree?"

"Certainly!" Tess replied promptly. "If that is what you wish, child! One could certainly marry into no higher rank short of royalty. I suppose it might compensate for a husband who is a trifle too starched-up, and a Medusa of a mama-in-law."

"*I* don't find Giles proud!" Clio was frustrated beyond bearing. "He is certainly a great deal more eligible that that dratted rake who is dangling after you!"

Tess was so bewildered by Sir Morgan's abrupt intrusion into the conversation that she failed to scold Clio for the use of language that was most unbecoming to a young lady of high station and tender years. "Believe me, Clio," she said wryly, "Sir Morgan hasn't the slightest idea of fixing his interest with me. There are other reasons—but I cannot speak of them!" She studied her sister's woebegone countenance. "I was teasing you, child. Truly, I haven't the least objection to Giles. He would do very well, in fact! I do not think he considers marrying again, but if you set your cap at him, I make no doubt you will change his mind."

Poor Clio ground her teeth at being so misunderstood. There was no opportunity to try and set things right; Lucille emerged from the apothecary's shop and consigned a number of parcels to the waiting footman.

Lucille, who had overheard the end of this conversation, thought Sapphira would be pleased that her plans for Clio promised to be fulfilled. Drusilla, too, would be relieved to learn that Sir Morgan's attentions to Tess were inspired not by lascivious intentions, but something else. But if Clio meant to marry Giles, she would have to mend her ways. Lucille might be timid and colorless, but she had two sharp eyes and a shrewd brain in her head, and unless she missed her guess, young Clio was wild to a fault.

"Now!" She took her young cousin's arm. "Your come-out is tomorrow night, and *Maman* has requested that I should tell you how to go on." Clio looked mutinous. Lucille plunged bravely on, though her spirits quailed. "You will be meeting a number of important people, and it is imperative that you make a good impression. You must not flirt, or appear coming, or indulge in unbecoming levity."

"It sounds," muttered Clio, who nourished dreams of Cutting a Dash, "like a dead bore."

"Well perhaps," admitted Lucille cautiously, "but it is the way of the world."

"In short, child," interrupted Tess, who despite her vast inexperience had more than a passing acquaintance with risqué French novels, "a young woman must be rigidly virtuous or be branded immoral. It is, of course," she added drily, "different for young gentlemen."

"But naturally!" While Lucille could find nothing objectionable in Tess's words, the tone in which they were spoken was highly suspicious, suggesting as it did not only disagreement but an inappropriate light-mindedness. "It is expected that young men will, er, sow their wild oats."

"You see, dear Clio," continued Tess, driven by a spirit of mischief, "it is quite the thing for a young man to keep a mistress, respectability being a virtue that can be acquired in middle age, and one that isn't really suitable to young men of breeding. A mother on the lookout for an acceptable *parti* for her daughter will happily overlook the habits of eligible young men. *You*, however, are not supposed to even suspect the facts of life until your wedding night." She glanced at Lucille's shocked face and smiled. "I believe in the word with no bark on it, you see!"

Clio, with unusual tact, swallowed her giggles and addressed her cousin. "You knew my mother, did you not, Lucille? I wish you would tell me about her." She spoke not from curiosity, but to prevent Lucille from forming a further adverse opinion of the woman whom Clio intended as her future sister-in-law.

"I cannot recall—she frittered away her chances—" gasped Lucille, then practically shoved her exasperating charges into Hatchard's, the Bond Street book dealer who had been established in the previous century, and abandoned them to turn over the pages of the latest books while she sank onto a chair and groped for her vinaigrette. Lucille was, as a married lady, acquainted with what Tess so blithely called the "facts of life"; but she did not care to think of such things, let alone discuss them. Heaven only knew what would happen if Tess chose to air her novel views so frankly in polite society! No doubt they would all be put to the blush.

Tess had already forgotten the matter, being absorbed in the pages of a book. Clio, unaware that her sister had just branded herself in Lucille's eyes as at least a bluestocking, if not a creature totally hardened to shame, studied the countess narrowly. Desperate measures were called for if Giles was to be ensnared. Despite the pang it caused her to think of the duke thus pledged to another, Clio considered the possibility of arranging that he and Tess somehow be closeted alone together for some time. The Duke of Bellamy was a gentleman and Tess was of noble birth; if he inadvertently compromised her, he was honor-bound to propose marriage in amends. If Tess would accept a proposal made under such circumstances remained to be seen; Clio could only plot her course one step at a time.

Rapt in thought, the sisters were unaware of the curious glances cast at them, a fair share of which were directed not at Clio but at Tess. The countess, had her attention been drawn to this unusual interest, would have thought it very odd, and would have supposed that the *ton* was rather startled to find in its midst a lady with a limp. She would have been mistaken; it was not her lack of perfection that earned comment, but the efforts of one Beau

Brummell, possessor of a keen eye and even keener wits and a diabolical sense of mischief. After making Tess's acquaintance in Hyde Park, that fastidious and vastly influential gentleman had, for reasons known only to himself, so far bestirred himself as to drop subtle hints about her beauty and cleverness into many ears, an unprecedented condescension that caused any number of lords and ladies to wonder if the Beau had at last lost his heart.

Lucille, belatedly aware of the speculation that was centered on her *protégées,* ushered them outside. "Famous!" cried Evelyn, who was waiting impatiently on the walkway, the faithful Nidget at his heels. "I made sure I would find you here. Sapphira says that you are to take me to St. James's Park so that I won't be setting everyone at sevenses or knocking the household on its ear." Since Bellamy House was in a state of severe upheaval due to preparations for the festivities of the following night, and since Nidget had an unhappy tendency to worry the flowers that lavishly adorned the ballroom and to snap at the caterer's heels, this command was not as callous as it might sound.

A lively discussion ensued as to their means of transport to the park, Lucille being of the opinion that they should all be taken up in the barouche, and Evelyn determined that he and Tess, for whom he had conceived a large fondness, even going so far as to inform his father that she was a "great gun," should proceed on foot. It was not to be expected that Lucille should withstand his blandishments, though she was not at all sure that such an excursion was quite the thing; and Tess and her young admirer set out, with a discreet footman in attendance.

"You don't mind, do you?" asked Evelyn, skipping at her side. "Lucille is so *stuffy*; this will be a great deal more fun!" His sparkling glance alit on her cane, and his face fell. "Aunt Tess, will you be all right? I forgot about your leg! Shall I send after the barouche?"

"Nonsense!" retorted Tess, who after that artless compliment would have cheerfully walked both her legs to stubs. "I will do quite nicely, providing you don't expect me to run."

"No one," said Evelyn admiringly, "will ever call *you* a pudding-heart, Aunt Tess!"

Thus the Countess of Lansbury made her way on foot through London's busy streets, while Evelyn pointed out to her such wonders as the elite gentlemen's clubs in St. James's Street—Brook's Club at No. 60; White's and Boodle's; Berry Brothers and Rudd at No. 6, dealers in wine and coffee, with the great scales where such customers as Brummell and Lord Petersham weighed themselves; Lock and Son at No. 3, where hats of the finest quality were made to measure; and St. James's Palace, built by Henry VIII on the site of a leper colony, the most glorious structure in the West End. She was introduced by the young viscount to such homely pleasures as the street-sellers who hawked meats and oysters and gilt gingerbread; she paused to observe fiddlers and hurdy-gurdies; she purchased an extremely improper pamphlet entitled "The Diabolic Practices of a Doctor on his Patients when in a State of Unconsciousness," which she promised Evelyn that he might read. At length, and without mishap, due primarily to the watchfulness of the footman, they arrived at St. James's Park.

Charles was not only an excellent footman, he was a mine of information, and was happy to inform his companions that James I had not only introduced the mulberry trees that flourished in the park, but had made a menagerie in which he kept exotic animals, among them a tame leopard from the king of Savoy, and camels and an elephant from the king of Spain. Charles might have waxed even more enthusiastic, had not Evelyn interrupted with a request that the rest of the party be found and brought to them. Tess, amused by his highhandedness, thought that the viscount was likely to grow up to be every bit as haughty as the present Duke of Bellamy.

But he was, after all, only a small boy, with his pockets filled with gingerbread and apples, and his nankeens already dirty and stained; and the smile he turned on her was pure mischief. "I didn't think," he explained, "that you wanted to hear about kings and things."

"Not at all," agreed Tess, who had enjoyed the footman's discourse very well. "Don't you think you should keep hold of Nidget? I doubt the park-keeper would be very happy if he, ah, tried to herd the cows." With a delightful giggle, Evelyn set off in pursuit of his pet.

Tess walked slowly between the trees that lined Birdcage Walk, musing over her sister's unaccountable behavior. Clio was not herself these days, and the countess wondered if that damsel's heart was truly set on Giles. It would be a splendid match, and Tess could think of no better husband for Clio; but she could not think Clio was acting like a young lady in love. Further occupying her mind was the diamond necklace. Sir Morgan had as much as admitted that he knew of its whereabouts, but had lacked time to say more. Tess determined to be more firm on her next meeting with that remarkable man, so that she might learn his plans.

Her ruminations were interrupted at this point; a villainous-looking individual in a greasy work-smock leapt out of nowhere to block her way. "Hand it over!" he demanded, extending a filthy hand as Tess stared. "Hand it over, I say, or it'll go the worse for you!"

"I don't suppose," Tess remarked, gripping her cane, "that you'd believe me if I said I don't know what you're talking about?"

The man swore a dreadful oath and spat on the ground at her feet, then reached to grasp her arm. That he meant her harm Tess was aware, but he was given no time to accomplish his evil intent. Nidget, who was as devoted to Tess as was his master, gave vent to loud and ferocious protest as he raced down the avenue. The villain took one look at the huge beast, whose large white teeth were exposed in a most menacing manner, and took summarily to his heels. Tess, weak-kneed with relief, moved off the pathway and sank down on the grass.

"Cripes!" said Evelyn, skidding to a stop in front of her. "What did that man want, Aunt Tess?"

The countess, not normally given to prevarication, had developed an outstanding talent for it in these past few days. "He didn't say," she replied and hugged Nidget who, having routed the enemy, had dropped panting at her side. "First highwaymen and now this! My life is fraught with excitement, I vow!"

Evelyn was not to be led off on a tangent. "I don't like it." He frowned. "You need protection, Aunt Tess. Perhaps you should marry me."

"I confess it pleases me beyond measure that you should wish to protect me," Tess responded, highly diverted, "but don't you think there's a rather large disparity in our ages? You would not wish to be shackled to a female when you are barely out of short coats! Think of all the fun you would miss."

"*I,*" Evelyn retorted indignantly, "am not a cabbage-head, Aunt Tess. It's perfectly obviously that you don't *wish* to marry me."

"Oh, no, no!" cried Tess, aware that the viscount's youthful pride had been stung. "I promise, Evelyn, that I am quite smitten with you. It is midsummer moon with me! But I do not think it proper that you should set up household with a lady who, if not precisely stricken in years, is at least at her last prayers."

There was a look of reluctant, and somewhat rueful, amusement on Evelyn's face. "Fudge!" he said. "Aunt Tess, you are the most complete hand! I confess I'd as lief not be married at all."

"Of course you wouldn't, and most sensible of you it is," the countess agreed cordially. "The wish to be leg-shackled is a piece of madness that generally comes upon gentlemen in later years, I believe. Now come here and sit by me!"

Evelyn did so. "He must've followed us, that man," he ventured, nibbling on a stalk of grass.

"I suppose so." Tess eyed him cautiously. "Shall it be our secret, Evelyn? Since no harm was done?"

A lad of the viscount's age might be expected to relish the prospect of such a conspiracy, but Evelyn shot Tess a glance that was surprisingly shrewd. "I've already said," he protested, "that I'm not bacon-brained. You needn't try and bamboozle *me.*"

"So you mean to tell all." Tess thought, rather grimly,

of the diamond necklace and of the rough man who had accosted her, whom she had recognized as being among those in the taproom at the inn. It appeared that she must make it clear to Sir Morgan that she would not give him away.

"No!" Evelyn was offended. "Not if you don't want me to, Aunt Tess. I wouldn't behave so shabbily! But it's plain as the nose on my face that you have windmills in your head."

# Chapter 11

*Lady Tess might have been unable* to avoid the formal dinner party which preceded her sister's coming-out ball, and which consisted of seventy dishes, among them four soups, four fish, four hors d'oeuvres, sixteen entrees, three joints on the sideboard including a haunch of venison, and six roasts; but she could, and did, hold herself aloof from the ballroom festivities. Many alcoves opened off that huge chamber, with its vaulted ceiling that was painted bright blue, and the walls that were paneled with ebonized wood inlaid with Amboina in a heavily gilded floral pattern, the center panels containing olive-colored Wedgwood plaques. Tess settled in one of these alcoves and watched with some amusement the antics of the *ton*.

Clio, who looked lovely in the simple white muslin gown deemed appropriate for the occasion, was a gratifying success. Though Tess knew well the mischief that hid behind that young lady's modest demeanor, she wasn't the least surprised that Clio should prove so popular. It would be no great marvel if Clio achieved her greatest ambition, and married a gentleman of rank and fashion in St. George's, Hanover Square.

But Tess—who considered herself so far removed from such ambition that she not only wore a gown of an unusual turquoise shade that exactly matched her eyes, but was virtually unchaperoned—was not long left on the sidelines, for no less a personage than Brummell himself sought her out, offered her his arm, escorted her through the glittering crowd, procured for her refreshment, and engaged with her in animated conversation all the while. The countess, unaware that she had received a supreme mark of approval, one that in itself was sufficient to establish her socially, laughed at his more outrageous remarks, parried his subtle efforts to learn more of her background with acerbic observations of her own, and in all concluded that the Beau possessed exquisite manners and an old-world courtliness and charm. At length—after sufficient time, in fact, that no person among the assembled guests had failed to note his marked preference—Brummell surrendered her, with nicely phrased reluctance, to one whom he claimed as a particular friend.

"So!" said Tess, her eyes sparkling, her heavy hair already threatening to escape its pins despite the efforts of the fashionable hairdresser who had with mingled praise and dismay drawn it into a huge chignon with curls escaping to caress her temples. "I suppose that I should have suspected some chicanery."

Sir Morgan quirked a brow. He looked very fine in evening dress, she thought, though he wore his long-tailed coat, frilled shirt, knee breeches, and silk stockings with an air of carelessness. "Brummell is in the way of being my good Samaritan. *I* could hardly rout you from your lair without giving rise to unwelcome comment."

"Heavens!" Tess was suddenly enjoying herself. "Is your reputation in such bad odor that you would be thought capable of ravishing a female in the middle of a crowded ballroom?"

"No, fair wit-cracker!" He chuckled. "Else I would not be standing here with you. However, I cannot say the gossips would be so tolerant were we to be closeted alone." Recalling their last encounter, Tess flushed, a fact which did not escape Sir Morgan's sharp eye. "I believe I owe you an apology, little one. It was not my intention to cause you embarrassment."

"Pray don't regard it; you did not." Tess looked up at him ruefully. "I think your life must be an exciting one, Sir Morgan, to attract such marked comment wherever you go! Doesn't it sometimes feel like living in a fishbowl?

I should think it would be uncomfortable to be forever under observation, with one's every action arousing comment."

"Do you?" inquired Sir Morgan, offering his arm. "I suppose you may be right, though I confess I hadn't thought of it. Tell me, do you think it too late for me to change my ways?"

"Certainly." Idly, Tess wondered where he was leading her. "Nor do I think you have the least desire to do so. Why should you? It is obviously a way of life that suits you admirably."

"I am glad you think so," he remarked, amused. "But you yourself are this evening exciting no little comment. Mistress Clio is like to be cast into the shade."

"How can you say so?" Tess was astonished. "If people look at me, it is because of my infirmity, not that I thank you for reminding me! For I have found that when I *think* of it, I limp much worse than I do otherwise."

Perhaps Sir Morgan did not realize that this frank reference to a debility that Lady Tess abhorred was unprecedented; he certainly did not treat the confidence with the respect that it derserved. "I don't know where you learned your fantastic notions," he said merely. "It is not because of your limp that all eyes are upon you."

"No," Tess retorted, then laughed. "It is because I am with *you!*"

Sir Morgan might be a man of dangerous reputation, a devil with the ladies, and a demon with the cards; but he was also the darling of the *ton*, and even those mamas who warned their daughters to have nothing to do with him were not beyond nourishing warm feelings for the Wicked Baronet. He might lay claim to the ensnaring of countless feminine hearts, but it was the ladies themselves who speculated upon such matters; no word of his conquests ever passed Sir Morgan's lips. His *amours* were confined to dashing members of the *demi-monde;* his flirtations were limited to well-born ladies of experience and discretion; he did not trifle with inexperienced girls who did not know the rules of the game. Lady Tess did not know that his marked pleasure in her company had given rise to vast curiosity among the members of polite society, who had never before seen the Wicked Baronet pay court to a female who was both unworldly and unmarried; Tess did not know that he paid her court at all. Nor did she realize that Brummell's intervention had prohibited her being considered "fast," or that even the unpredictable Sally Jersey, long accustomed to numbering Sir Morgan among her beaux, only laughed and said that Drusilla's nose was being put out of joint, as indeed it was, but that too Tess did not know.

"I have wished to speak with you," she said, awarding Sir Morgan her clear pure glance. "First, I must thank you for having my cane mended after the incident at the inn. It is shockingly remiss in me not to have done so before."

"It is," agreed Sir Morgan, "the height of ingratitude. Fustian, little one! Had I more time, I would have effected further repairs. Where came you by the thing? It is entirely the wrong height for you."

Tess paid little heed to this intimation that Sir Morgan himself had made the repairs; it was not the cane that occupied her mind. "I had an odd encounter in St. James's Park," she announced abruptly, reaching a decision, "a couple days past, with a villainous-looking man who demanded that I hand over some unspecified item to him." Suddenly she realized that she was being guided onto the dance floor. "What are you doing? You must know that I do not dance!"

"I suspected you did not," Sir Morgan disclosed. "Nevertheless, you will."

Having been accorded little choice in the matter, Tess danced, and due to Sir Morgan's firm support, did so very well. She was no stranger to the steps, having witnessed Clio's lessons. But the countess was not one to gloat over every new accomplishment. Having determined that Sir Morgan would not let her fall, Tess returned to the attack. "You are the most vexatious man! I must tell you that I recognized my would-be assailant as a *habitué* of that dreadful inn."

"You intrigue me," remarked Sir Morgan, and nothing would do but to recount to him the whole. "You have no idea," he inquired when she had finished, "to what the man referred?"

"I have every idea!" retorted Tess. "That's what I'm trying to tell you. Pretty companions for a man of honor! It is not at all necessary to offer me violence, you know."

"Believe me," Sir Morgan protested sincerely, "violence is not among the things I have considered offering you."

"I suppose," said Tess, fast finding herself out of charity with this aggravating man, "that you are playing some devilish deep game. I see that I must not be vulgarly inquisitive! I only hope that I may not get my throat cut over this business."

"Oh, not that, surely." Sir Morgan wore his crooked smile. "Though there are those, I'm sure, who would consider it a preferable fate."

Perhaps, thought Tess, the threat of recrimination might induce him to confide in her. It was not a question of how the necklace had come into his possession that concerned Tess; she could not imagine that Sir Morgan, despite his reckless reputation, was less than honorable; she only sought to learn what he wished done with the gems. "I know little of such matters," she added, holding his eyes, "but I would think that the penalty for such a thing would not be inconsiderable."

"Not at all inconsiderable," agreed Sir Morgan cheerfully. "I shouldn't settle for less than life, I think."

"So long!" gasped Tess, astonished. "You are a gambler indeed, if you can speak so calmly."

"Do I seem calm?" Sir Morgan tightened his grasp and twirled her about expertly. "Then there is a great deal to be said for experience. May I hope that you will not hold it against me, little one?"

Tess was feeling slightly giddy, but whether it resulted from the movements of the dance, or the novel sensations attendant upon being clasped in a man's arms, or the disclosure that her partner was no novice at skullduggery, she could not say. "Apparently I do not," she mused, incurably honest, "since I am ready to assist you. I do wish you would tell me what to do!"

Sir Morgan wore an arrested expression, in his amber

eyes a look so warm that even Tess understood its significance. "I have told you already that I await your pleasure!" she said crossly. "It is not at all necessary that you should get up a flirtation with me!"

The dance had ended; Sir Morgan escorted her from the floor. "You misunderstand," he murmured, "but I fear we cannot discuss the matter further at the moment without suffering dire consequence." He gazed upon Drusilla, elegant in a gown of pink tulle adorned with myriads of silver stars and an extreme *décolletage*. She peremptorily beckoned him. "Accept my assurances that I do not mean to flirt with you, my beautiful bluestocking."

"Hah!" replied the countess.

And then she was given over into the keeping of the dowager duchess, who appeared quite in charity with her until Giles, having done his duty by Clio, took a place by her side. "Crowded as the very devil, isn't it?" he commented, with obvious boredom. "I suppose my sisters will account it a great success."

Tess studied him. The duke was very correctly attired in a corbeau-colored full dress coat with covered buttons, a white marcella waistcoat, light sage-colored breeches, and an exquisite cravat; and so aloof as to appear unapproachable. Then he smiled at her, with the effect of ice melting. "You will think me impertinent," he said, "but I would consider that I had done less than my duty if I did not drop a hint or two." He glanced at Drusilla, who, her anger temporarily forgotten, was coquetting outrageously with Sir Morgan.

"You mean to warn me once more about your friend," Tess responded serenely. "I wish you would not! I have heard too much of the wretch already, fiend seize the man!"

Giles lifted his gold-handled quizzing glass and studied her as if she were a rare specimen that had hitherto never come his way. "You do that very well!" approved the countess, returning his regard. "I suppose it has quailed countless encroaching mushrooms and sent many an erring servant away in tears. Truly, I myself feel as if I'd been dealt a crushing set-down, which is I presume what you intended, though I must confess I find it just a trifle rag-mannered, Your Grace!"

Those doughty individuals who had already remarked the lovely stranger's popularity with such disparate, yet discerning, gentlemen as Beau Brummell and the Wicked Baronet, were further astounded when by a remark she sent the haughty Duke of Bellamy into peals of laughter. But whatever warning Giles had meant to offer went unvoiced: no sooner had he recovered himself than Clio interrupted to draw her sister aside.

"Tess, it is the most famous thing!" said that damsel, so flown with the compliments she'd received from numerous young courtiers that she didn't begrudge an instant of her sister's popularity. "There is someone here who wishes particularly to speak with you." Tess was awarded a sly look. "Isn't Giles the most *amusing* gentleman?"

"If you think so, child," agreed the countess, still wrapped in contemplation of a certain diamond necklace.

"Of course I do!" enthused Clio, "and you must also. He is certainly far more agreeable than that odious Sir Morgan! It is Drusilla's business, I suppose, if she meant to settle in matrimony with him. I shouldn't think he'd be a *comfortable* husband, but he has been accepted by the family, and I suppose it will be an unexceptionable match." Again she glanced sideways, hoping to see the seeds of doubt take root in fertile ground.

Mistress Clio, if she had expected to see a face of despair, was disappointed: Tess thought only that though Sir Morgan might not make a comfortable spouse, he would be an exciting one. And then she spied a familiar face. "Good God!" ejaculated the countess, fit to leap out of her skin. "It can't be Shamus! *Here?*"

"But it is," giggled Clio, ruthlessly urging her sister forward. "Your curate has come all the way to London to renew his suit. You have made a conquest, Tess! What's more," she added primly, "he promises to use the knowledge of your altered status in only the most discreet manner, though this deception is something of which he can hardly *approve!*"

Tess did not argue with this patent disrespect, secretly

agreeing with Clio that the curate, though undeniably well-meaning, was a most tiresome, prosy man. "Here!" she repeated unhappily. "I cannot credit it."

With a flourish, Clio presented her to the gentleman. "Shamus will explain all!" she promised. "Now, if you will excuse me, I am engaged for the next set."

"Well," said Tess, callously abandoned to her fate. "Here we are, it seems."

The curate, one Shamus O'Toole, found nothing lacking in this remark, which he took as an indication that her ladyship was, on discovering his presence, quite properly overwhelmed. "You are surprised to see me, Lady Tess!" he stated. "But I must not call you that! I cannot think this charade is quite the thing—I believe I know you a little too well to stand on ceremony with you, after all!—but I understand perfectly why you embarked upon it, and I cannot but applaud your motives."

"Oh?" Tess regarded her suitor quizzically. He was a very presentable young man with reddish hair and a fair complexion to which the blood rose rather too easily, and a physique that would in time tend to corpulence. "You surprise me, Shamus!"

"I hope I do not lack for sense," he responded archly. "It must be evident to all who know you, dear—ah—Tess, that you have chosen to remain in the wings so that your sister may claim the center of the stage." The curate, though eschewing such frivolous matters, was prone to claim a certain knowledge of the world. "It does you great credit!"

"How little you know me, Shamus!" Tess replied ruefully. "Were it in my power, I would gladly upstage Clio. It might prove a salutary lesson for the minx!"

The worthy Shamus, a younger son destined from birth for the church—a calling that admirably fitted one of his moralistic bent and innate pomposity—raised his sandy brows, tsk-tsk'd, and avowed that the countess spoke in jest and that he knew her far too well to believe a word of it. "You haven't told me what brings you to London," she interrupted, lest he elaborate further on the esteem in which he held her various sterling qualities. "Have you suddenly discovered in yourself a taste for the trivialities of life?"

Shamus, who had no sense of humor whatsoever, a fact of which he was inclined to boast, disclaimed this shocking suggestion at some length. "Since the living is in the keeping of the Churchills," he concluded, "I could hardly refuse the squire's request. So here I am, dear Tess, rubbing shoulders with the nobs."

The countess, who usually accorded her suitor an exasperated tolerance, now gazed at him with such ferocity that he blushed. "The squire?" she repeated somberly. "Do you know, Shamus, I feel as though I have stepped into a horrid dream."

Had Lady Tess been hale of limb, the curate would never have dared aim so high as to marry her; but crippled as she was, and thus with little hope of making a better match, he considered himself eminently eligible. That the countess was very wealthy was not of great significance; Shamus hoped he was not an overly ambitious man; he wished only to command the elegancies of life—a small mansion, a comfortable bankroll, and a wife connected with royalty. Her lamentable tendency to light-mindedness would in time be tempered by his own sobriety, and her inclination toward bookishness would be forgotten once she was otherwise occupied by parish matters and a great many offspring.

"Well?" demanded the countess, happily unaware of this proposed fate. "What *about* the squire?"

She also had, reflected Shamus, an unhappy tendency toward temper. It was doubtless because he had not professed himself delighted to see her once again. Taking her hand, he promptly repaired that omission.

"Shamus," hissed Tess through clenched teeth, "if you do not tell me instantly *why* you are here, and what the *squire* has to do with it, I swear I shall scream!"

"Come, come, my dear, you will do no such thing!" Shamus patted her hand. "But it is no great secret, after all! I thought your sister would have told you."

"My sister," muttered Tess, glancing irately about for that devious miss. She saw Clio, at last, on the arm of an

Exquisite clad in a light brown coat with absurdly long tails, a white waistcoat, nankeen pantaloons, and yellow stockings with violent purple clocks. "Oh, my God!" she cried, with abject horror. "Ceddie!"

"I, too, lament the idle tendencies of English youth," the curate responded gravely, "but I believe you are too harsh. The lad is a trifle high-spirited, perhaps, but nothing to signify. And," he preened, "young Cedric is hardly like to fall into bad company with *me* in attendance. It was for that exact purpose that the squire decided I must accompany his son to town."

That Cedric—who was, at the age of twenty, already excessively imprudent, a spendthrift, and firmly entrenched in sporting ways—was hardly likely to be prohibited by the presence of a bearleader from embarking upon every sort of lark, Tess forbore to say. Shamus, grateful at his young age to have fallen into a very comfortable living, was deaf to any criticism of his patron's family. "You have been set an awesome task," she commented, watching with despair as Clio spoke in apparent earnestness to the young man.

Shamus did not consider this remark worthy of reply. He gazed disapprovingly about him, his censorious glance resting on a lady so covered with jewels that she could barely stand erect, and then on a dashing young matron whose gown was so low cut that it would surely slide right off her shoulders if she so much as sneezed, and then once more on the countess. He could not help but feel that she had altered in some incomprehensible manner since they had last met. There was an indefinable difference in her tonight, one that could not be accounted for simply by the modish gown. Perhaps, he thought with disapproval, Lady Tess's head was being turned by so much frivolity. And so much attention! he added, as before his offended eyes Lady Tess caught the gaze of a swarthy, reckless-looking gentleman, and smiled.

There was only one thing to do, Shamus decided. He must press his suit and remove his intended wife from the temptations of the metropolis before further damage was done. He determined to put his luck to the test at the first opportunity. That the countess had, on the previously mentioned last meeting, unequivocally refused his nicely phrased proposal of marriage for the umpteenth time not a whit disturbed the curate's conviction that she was destined to be his wife.

# Chapter 12

*Cedric Churchill was a very handsome young man* of slender physique with green eyes, dark gold hair, and luxuriant side whiskers extending down toward his chin. Already he was earning a crude reputation for racing, gaming, and extravagance of dress; already he was spending his existing capital at an alarming rate, though since his father was a mere forty-five years of age, he had no expectations of any quick inheritance; already he was exciting no small interest among the various young misses who stood with their families, watching the great ladies in their jewels, the ambassadors and generals in their decorations, and wishing fervently for an introduction to this dashing young man, that his name might be inscribed on their little cards for at least a country dance.

Ceddie might have obliged at least some of those hopeful maidens, had not Clio had him firmly in tow. It was not an exceptional action; after the conclusion of a dance, a gentleman customarily took his partner on his arm and walked about with her until the next set began; but Cedric exhibited no great gratification at being so honored by the belle of the evening, who was tormented on all sides to dance by an astonishing number of young hopefuls. He considered himself a man of the world, one who had broken irrevocably away from his mother's apron strings to drink excessively, seduce freely, and gamble lavishly, if unwisely; and it in no way suited his self-image that a young lady who, though certainly lovely, was little more than a schoolgirl should thus monopolize him.

"Ceddie!" hissed Clio. In exasperation, she pinched his arm. "Will you *please* listen to me?"

Cedric winced. "Dash it, Clio!" he protested. "Take care you don't crease my coat."

"The devil with your coat!" snapped Clio. "Now pay attention to what I tell you or you will land us both in the suds!"

In truth, Cedric was not far from a standstill himself, being in need of a substantial windfall if he was to keep up his existing standards. Life in London promised to be not inexpensive for a young man set on Cedric's path. To start with, there were his rooms at Fenton's Hotel in St. James's Street, which had started life as a fashionable lounge known as Pero's Bagnio, and now was a favorite resort of dandies and Guards officers, and where a warm bath cost an astonishing five shillings. Then there were the gentlemen's clubs where one sat, hour after hour, with hat tilted to shield one's eyes, stooped over the green baize tables until fuddled with exhaustion and drink; the expensive shops where one procured a fashionable wardrobe; Tattersall's and cockpits, prizefighters and lessons in the noble art of self-defense. It was not that Cedric counted the cost of such gentlemanly pursuits; Cedric didn't count the cost of anything, or dream of living within his means or of practicing the dreary middle-class virtue of economy. He did, however, recall his parting confrontation with his irascible sire, and that the squire had bluntly told him that there would be no further forays on the family purse. Therefore, with a great deal of fellow-feeling, Cedric engaged himself to listen to what Clio had to say.

It was a disjointed narrative, consisting of odd references to intruders and rakehells and highwaymen, and Cedric's attention quickly wandered. "Gad!" he interjected suddenly. "Why the deuce is your sister looking daggers at me?"

"*Not* my sister!" said Clio despairingly. "I thought you were listening to me!"

"*Not?*" Cedric stared at Tess. "I must say *that* was a

119

proper take-in! None of us would've guessed." His forehead wrinkled. "If not your sister, then who *is* she?"

"Of course she's my sister!" Clio cast her eyes heavenward. "We are only pretending, Ceddie! Now listen well! Tess is thought to be my companion, and you must not address her by her title or you will give us away." She pondered upon Cedric's legendary absent-mindedness. "Better yet, you'll not speak to her at all."

"A companion?" repeated Cedric. "I see what it is, you're cutting a wheedle! But to have your companion at a ball? Don't seem quite the thing to me."

"Never mind!" Clio lacked sufficient energy to explain the circumstances of her sister's presence to one who, if not precisely dicked in the nob, was definitely cocklebrained. "You must give me your word that you won't betray us."

"As if I would!" Ceddie was offended. He glanced again at the countess. "That don't explain why she's looking murder at me."

"Well," and Clio giggled, "it's understandable enough. I told Tess you wished to marry me."

This simple statement affected Cedric most extremely. "You told her *what*?" he croaked, in froglike accents.

"Don't go into high fidgets!" Clio advised soothingly. "It was only so she would allow me to come to London. I said if she wouldn't accompany me, *you* would."

Cedric was not appreciably impressed by this clever ploy; he looked very much as though he doubted the fidelity of his own ears. "Dash it, Clio! I don't *want* to be married!" At least not to anyone without the handsomest of dowries, he amended silently.

Mistress Clio tossed her head. "And so you shan't be!" she retorted. "I think, Ceddie, this attitude is very shabby of you! A person would think I'm an antidote."

"No, no!" protested Cedric, looking harassed. "I vow I'm devoted to you, Clio! But you gave me a nasty turn, saying I was pledged to step into parson's mousetrap."

Clio might have made any number of sharp rejoinders, among them that her companion's mind was of a mean and little structure, and that she had no wish to acquire for herself a husband who was, despite empty pockets, hell-bent on living high; but she said none of these things. "Come!" she murmured, leading him firmly through the crowd. "You must meet the other members of my family. Then, Ceddie, you must engage me in conversation, for I wish especially to speak further with you!"

Cedric obeyed meekly enough, if gloomily. He knew perfectly well that if he refused, Clio was capable of ringing a regular peal over him, even in the midst of a ball. He made the acquaintance of the Dowager Duchess of Bellamy—who shot him a keen glance, announced him a "fashionable fribble," and then studiously ignored him—and of the various members of her family. Lucille, who looked insignificant even in formal dress, earned only a brief glance, though Cedric's eyes tended to linger on Drusilla's *décolletage;* and he was rendered hideously uncomfortable by the duke, immediately recognizable as that most intimidating of creatures, a Perfect Gentleman. Clio was borne away by one of her many admirers, and Cedric found Constant by his side.

"You are an old acquaintance of our dear little Clio?" queried that sly gentleman, conjectures wriggling like eels through his fertile brain. "Such a charming girl! She has stolen all our hearts, little minx that she is. I would wager that she was quite a belle, even isolated in the country, and broke many a heart."

"I suppose so," replied Ceddie absently, so bemused by Drusilla's low-cut neckline that he forgot that he had been among those young men who vied for Clio's favors and professed themselves ready to expire for one of her smiles.

"An uncommonly lovely girl" proclaimed Constant, wondering if in this young sprig he might find a means to thwart his scheming mother-in-law's plans for Clio and Giles; or if Cedric might be the tool by which Clio could be bent to his own will. If push came to shove, the girl could be disgraced, but Constant hesitated to go to such dire lengths despite Drusilla's insistence on something of the kind.

Ceddie made no response; Drusilla, having become aware of the direction of his fascinated gaze, had shot him a smile so brilliant that it rendered him half-senseless. He watched with some envy as a military gentleman led her away, and Constant adjudged it time for his next move. "So this is your first visit to town," he said expansively, as befit one already well-versed in the ways of the world. "You will find it vastly diverting."

"I already have," Cedric replied wryly. The squire's son did not care to be patronized. "You must not think me a flat."

"I see I must not!" the other man said jovially. "But I daresay there are things you have not yet seen." Constant may not have been particularly clever, but he possessed sufficient wit to see in Cedric not only an aspiring tulip of fashion, but a young buck ripe for any spree and concurrently a pigeon to be easily plucked. He mentioned various expensive and well-appointed brothels in King's Place and the Haymarket; he spoke with amused tolerance of the prostitutes who stood naked in indecent postures at their windows, or rushed out in their underclothes to drag gentlemen inside; he waxed enthusiastic about the well-known courtesan who had recently appeared undressed at a fancy ball. From there it was but an easy step to the East End's gambling halls, though Constant refrained from elaborating on the Greeks and Captain Sharps who were forever on the alert for unsuspecting young blood.

Ceddie did not lack for experience of the more titillating varieties, but he quickly became aware that his most outrageous undertakings—such as being taken to court and fined £5 for fighting a main of cocks in his private rooms on a Sunday—would be seen by knowledgeable gentlemen as mere schoolboy pranks; and with each word he heard he grew more anxious to remedy the serious gaps in his education. By the time Constant's masterful dissertation came to an end, Cedric was so much impressed that he believed Constant to virtually possess the keys of the town, and professed himself more than willing to undertake an expedition to Ratcliffe Highway in Shadwell, scene not only of horrid murders that had taken place recently, but gathering-place for lower-class prostitutes. Constant turned away, pleased with his work, and exchanged a glance with his sister-in-law.

Cedric, lost in visions of rather unfeasible debaucheries, returned to the present when Clio tugged impatiently at his sleeve. "I have come to a conclusion!" she hissed, completely unaware that Cedric had fallen into Constant's clutches or that Constant and Drusilla were regarding her with a certain complacency. "Ceddie, you must help me!"

"Help you *what?*" demanded that suspicious, and unobliging, young man.

"Lower your voice!" begged Clio, looking mournful. "It's Tess. She's behaving in the most bird-witted manner. If we don't contrive to stop her, she'll land herself in the briars."

"*Tess?*" repeated Cedric, with such shocked incredulity that heads turned. Clio kicked his shin, and he attempted an unsuccessful look of innocence. "Why should I help *her?*" he demanded, in lower tones. "She don't even like me above half."

"Of course she does!" blatantly lied Clio. "She only thinks I should not marry you. Listen, Ceddie! I fear Tess may form a lasting passion for a *most* unsuitable man. Heaven knows he's making a dead set at her."

"So?" inquired Ceddie, who, though far from needle-witted, was perfectly aware that the countess had taken an implacable dislike to him. "That's no bread and butter of mine."

"Oh, yes, it is!" Clio was an enterprising miss; if cajolery would not serve, coercion would. "In short, dear Ceddie, if you do *not* assist me, I shall tell your papa about your intimate acquaintance with a young married woman of excellent family. He would be very angry, I imagine, that you had dallied *there,* and would probably cut you off without a farthing."

Never had Cedric thought, when he came to town, that he would find himself engaging in a brangle with Clio in the Bellamy ballroom. He had no notion of how she could have come by such damning information. In Cedric's admittedly limited experience, young ladies weren't supposed to know of such things. He gaped at her, speechless, as he struggled with an ignoble impulse to bid her go and be damned. "I'll do it, too!" added Clio grimly. "Don't think I won't."

Having been acquainted with the young lady for the greater portion of his life, Ceddie did not doubt that she would not fail to make good her threat. For a young man already in the hands on those unscrupulous moneylenders known commonly as Bloodsuckers, the prospect of disinheritance was much too dreadful to contemplate. "Oh, very well!" he gloomily agreed. "I must say, Clio, I think it very hard of you!"

Clio shrugged. "What would you have me do?" she inquired mournfully. "When the fate of my beloved sister is at stake? I cannot stand idly by, surely, while she condemns herself to a life of misery, or worse!"

Cedric's long experience of Mistress Clio had hitherto left him unacquainted with the sisterly devotion she now professed. "Worse?" he asked cautiously.

"Worse!" Clio was tragic. "I very much fear, Ceddie, that the odious man is a fortune hunter. Look! There he is, and talking with her *again!*"

Cedric obediently gazed upon the countess, laughing up at a dark-skinned man. *Had* she a fortune? he wondered. If so, how had he failed to know of it? It was growing obvious to Cedric that he had in the past failed to award Tess the attention she so richly merited. She was extraordinarily lovely, now that he took a close look. "A fortune hunter," he repeated thoughtfully.

"Yes!" Clio was pleased by this indication that her fellow conspirator was not entirely want-witted. "I'm sure of it! Tess is *very* wealthy, you know, and that brute has her positively bewitched, though there is Another who looks upon her kindly, and who is perfectly eligible."

"Aha!" said Ceddie. "Another." Cedric was in great need of wealth, and not one to boggle at a certain unscrupulousness. He wondered if the Countess of Lansbury, who was growing by the second more attractive to him, might be induced to alter her unhappy estimation of his character. Barring that miraculous conversion, he wondered if she might be susceptible to some polite blackmail, either on her sister's or her own behalf.

Clio, long used to Cedric's little mannerisms, paid scant heed to this indication that he was preoccupied. "Or there *will* be Another," she added somberly, "once I can put into effect a certain Plan. I think you may also help me with that."

"Humm." Cedric, in the process of evolving a Plan of his own, tugged thoughtfully at his side whiskers. "What would you have me do?"

"I'm not sure." Clio was gratified by his capitulation. "I think you might dangle after me once again. That will distress Tess, and she will seek to reason with me; I shall pay her no heed, and she will turn to—ah!—Another for comfort. And we must strive above all to keep her safe from Sir Morgan!"

Cedric, who couldn't imagine Lady Tess behaving in such a vaporish manner, looked doubtful. "That's all well and good," he protested, "but what's to stop her from keeping *you* safe from *me?*"

"You forget." Clio grinned. "Tess is a mere companion, and her wishes little signify—particuarly since Sapphira thinks you an old friend of the family! She doesn't like Tess at all, and should Tess protest, will do the exact opposite. It will work very well, you'll see!"

Cedric expected to see nothing of the sort, and considered this hubble-bubble scheme all that one could expect from a hoydenish miss with more hair than sense; but Cedric possessed a strong sense of expedience with regard to himself. Therefore, when Mistress Clio demanded his presence in Berkeley Square on the following day, he thought of the measures he meant to immediately set into effect regarding the countess, and of the opportunity of gazing once more upon the exciting Drusilla, and promptly agreed.

"Here comes Shamus!" he added, a wary eye on his mentor, whom in kinder moments he termed a "crashing bore." "I've no wish to hear him prosing on about my responsibilities." Clio received an extremely cheerful smile.

"I'm off, then! Don't worry your head about your, er, Tess. We'll fix it up all right and tight between us. Until tomorrow, then!"

Clio, who had not expected such a great degree of co-operation from Cedric, looked after him with a little frown and a large suspicion that he had fish of his own to fry. However, so did she.

"Shamus!" Mistress Clio smiled at the curate. "How lucky it is that you have come to Town. Tess was remarking just the other day that London only needed *your* presence to make it most agreeable!"

This artless comment accorded well with the curate's own estimation of himself. He blushed and smiled and remarked gravely that though he could not precisely care for the *tone* of town life, he was at all times ready—nay, eager!—to oblige his dear Tess.

"Yes, and she is very grateful for it!" said Clio, spreading her eggs among a great many baskets. "You must call at Bellamy House tomorrow, Shamus, so that she may tell you so herself!" Beaming, the curate agreed.

# Chapter 13

*It was not surprising,* after a night passed in such gay dissipation, that the inhabitants of Bellamy House should the following morning keep late to their beds. There was, however, an exception to this general air of exhaustion and *ennui:* Lady Tess had not only wakened early but had dressed herself and slipped rather stealthily out to the stables, there to collect her dappled mare and her faithful groom. Perhaps this rather unbecoming amount of enterprise—ladies were expected to be languid creatures, robust constitutions and energetic dispositions being considered rather vulgar—may be partially explained by the fact that Lady Tess, fed up to the teeth with her earnest swain's solicitations and driven half-wild with anxiety prompted by Cedric's presence in town, had remained at the ball only until midnight, when the footmen passed around champagne punch and lemonade and sandwiches; and then, after a clandestine supper with Evelyn and Nidget, neither of whom could be expected to sleep through such excitement, had retired gratefully to her bed.

The countess's spirits, alas, had been in no way elevated by a night enlivened by unhappy dreams, the gist of which can easily be imagined; her fine eyes were shadowed, her face pale beneath her elegant hat. Her companion cast her a searching glance. "Come out of the mopes!" he urged. "Surely it can't be *that* bad."

"Hah!" retorted Tess. "It is easy to see that you do not know Clio. I vow I could murder the little wretch!"

An odd way for a lowly companion to speak of her employer, perhaps, but Sir Morgan made no comment. Instead he pointed out various items of interest as they rode through London's cobbled streets, the groom following at a discreet distance behind.

London was deserted at this early hour, few signs of life stirring in the fashionable mansions that lined Piccadilly, or in the pretty little shops that displayed such disparate delicacies as stuffed birds of paradise and funerary urns. Tess had assumed that Sir Morgan meant to guide her to Hyde Park, but they rode in an altogether different direction, down a narrow and picturesque little street lined with small inns and livery stables once, as he informed her, the haunt of highwaymen.

"I'm sorry!" she said abruptly. "I'm very poor company, I fear."

"What you are," replied Sir Morgan, "is blue-deviled, and it takes no great intellect to deduce that Mistress Clio is the cause. What has that abominable brat done now?"

"I'm not sure," Tess replied ruefully. One thing she didn't have to worry about, at least, was that Clio would catch this particular rogue's eye. "When we had decided she was to come to London, I distinctly remember feeling free from much alarm—and I'll swear I haven't known a moment's peace since!" She recalled her supposed position. "But I should not speak so frankly."

"No," agreed Sir Morgan. "Not if you mean to keep up this ridiculous pretense! I shan't tease you about *that;* I'm sure you have your reasons and I have a good notion what they are. Not that I don't think they're also absurd, mind, but the way in which you live your life is up to you."

"So one would think," murmured Tess noncommittally, then lapsed into reverie. At first Sir Morgan's words seemed to refer to her imposture, and then to hint at something else. Heavens! thought Tess suddenly. Perhaps he thought she truly *was* an adventuress and that, having discovered the necklace among her possessions, meant to keep it for herself.

"Don't worry," soothed Sir Morgan, with kind intentions but an unfortunate choice of words. "As I have previously told you, you are safe with me. Now, little one, pay heed, for I am going to show you parts of London that are not considered strictly fashionable."

Thus Tess was privileged to gaze upon Fleet Street, center of the newspaper world, a street overhung by tall houses and lined with plate-windowed shops displaying books and engravings and silverware; the slender towers of Saint Martin's-in-the-Fields, the tall columns of Charing Cross and the Temple, where rooks roosted and cawed; and the sleepy Thames, sparkling silver in the early morning sunlight.

"You are fond of this city, aren't you?" she asked, interrupting Sir Morgan's somewhat irrelevant dissertation on Nell Gwyn, the flower girl who had risen to eminence as the favorite of Charles II, and who had once resided in Pall Mall in close proximity to the royal apartments in the Palace of Whitehall. "Despite its rather grotesque contrasts, the haunts of the aristocracy and the dreadful slums?"

"I am fond of many cities," replied Sir Morgan, apparently unconcerned at this lack of appreciation for his efforts as a tour guide. "London, Paris—although I have not been *there* in some years!—Vienna, Saint Petersburg, Moscow. And you?"

Tess shrugged. "How should I know? I am a country mouse. I had not expected to enjoy this visit, having unpleasant memories of London, so it comes as no great surprise that I am not deriving any great degree of pleasure from the town. However, a great deal of that can be laid at Clio's door."

She had expected, once the words were said, that he would ask her about those unpleasant memories, and had steeled herself to make him a rebuff. Tess remembered all too clearly the accident that had left her lame; and the rough young man, several years older than herself, who had dragged her from beneath the wheels of the carriage; and her father's expression when she had been returned, bleeding and hysterical, to him. Lord Lansbury had blamed himself for the accident and taken upon himself the brunt of a negligence that did not, in fact, exist; for it was Tess's own waywardness that had prompted her, while her father was engaged upon a business matter, to go adventuring. It was a waywardness for which she had paid, and dearly; and a trait which, alas, Clio shared. Tess doted on her young half-sister, aggravating as that damsel was. She did not wish to see Clio suffer, as she had, from the results of rebelliousness.

"Have you no wish to travel?" inquired Sir Morgan. "I should have thought you would enjoy it very well."

"Having an adventurous spirit?" parried Tess. Did he think she meant to take the diamonds and make a midnight flit to some exotic clime? "The opportunity has not come my way." Sir Morgan remained silent, and again she glanced at him. "I envy you," she said. He quirked a brow. "You sweep so magnificently through life, going where you please and doing as you will. It must be marvelous to be so unfettered." A thought struck her. "Oh! Clio has told me about Drusilla. Are we to wish you happy then—or am I guilty of impertinence?"

"I suspect it is Mistress Clio who is guilty," Sir Morgan retorted, looking rather diabolical, "and of spinning shocking fibs!"

"Oh?" asked Tess, confused. "She does tell the most dreadful clankers. Why should she tell me you are to be married if it isn't true?"

Sir Morgan was not inclined to be helpful. "Drusilla knows just how close she can sail to the wind without disaster, but Clio evidently does *not!*" he said with emphasis, then deftly turned the subject. "Who is that young sprig who paid her such marked attention last night?"

"Ceddie!" ejaculated the countess, with loathing. "Not a sprig, but a basket-scrambler, sir! It was because of Ceddie that I—that *we* thought it expedient to remove Clio to London, lest she contract a most imprudent match. Now what must happen but that he follows her? It utterly sinks my spirits!" She glowered. "As if that were in itself not bad enough, he must bring Shamus along!"

"Ah," said Sir Morgan. "*Your* admirer, I apprehend."

"Bah!" Lady Tess's tone was so venomous that her mare danced nervously. "He is the most tedious man!"

She flushed guiltily. "I should not say so, of course. Shamus is possessed of many admirable traits. He is kind, and considerate, and always willing to take one's problems onto his own shoulders."

"Even if you don't wish him to," concluded Sir Morgan, who was guilty, at least in this instance, of a similar sin. "A dead bore, in fact! Shall I warn him away?"

"Lord, no!" protested Tess, somewhat regretfully. "It would be the most shabby thing." She sighed. "Nor would it serve; Shamus is most tenacious, as I know only too well. But I should not be speaking like this to you! You will think me a ramshackle creature, ungrateful and incapable of comprehending a man's good qualities."

"What I think you," responded Sir Morgan, with a distinct warmth, "must be reserved for another day." He smiled at her puzzlement. "I *don't* think, by the way, that you need fear young Clio will suffer any harm from her provincial Romeo. If anything, she is more likely to inveigle him into some scheme."

"Do you think so?" asked Tess doubtfully. "I'll own his manner last evening didn't appear that of an ardent swain." Her eyes kindled. "If that little minx has lied to me—she vowed she'd elope with Ceddie if she wasn't allowed to come to town—I vow I'll wring her neck!"

Sir Morgan seemed to accept this indication of a violent nature as perfectly justifiable. "I think you may assume she has," he remarked. "Clio seems to possess a remarkable deviousness of mind."

Tess did not pause to wonder what had led him to this conclusion; she was stricken with remorse at the freedom she'd allowed her wretched tongue. "You must pay me no mind," she begged. "I have said the most improper things. The truth is that I am cross as a cat because Clio has pitchforked me into the *ton*."

That Mistress Clio had had help in that endeavor, Sir Morgan did not admit. "You would have much rather stayed in the background," he suggested smoothly, "as befits your position."

"Of course I would!" Tess mourned her laggard memory. "Who am *I* to hobnob with polite society?" Sir

131

Morgan looked very much as if he would answer this hypothetical question, and she hastily continued. "It is done now, and I perfectly see that to remain in the background would not have served. The Bellamys are very fine, and very proper I'm sure, but I cannot think they will deal successfully with Clio, particularly since I'm sure she's up to her tricks." She frowned. "Why, I wonder? But I have bored you far too long with all this! Tell me, where are we?"

Sir Morgan, who wisely made no mention of his impulse to take Miss Clio in hand and thus prevent her supposed companion from becoming worn out with fuss, fatigue, and rage, obligingly pointed out the various wonders of Mincing Lane, which boasted shops providing tea, coffee, sugar, and spices from the East, and where rich brokers lived above their tasting-rooms. The name of the street had derived from some houses belonging to the "Minchuns," or Nuns of St. Helen's, Billingsgate Street. Once Genoese traders or galleymen had dwelt in the narrow lane, and had brought their wares to Galley Wharf in Thames Street. Lady Tess inhaled the fishy air that wafted in from Billingsgate, and professed herself enchanted.

From there it was but an easy step to the Mansion House, residence of the lord mayors of London, a building of Portland stone with a portico of six fluted columns constructed in the Renaissance style; and an animated discussion of the regent's most recent activities, most unremarkable among which was a speech given after an inspection of the annual Royal Academy exhibition and a bronze lamp commissioned by the regent from Mr. Gullaimy of Pall Mall, to be presented to the Academy as a handsome reminder of the princely patronage. This, and Lady Tess's somewhat irreverent comment that the officers of the prince's regiment looked like hurdy-gurdy monkeys in their red breeches with gold fringe and yellow boots, occupied them pleasantly all the way back to Berkeley Square.

Sir Morgan did not leave the countess there or offer to help her to dismount, but instead led the way around to the stables as if it were only natural. "It is time I paid my respects to Sapphira," he said in response to her quizzical glance. "And I have something further I wish to say to you."

"Ah!" The diamond necklace, thought Tess, pleased beyond measure that he had at last decided to speak of it. "Shall we walk in the garden? You would not wish to be overheard."

From any number of other women, Sir Morgan would have taken this as an invitation to indulge in some early-morning dalliance, but he was far too knowledgeable in such matters to think Tess had any such pastime in mind. "Certainly," he replied, and swung her easily to the ground, then took from a goggling stableboy her cane.

Tess, well aware that Sir Morgan's presence in the stables, in companionship with herself, had given rise to no small amount of comment, launched upon an enthusiastic discussion of the various varieties of flowers and shrubs to be seen in the gardens. She furthermore assured him that she had it on very good authority that botany was among Drusilla's ruling interests, and advised him that he might further his suit by discussing such matters. "Doing it a little too brown," said Sir Morgan, when they were out of earshot. "You need not go to such lengths to protect my reputation."

Tess, considering the proprietary air with which Drusilla regarded this gentleman, rather thought she did. "I confess," she admitted, doubtfully surveying a rather neglected-looking bush, "that gardening is not among my ruling interests." She cast about in her head for a topic of conversation. Now that the moment for enlightenment had come, Tess found herself oddly reluctant to hear the truth of the necklace. It was *not*, she told herself firmly, that she regretted Sir Morgan's unavoidable waning of interest in her—for, once the secret was out and he was assured of her complicity, he would need no longer go to such lengths to maintain her goodwill—but that she did not wish to be possessed of information that would make her think poorly of him.

"I have," he said suddenly, taking her hands, "a confession to make. I should have told you before, but I was waiting to see if you remarked on it yourself."

"Pray, don't!" interrupted Tess, trying ineffectively to withdraw from his grasp. "There is no need—I do not wish to know! Consider, even here someone could overhear, and think of the consequences!"

"Surely," objected Sir Morgan, a rather startled expression on his swarthy face, "it would not be so bad."

"Not *bad*!" Tess cried. "To be taken off to Bow Street, to maybe stand your trial? You yourself said it could mean as much as life imprisonment!"

"So I did." Sir Morgan looked very stern. "I think you had better tell me exactly what you mean."

"You must not think," Tess assured him, for he obviously thought she was untrustworthy, "that I mean to tell on you, or to keep the gems for myself! I do not know how you came by them, or why, or even why you entrusted them to me, but I am sure you had a *very* good reason."

"I see," said Sir Morgan thoughtfully. Again Tess experienced that odd little twinge of memory, as if she'd seen that particular expression on those dark features at some long-previous time. It was impossible, of course; had they met before, Sir Morgan would surely have remarked on it.

"You may rely on me," Tess promised. "I had wished to tell you so earlier and blame myself that I did not, for then you would have been spared the bother of bribing those highwaymen and that man in the park. Just tell me what you wish me to do with the thing! I will be glad to hand it over to you."

"I think," and Sir Morgan looked grave indeed, "that perhaps you should. Where is, er, it now?"

"Hidden in my room." Tess tried once more to free herself, but he gripped her so tightly that her hands ached. "In fact, it's where your accomplice put it, in my portmanteau. It must have been a shock to you that I overpowered him, and I am very sorry if I inconvenienced you, but how could I know?"

"How, indeed?" murmured Sir Morgan. "You are a continual surprise, are you not?"

"I am?" Tess's brows flew up. "Why?"

"You have known me to be so reprehensible, yet seem to find no great danger in my company. Aren't you afraid that a man like myself will offer you harm?"

"I don't think," Tess replied judiciously, "that I should call you reprehensible. A trifle rash, perhaps, but I'm sure you had very good reasons for what you did. And how could you tell me what you wished me to do with the thing if I avoided you?" She smiled. "I am hardly a green girl, Sir Morgan!"

"You are exactly that!" he retorted. "If you think you stand in no danger for possessing something that was obviously stolen, you are in addition all about in your head!"

That this was an odd way in which to express one's gratitude, Tess did not pause to consider. "I'll admit the whole thing is a little shady," she replied cheerfully, "and not a situation that I would have expected to come my way, but it has been vastly exciting! I will be almost sorry to hand the bauble over to you." He frowned. "I will, of course!" she added quickly. "Don't look so grim! I only spoke in jest."

"And you call me rash!" Sir Morgan shook her, with no particular gentleness. "Next you will tell me you have enjoyed yourself so much that you mean to set up as a receiver of stolen goods!"

"What a wretch you are!" Tess's hands, released when he'd grasped her shoulders so roughly, flew up to catch her bonnet before it tumbled off her head. "Naturally I mean to do no such thing! I daresay I would have turned over the gems to Bow Street immediately, had you not been involved!"

"I?" Sir Morgan ceased to shake her. "Explain!"

"One does not lay information against one's friends," Tess replied, surprised that he should have to ask. "I did not wish to get you into trouble, for even though I had just met you, I liked you very well."

It was natural that this innocent little speech should prompt Sir Morgan to a belated expression of gratitude for her efforts in his behalf; it was equally natural, considering the man's rakish propensities, that his gratitude should be expressed by way of an extremely fervent embrace. The countess saw nothing remarkable in this, and in fact gave herself up wholeheartedly to the unique sensations resultant upon being clasped firmly in a pair of strong arms and kissed most ruthlessly. She had nothing with which to compare that kiss, it being her first experience with such things, but she thought—rather fuzzily—that she at last understood why some ladies were so addicted to the pastime.

# Chapter 14

*The dowager duchess was far too well aware* of her own consequence to be the least gratified by the stream of noble visitors who presented themselves at Bellamy House on the day after Clio's coming-out ball, and gazed unawed upon such illustrious and influential callers as Lady Jersey, the Countess of Lieven, Lords Petersham and Alvanley, and even Beau Brummell. Though totally devoid of any of the more praiseworthy virtues, Sapphira did possess a very lively appreciation of the absurd. With her favorite caller of them all seated nearby, and privy to her various acerbic comments, Sapphira allowed herself to be entertained by the raree show that was being enacted in her front drawing-room.

Excepting the duke, the entire family was present, though Evelyn and Nidget were speedily banished when the mongrel took loud exception to Lady Jersey's bonnet; but Sapphira had no thought to spare for the volatile Silence's sensibilities. She was far more interested in Tess, who was commanding much more attention than young Clio, a state with which neither of them seemed particularly pleased. Tess looked well enough, Sapphira conceded charitably, in that round robe of lilac cambric, but she couldn't hold a candle to Clio, exquisite in a morning gown of fine white French lawn. All the same, Tess was being besieged by the gentlemen while Clio sat talking in a desultory manner to Lucille. It was deuced queer, concluded Sapphira, wondering what it meant.

The dowager duchess was not the only one to ponder Tess's apparent success, and not the least of the others thus puzzled was Tess herself. It did not surprise her that the gentlemen were polite to her, for she knew them all to be friends of the Duke of Bellamy and Sir Morgan, and assumed that they had been asked to be kind to the country mouse. She thought nothing of it, though she appreciated the effort to make her feel comfortable, and when Brummell engaged her in a discussion of Wellington's progress in the Peninsula, acquitted herself quite nicely with a knowledgeable discussion of the situation at Badajoz. The Beau—who, unknown to Tess, neither held a kindness for country bumpkins nor made a practice of obliging his friends—listened and smiled rather enigmatically, then with professed reluctance and an odd glance at Sir Morgan took his leave. This was the sign for a general exodus. Only Sir Morgan, Shamus, and Cedric remained behind. Conversation briefly lagged, then Drusilla—stunning in a Spanish robe of pea-green muslin for which she had not yet paid—suggested getting up a party to attend the Royal Opera House. The idea was seized upon eagerly.

One of the visitors, however, could not look upon such dissipation complacently. "I have a poor view of music," stated Shamus for Tess's unwilling ear alone. "I fear it often draws a person to mix with much company he would otherwise avoid."

"Ah!" replied Tess, who had been hard pressed to greet his more inane utterances with civility. "Then I must allow myself to be guided by you, and refrain from exposing myself to contamination by remaining safely at home."

The sarcasm was entirely wasted; Shamus looked gratified. "I wish you would!" he murmured. "You know it is my dearest wish that you should place yourself in my hands. Nor am I alone in that desire, as your—but I must not give *that* away!—as Clio has intimated to me."

Tess cast a fulminating glance at that young miss, who was looking rather subdued. Surely Clio didn't wish her to marry a dullard whose conversation was flat as a street pavement! "I am not," she retorted repressively, "in the habit of considering Clio's wishes above my own. I beg you will say no more on this subject, Shamus! It is very bad of you to plague me when I have already told you that it is impossible."

"Nothing," reproved the curate playfully, "is impossible! You do not know your own mind. But I will say no more on *that* matter now!" He did not, but he elaborated on any number of other topics, discussing them with a thoroughness that Tess found exceedingly tiresome.

The countess was not the only one to be acutely ill at ease; Mistress Clio nurtured a burgeoning suspicion that things were not going at all as she had planned. Even the forty invitations that were already lying on a table in her room had no power to lift her spirits. Clio pondered Cedric's inexplicable behavior. Although he had appeared, as requested, at Bellamy House, he made no attempt to address his attentions to her, but gave every indication of wishing to dangle after Tess. Clio, recalling her hapless comment to him about her sister's wealth, glowered so terribly that Lucille, feeling the onset of a spasm, fled the room in search of her cordials and her laudanum.

Drusilla quickly claimed the abandoned chair. "My dear," she said, touching Clio's hand, "you are looking sadly knocked-up! It will not do! I have some excellent complexion powders that will quickly bring the roses back to your cheeks."

"You are very good," murmured Clio, bewildered by this unexpected friendliness.

Cedric, perfectly aware that he had aroused Clio's wrath, studiously avoided her gaze. He had dressed carefully for the occasion, and knew that he was positively eye-catching in his exquisite raiment, the *pièce de résistance* of which was a pristine cravat arranged in the intricate folds of the Mathematical, a feat which had taken countless ruined neckcloths and two hours to achieve. He also knew that the countess regarded him with abhorrence despite his efforts to be charming, but Ceddie did not easily despair. He could not, lest he be arrested and imprisoned in King's Bench prison for his debts. Cedric had that very morning—having adjourned after the ball to visit Mother Windsor, a notable procuress in King's Place—

heard a harrowing tale of a young gentleman who, after giving a splendid supper party at his club, had returned home to swallow a lethal dose of prussic acid rather than face arrest and ruin. Though Ceddie would not go to such lengths, he foresaw that he might have to follow the time-honored tradition of fleeing the country if his luck did not soon change. Lady Tess, wealthy and unworldly as she was, seemed the answer to his prayers. Clio would surely forgive him after the *fait accompli*.

But the worthy Shamus was grievously interfering with the execution of Ceddie's schemes, and he considered it nothing less than an exhibition of boundless effrontery. Cedric smoothed his golden locks, cropped short in the fashionable Brutus, and once more interrupted the conversation with a nicely phrased compliment. It earned him only a glance of pure dislike from the countess. Disgruntled, he turned away.

Constant, who had been watching his prey with mingled anticipation and curiosity, saw his opportunity. In no time worth mentioning Ceddie had forgotten Tess in an animated discussion of the turf—the barren heath at Ascot, the horseraces at Newmarket—for like many an aspiring young aristocrat, he dreamed of proceeding to the unsaddling enclosure at Epson as the owner of a Derby winner, and of bringing an illustrious career to culmination by being elected a steward of the Jockey Club. Constant played cleverly upon these boyish visions, and soon had convinced Cedric—whom he mistakenly judged to have more money than brains, neither of which commodities Ceddie owned in abundance—that he was most knowledgeable in such things.

Drusilla, piqued that Sir Morgan should have so long ignored her in favor of her mother, and angered to have learned from her abigail that Sir Morgan had gone riding that morning with Tess, stirred restlessly and temporarily shelved a half-made plan to spread a tale that Clio was so hardened to shame that she engaged in brazen flirtations with young officers. *"Maman!"* she called out, nicely silencing the various conversations. "I have heard the strangest thing!"

"Eh?" inquired Sapphira, who thought nothing could be more droll that her daughter's efforts to ensnare the Wicked Baronet.

"You will barely credit it." Having secured a unanimous attention, Drusilla paused dramatically. "Bianca has suffered a robbery." She glanced at Sir Morgan, animated by a very bad spirit indeed. "She is mighty careless, it seems, and has lost that diamond necklace you gave her, Morgan. I wonder that you will treat your flirts so generously!"

No one exhibited the least surprise at these words; it was common knowledge that generous as he might be with his inamoratas, the Wicked Baronet had never given Drusilla any presents at all. Ceddie eyed her with open admiration; Sir Morgan smiled. Shamus, alas, was a great deal more easily shocked. "I am astounded," he muttered, "at such familiarity and upon such a subject! It is not at all, I think, what we are either of us used to, dear Tess."

The countess, distracted by that mention of a diamond necklace, thought if she had to listen to one more word from her worthy suitor they should come to cuffs. With vast relief, she saw Giles paused on the threshold, looking excessively handsome in a fashionable blue coat with brass buttons, a buff-colored waistcoat, pale yellow breeches, and gleaming top boots. "Excuse me!" she said, rather disjointedly. "I must speak with the duke! About his son."

Shamus stared after her, indignant at having been interrupted in mid-soliloquy. Not a clever man, as he himself would be the first to rather ponderously admit, Shamus saw nothing remarkable in Ceddie's pretty attentions to the countess, and thought it admirable that the young man conducted himself so nicely toward the curate's intended bride. Tess's continual refusals of his hand were, of course, nothing more than maidenly modesty. However, Shamus—as he was also fond of saying—was far from a dunderhead, and therefore saw in the Duke of Bellamy a rival of the first magnitude. He did not even briefly consider that the duke would have Tess, with her disfigurement, but he thought it not at all unlikely that she might develop a *tendre* for him. As Shamus watched, Tess reached the duke's side, and he smiled at her in a manner that convinced the curate that the case was desperate.

Drusilla was still speaking of the necklace, which had been blatantly removed from its owner in the lobby of the Drury Lane Theatre, despite the Bow Street Runner who was engaged by the management to prevent that very thing. "You have just heard of this?" inquired Giles absently, his attention fixed on Tess. "You are behindhand, sister! The news has been for some time all over town."

"I had it from Bianca herself. She now believes that the robbery was planned—and perhaps executed!—by one of her acquaintance." Drusilla looked pointedly at Sir Morgan. "Perhaps our friend can tell us more."

"Not I!" responded Sir Morgan. "Bianca and I are not, er, precisely on terms."

Much as Clio deprecated the presence in Sapphira's drawing-room of the Wicked Baronet, she was not thinking of either Sir Morgan or diamond necklaces. Instead, she covertly watched her sister and the Duke of Bellamy, engaged in a murmured conversation that, from the duke's expression, was both lively and humorous. It seemed, she thought with oddly deflated spirits, that there was yet hope for her scheme.

Sapphira was not similarly encouraged. "That chit," she observed to Sir Morgan, "is one of the greatest curiosities I have ever seen! I wish you would make an effort to disentangle my son from her coils."

"Don't get on your high ropes." He looked uncommonly amused. "She won't have Giles."

"Little you know about it!" snorted Sapphira, blandly overlooking the fact that Sir Morgan possessed a far vaster knowledge of the opposite sex than was seemly. "That's an artful woman who will take him in as far as it lays within her power."

Sir Morgan wasted no time in pointing out that the duke had for many years avoided far more practiced snares. "What would you have me do?"

"Surely you don't need *me* to tell you that!" Sapphira cackled. "Set her up as your fancy-piece, you seem to like

142

her well enough. Though for the life of me, I can't see why!"

"I didn't expect you to." Sir Morgan glanced at Clio who, from all appearances, was reading the unhappy Cedric a thundering scold. "What of the other one?"

Sapphira followed his gaze and glared at Cedric, who happened to look up at that unpropitious moment. "Coxcomb!" she announced, in tones that were more than audible. He flushed. "Clio," she added, for Sir Morgan's ears alone, "is an unconscionable little liar, but not for the likes of you! I have plans for her."

"I thought you might." Sir Morgan was bland.

"Humph!" Sapphira smirked. "I always said you were a downy one. You don't want Clio anyway. She's a mere dab of a girl."

"You might say the same of the other one," Sir Morgan pointed out. "She isn't in my style either. Furthermore, she limps."

"Since when are you so nice in your tastes?" inquired Sapphira. Exchanging barbed insults with Sir Morgan was her favorite pastime. "I'll warrant you already have seduction in mind. You may proceed, and with my blessing! Remove the wench from my house before she takes all kinds of encroaching fancies and sets my plans at naught." She studied him. "By the by, why the devil were *you* putting up at that inn? Some discreet rendezvous, I'll wager!"

"Sapphira," said Sir Morgan in admiring tones, "I am every day more struck with the endless mine of your intellectual resources! After I have ruined the girl, what would you have me do?"

"Lud, *I* don't care!" Sapphira shrugged. "I want only that you should place her beyond the pale of society. It won't take long, I vow! You're as plausible and cunning as the devil himself."

"And," added Sir Morgan, "according to you, I am also cruel to the greatest degree.'"

"Where are you going?" Sapphira demanded suspiciously.

"To do your bidding, you old griffin!" Sir Morgan swept

her an elegant bow. "You must have known I would not refuse."

It was with no little trepidation that Tess observed the approach of her fellow conspirator, for she anticipated that her next interview with Sir Morgan would be highly unpleasant. With reluctance she broke off her conversation with the duke—which, had Sapphira but known it, concerned nothing more potentially dangerous that Nidget's encounter with Lady Jersey's bonnet. "You're leaving?" inquired Giles.

"I am. We'll meet later at White's? Good!" Sir Morgan's golden gaze fixed speculatively on Tess. "Come, little one, and show me to the door. I wish to speak with you."

Tess considered refusing this rather odd request but was given no opportunity; Giles smoothly and firmly thrust her forward. It was a departure that went unnoted by no one in the room. Drusilla seethed with indignation, and Constant stifled malicious laughter only with great effort; Clio's spirits sank right to her toes; Sapphira wore an evil little grin, and Cedric looked thoughtful. Of them all, Shamus was the most strongly affected, and his withers were positively wrung. A man of insuperable vanity, the curate didn't briefly consider that from the countess he would receive a final rebuff, but he did feel that she was shockingly unappreciative. When Shamus considered his flawless character, the faithfulness and extent of his attachment to her, and the lengths he had gone to in making that preference obvious, he thought that the countess was behaving in a monstrously ungrateful manner.

The countess had no thought to spare for the others; she stood in the deserted hallway, looking up at Sir Morgan, and waited for the axe to fall. "My treasure!" he said, rather gruffly.

"Well, yes," Tess agreed cautiously, "I know I said I'd give it to you, but I have changed my mind." She read anger on his swarthy features, and stepped back hastily. "Surely you must see why! But we cannot talk here."

"On that head, at least, we are in agreement." Sir Morgan moved down the hallway and threw open a door. "If you will, madam?"

Silently, Tess proceeded into the book-room and watched him close the door. "It will not serve to offer me violence!" she said hastily, when he turned. "I retain possession of the diamonds, remember."

"So you do." Sir Morgan looked no less forbidding. "However, you have already told me where they are hidden. I could very easily dispose of you, reclaim them, and make a getaway with no one the wiser. You might consider *that*, Tess!"

The countess did so, judiciously, then burst into laughter. "You are the most absurd man!" She moved across the room toward him. "I see that I have offended you, and I am sorry for it! But you did look rather diabolical, you know, and I expected you would be angry when I refused to return the gems."

Sir Morgan did not appear to share her amusement. "Very perspicacious of you," he replied, in tones totally devoid of praise. "Would you mind telling me why you changed your mind—although I think I can guess!"

"You could," agreed Tess, watching as he folded his arms and leaned against the wall, "but I don't think you have! When I first learned that the necklace had been given by you to one of your, er, friends, I thought perhaps you had reclaimed it when your, ah, relationship had come to an end—and I couldn't blame you for that at all, though it does seem a trifle nipfarthing to take back a gift! Then I wondered if perhaps she hadn't given it back to you and then regretted the action, so claimed it had been stolen so that *you* would give it back to *her*. But then, I fancy I hit upon the truth!" Tess smiled triumphantly. "It *was* stolen from her, by persons unknown, and she called upon you to bring about its return!"

Sir Morgan might have a quick temper, but his lips twitched at various points throughout this narrative. "Oh?" he inquired. "Why should she turn to me instead of trusting to Bow Street?"

"I don't know." Tess looked rueful. "I thought perhaps you might tell me that."

"If you don't mind," Sir Morgan retorted, with greatly strained severity, "I think I will not! You already know entirely too much for your own good. Having determined that I am prompted only by the most praiseworthy of motives, why do you now refuse to return the gems to me?"

"You must see that it is much too dangerous!" Tess was stern. "I hope you will forgive me for saying that this lady sounds to me most untrustworthy. You heard what Drusilla said! She as much as accused *you* of being responsible! Think what would happen were you to be caught with the necklace! Only this Bianca knows you have it at her express request, and if she chose not to remain silent, your conduct would be exposed to such recrimination as to make you unpopular beyond measure!" She shook her head. "No, Sir Morgan, it simply will not serve. You must see that!"

"Oh, I do!" replied the Wicked Baronet, in somewhat strangled tones. "What then do you mean to do?"

"Why, I must take the necklace to her myself!" said Tess, with widened eyes. "What else? It should prove easy enough."

"Not so easy as you might imagine." Sir Morgan regarded his benefactress with fascination. He tried without success to imagine a meeting between Tess and the volatile Bianca. "The lady, prostrated by her loss, has retired to Bath."

"Bath!" Tess's face fell. "Then I suppose we must wait until her return. How unfortunate!"

"We have little choice," agreed Sir Morgan, detaching himself from the wall, "since you do not appear inclined to entrust the gems to me. There is one thing you have not considered! Since I have been acquitted of the theft, I must also be acquitted of plaguing you with footpads and highwaymen."

The countess was far from unintelligent. "Ah!" said she.

"Precisely. Someone knows you have that necklace, and is anxious for its return."

Nor was Lady Tess easily daunted. "Then," she replied

easily, "we shall simply contrive to see that their efforts are thwarted, shan't we?"

No doubt impressed by so stalwart an attitude, Sir Morgan placed his fingers on her throat and tilted up her chin. "You are not the only one who is perspicacious!" he remarked, somewhat inconsequentially. "I myself possess no little foresight, having broken off with Bianca before I ever encountered you at the inn. I suppose I must have known that fate held in store for me a charming nitwit who would remove all other considerations from my mind!"

"You are flirting with me again," Tess said severely, though she made no effort to move away. "I have told you it is not necessary."

"I *never*," retorted Sir Morgan, offended, "flirt because it's necessary." With an idle finger, he traced the outline of her nose. "Don't you like it, little one?"

"Well, yes, I rather do," admitted Tess, in a husky little voice. "I suppose I should not say so, but such things have never come my way before. And I see it must be perfectly natural for you to behave so, being a rake, and I should not wish you to be uncomfortable because I asked you to refrain! But I should not wish you to think you *had* to do so to protect your interests."

A man of less worldly wisdom and greater sensibility might have been totally dashed by this forthright little speech, but Sir Morgan only smiled crookedly. "That will teach me!" he said. Tess's puzzled look did not prompt him to explain.

"If you *do* wish to flirt with me," Tess added, afraid she had somehow wounded him, "you may do so, of course! I haven't the least objection!"

"But I *don't* wish to flirt with you!" Sir Morgan replied. This was an odd comment in view of the fact that he still held her face between his hands.

"Oh," said Tess, absurdly disappointed.

"You are not at all the sort of female," explained Sir Morgan, drawing her closer, "whom I engage in flirtation." Tess looked up, bewildered, and the Wicked Baronet suffered an unprecedented pang of conscience. "Poor puss!" he murmured. "It is not at all kind of me to tease you. But I am *not* kind, Tess, or considerate, and I have a vile temper and an even viler tongue."

"I know," she said, trying desperately to summon rational thought, "but—though I brand myself reprehensible by admitting it!—I have always considered virtue very dreary when not tempered with at least a little practiced vice. Well, look at Shamus! *He* possesses every conceivable virtue, and he is a dead bore! You are a much more interesting man." Sir Morgan was so taken with this unusual outlook that he stood rooted to the floor, and she ventured to touch his lean cheek. "Truly," begged the countess, "you must not berate yourself! Think how highly you are valued by all your friends! Even Sapphira admires you, and I don't think she approves of anyone else except Giles." She studied his cravat. "As for myself, I admire you, Sir Morgan, and I like you far more than any other gentleman I have ever known."

Conscience was snuffed out like a candle. Without the slightest compunction, Sir Morgan kissed the countess again.

# Chapter 15

*The Dowager Duchess of Bellamy's berlin rolled* with dignity through the streets of the West End, pausing briefly so that its occupants might gaze upon such entertainments as conjurers, fire-eaters, and Punch-and-Judy men. Despite these rare treats, the expedition was not proving felicitous: the occupants of the carriage were at distinct odds with one another. Even Evelyn, having been denied the pleasure of viewing the famous elephant Clunee at the Exeter 'Change, had succumbed to sulks. Nidget lay on the floor at his master's feet, equally abject; Delphine stared stonily out the window, having received a most emphatic set-down from her mistress when she dared broach the subject of Sir Morgan; and Clio gazed gloomily upon her neatly gloved hands. Impervious to the discontent that she had roused in her companions, the countess enlivened the rather brooding atmosphere with a lively discussion of the Royal Institution, which was more the *ton* than anything, the regent having been elected president. There, she announced, ladies of all ages submitted to a shocking squeeze to hear morning lectures on the Human Understanding, Experimental Philosophy, Painting, Music, and Geology. No one paid the slightest attention to her words, and Tess fell silent. She looked at Clio, who appeared burnt to the socket, and frowned.

Despite the pleasure of wearing a brand new walking dress of muslin with a waistcoat bosom, a gypsy hat and veil, Mistress Clio felt as unhappy as she looked. There was more than ample justification for her malaise—to wit, an unnerving interview with Sapphira, which had left Clio so overset that she had fled in total confusion and had swallowed Drusilla's complexion powders without demur. Sapphira was out of charity with her entire family and had made no bones about saying so: Drusilla was a fast piece of goods, so lost to reason as to hang on Sir Morgan in the most revolting manner; Lucille was spineless and a damned nuisance, giving way to nervous fancies such as the imbecilic notion that sinister characters were lurking about Bellamy House and consequently rendering herself hysterically useless when her mother needed her most; and Constant was worse than worthless, being a curst loose fish. Having nicely disposed of those of her dependents, the dowager duchess had turned her guns on Clio, informing that astonished miss that *she* was to marry Giles, and without further nonsense. Whether the duke had been informed of his fate, and what he thought of it, Clio had dared not ask, and in fact had been given scant opportunity to do so, Sapphira having launched into a lamentation over past errors, and a panegyric upon the rapturous future which Clio might expect as the duke's wife. In truth, the notion did not displease Clio, who had never seen a greater appearance of worth and honor than she saw in Giles; but she remembered the way he looked at Tess and the mutual pleasure that they appeared to derive from one another's company, and knew that she would not allow herself to be instrumental in breaking up such a promising romance. Her decision was made and she was honor-bound by it, even though it must inevitably condemn her to a lifetime of unhappiness.

Nor would Sapphira disapprove, once she learned Tess was the Countess of Lansbury. Had she not been so shocked, both by Sapphira's plans for her future and the discovery that she liked those plans exceedingly well, Clio would have informed the dowager duchess of the truth—but she had not, and therefore had sunk even deeper into the morass.

Clio had come to view Sir Morgan as the only obstacle on her sister's roadway to happiness, and there seemed no alternative now but to attach that audacious gentleman to herself. Ceddie having proven himself next to useless, Clio had sent that young man off with a flea in his ear. He was furious with her as a result but he would come about again, and when he did Clio thought she might have some use for him. For Shamus, she had none at all. A brief moment's conversation had been sufficient to show her that the curate had more chance of driving Tess to murder him than of winning her heart. But he would serve as distraction, if nothing else; while engaged in elevating conversation with the curate, Tess could hardly further her acquaintance with the Wicked Baronet.

It was not that Clio suspected Sir Morgan of harboring improper intentions toward her sister; she never considered his intentions at all. She only knew he was a heartless man, one who would flaunt convention at a whim, wager all his possessions on the turn of a card, and merely shrug if he lost; and she feared that Tess, so inexperienced as to not realize that Sir Morgan was capable of ruining her without the slightest twinge of remorse, was so blind as to overlook his faults. Clio, who had taken an unreasoning dislike to the man, would have been startled to learn that the countess was very much aware of Sir Morgan's faults, and found in them nothing particularly worthy of censure; she would have been thoroughly scandalized had she known that the countess had already been twice embraced by that swarthy rake and was rather hoping he'd find occasion to do so again.

The barouche drew up outside the British Museum, which Sapphira had decreed was sufficiently absorbing to keep the various members of the little party out of mischief for a while, and disgorged its passengers. A brief altercation ensued when it transpired that Nidget would not be permitted inside, but at length he was sent off in the barouche, and the others crossed the threshold.

Within was a strange mishmash of works of art, natural curiosities, books, and models in random display. Evelyn went off immediately to inspect two enormous stuffed giraffes that stood like guards at the top of the staircase, but his companions were less enthused.

"You are looking positively haggard, child," said Tess to her sister. The countess had some faint hope of healing the breach that had opened up between them. "Is something troubling you? Won't you tell me what it is?"

Clio could hardly announce her appalling discovery that she was more than a little fond of the man whom she meant her sister to wed. "Nothing," she replied sullenly. Giles must be shown that Tess would be a wife worthy of his rank and station, and Tess must be shown that Sir Morgan was unworthy of her affection. What a hobble! thought Clio, wondering how she was to attach a gentleman who preferred to remain unaware of her existence.

"Bah!" muttered Delphine. "Something is very wrong, you needn't bother denying it, *poupée*! You are white as a ghost, and trembling, and starting at a sound. That *you* should be afraid of your own shadow is of all things incomprehensible!"

"I have said it is nothing!" snapped Clio, glowering at a bust of Hippocrates. She was well aware of how she looked, and for that reason had resorted to the complexion powders, bitter as they were, and not that they seemed to be particularly effective. However, as Drusilla had pointed out, such things took time.

"If it's Ceddie," remarked Lady Tess, a trifle tactlessly, "then it *is* nothing. I suppose he followed you here? Forget him, child! He is not the husband for you."

This callous attitude could not but set up Clio's hackles, particularly since she was making such sacrifices on her sister's behalf. "I'll marry whom I please, Tess, with or without your consent!" she retorted waspishly. "You've never given poor Ceddie a chance."

The countess reflected that she had given Cedric every chance, allowing him the run of her house for many years; she further thought that it was Clio who had given Sir Morgan no opportunity to prove *his* value. She said none of these things, lest she inspire her sister to further exhibitions of temper. "Don't make a piece of work of it," she said, gazing unappreciatively upon the celebrated Portland vase. "Think of all your other beaux, Clio. I'm sure the majority of them are perfectly unexceptionable."

This was true; Mistress Clio had not allowed her various schemes to interfere with her social life. She had attended brilliant dinners at which the company was drawn from the highest in the land, where the wine and food was of the best quality; she had graced a breakfast given in the Horticultural Gardens and surveyed the exhibition of prize fruits; she had witnessed concerts where only the very first talents in the metropolis were engaged; she was promised that very evening for a great *fête* where the fashionable world would be entertained by musicians, a ball, and a French play. In so doing, she had amassed a great many admirers, a gratifying number of whom gave every indication of coming up to snuff. A few scant weeks before, Clio would have been in high flights at her success; now she was depressed. But she roused herself to make an effort, and was so successful that Tess, against her own wishes, agreed to accompany her sister to Almack's. "Good!" said Clio, and promptly plunged again into gloom.

Tess and Delphine exchanged a worried glance, both considering it decidedly queer that so highly capricious a damsel should turn so lachrymose. They did not discuss the matter, however, being themselves barely on speaking terms. Tess regretted the estrangement from her abigail, of whom she was fond; but she dared not acquaint Delphine with the truth of Sir Morgan's association with her. Were Delphine to learn of the necklace, the fat would be in the fire. The abigail already had the lowest opinion of Sir Morgan's character, as Tess had every reason to know, and no consideration would prevent her going to Bow Street, which would land Sir Morgan—and perhaps Tess herself—in prison for theft.

There was one thing Tess could do something about, much as she disliked the idea. "Clio," she ventured. "Listen to me, child! I suppose Ceddie may have good qualities of which I am unaware. Indeed, he must! Even the worst rakehell must have *some* redeeming qualities. Perhaps my dislike—it would be absurd to deny that I dislike him!—has blinded me to Ceddie's merits."

Clio remained silent. She could not think that Ceddie possessed any virtue whatsoever, or that Sir Morgan, the greatest blackguard of her acquaintance, was otherwise blessed.

"All I wish," added Tess, daunted by this uncooperative attitude, "is your happiness, child! If you must have Ceddie, so be it! I only ask that you give yourself time to know him—and to know your own heart. I would not wish you to contract a marriage that would in time make you miserable."

Clio, who hadn't the slightest wish to marry Ceddie, and who had no hope of contracting a marriage that wouldn't make her miserable, being as the only man for whom she nourished the slightest *tendre* was destined for another, greeted this generosity with less than gratitude. "Thank you!" she sniffled. Tess, totally baffled by such bizarre behavior, shrugged and allowed Evelyn to lead her off to the huge shed that housed the noble Elgin marbles.

"Oh, Daffy!" wailed Clio, staring at her sister's departing back. "Whatever am I to do?"

"We shall contrive," soothed Delphine, though she hadn't the slightest idea how.

With little idea that her two closest companions considered her almost past praying for, Tess gazed upon the famous marbles, and then at her youthful escort. "Ugly, aren't they?" inquired Evelyn. "I think it was a waste of time for Lord Elgin to bring them from Greece! You are looking fine as fivepence, Aunt Tess."

The countess twitched her fawn-colored sarsenet pelisse trimmed with mohair fringe, adjusted her straw bonnet, and smoothed her Limerick gloves. "Aren't I just?" she agreed. "A nonpareil, in fact! Gammon, young man."

Evelyn laughed and grasped the hand that was unencumbered by a cane. "Are you going to marry my father?" he asked bluntly. "I wish you would! Sapphira wants Clio

154

to marry him, and I suppose she's a good sort of girl, but I'd much rather have you."

"How nice of you!" responded Tess. "Just how do you know what Sapphira wants, Evelyn? I don't suppose she told you."

"Well, no!" The young viscount was totally unabashed. "They forget I'm around, you see! I was in the hallway this morning when she told Clio."

"You just happened to be passing," said Tess, considering herself hardly of sufficiently untarnished moral character to chastize Evelyn for eavesdropping.

The boy grinned. "And I heard Drusilla tell Constant that Clio is every bit as bad as her mother was, and will probably go the same way." He looked puzzled. "What does that mean?"

"I don't know." Tess was mortified by the realization that she hadn't thought of Mirian for several days. "But I think, Evelyn, that we must find out."

This sounded quite reasonable to the viscount. In perfect accord, they proceeded outside. "Aunt Tess?" he said, exhibiting a laudable tenacity of purpose. "If you won't marry my father, who will you marry? Sir Morgan?" Tactful beyond his years, he refrained from telling her what Drusilla had said about *that*.

"Dear Evelyn," Tess responded gently, "it is very good of you to think that I am so irresistible!" She glanced at her cane. "Females like myself do not think of marrying."

"Fudge!" remarked Evelyn, but did not argue. A precocious lad, he had already deduced that even the best of females were prone to queer notions. Gaily he skipped into the street. Tess followed more slowly, pausing to gaze into the window of a shop where the best English glass was displayed, and admiring an exhibit of sapphire- and ruby-colored glass tastefully combined to look like a cluster of flowers from an Oriental garden.

Later she could not say exactly how it happened, but one moment she was staring at the glittering glass and thinking inevitably of diamond necklaces, and the next a rough hand had grasped her arm and thrust her into the street, right into the path of an oncoming carriage. The countess gasped and wielded her cane, only to have it knocked out of her hand. Clio, emerging from the museum, shrieked; the spectators gaped and murmured, but made no attempt to interfere. It was left to Evelyn to grasp a handy rock and hurl it with great accuracy at the assailant, who took quickly to his heels, and to Tess to throw herself out of the way of the murderous carriage-wheels. Revelation, if not the carriage, struck her then: she had the answer to at least one of the questions that puzzled her. No wonder Morgan seemed familiar! She grinned.

An understandable pandemonium ensued, the spectators expressing belated concern and the driver of the carriage uttering mingled oaths and apologies, but at last the crowd was dispersed, the barouche summoned, and the countess placed tenderly within. "It was the man in the park," hissed Evelyn. "I recognized him."

"*Voyons!*" erupted Delphine.

"It was nothing!" Tess said, almost euphorically. "A mere accident! I have taken no harm. You will all oblige me by not speaking of it."

Evelyn, alarmed not a little by the possibility that Tess might extract from him a promise to keep silent about *this,* rattled into quick praise of the antediluvian remains he had observed at the museum, chief among which seemed to be—according to him—an enormous and remarkably perfect pair of stag's antlers. The young viscount was a clear-sighted lad, and he didn't like the appearance of things.

Since Evelyn was not the only one to harbor misgivings, and since Tess had effectively forestalled further comments by the simple expedient of closing her eyes, the trip back to Bellamy House was accomplished in a tense silence. Their arrival coincided with that of Sir Morgan, who was ascending the steps. The Wicked Baronet was a man of legendarily quick action; no sooner did he set eyes on the shattered cane, which Evelyn bore aloft like a trophy of war, than he was down the steps, across the courtyard, and firmly clasping Tess in his arms. Before Delphine could utter so much as a single word regarding *les covenances*, he had carried the countess inside. Clio stared glumly after them, wondering what Tess could possibly see in a monstrous man who treated her with as little respect as if she were a member of the frail sisterhood.

"Truly, I'm not hurt!" protested Tess, having acquainted Sir Morgan with the details of her misadventure as, to the scandalized amazement of various servants, he carried her up the stairs.

With a booted foot he kicked shut the door and dumped her unceremoniously on the bed. "You should be!" he thundered, his dark face forbidding. "Of all the bird-witted things to do! I could throttle you."

"It seems an odd way to conduct a flirtation!" replied Tess, fascinated. "But I will concede you must know far more about such things than I."

"I would like," uttered Sir Morgan wrathfully, "to turn you over my knee!"

"Then by all means do so!" Tess invited cordially. "*I'm* not one to flinch away from a new experience."

Sir Morgan regarded the countess, a rueful expression in his golden eyes. She had lost her bonnet, her pelisse was in a shocking condition, there was a smudge of dirt on the end of her nose, and her hair had again come unpinned. "You must now admit," he said, in gentler tones, as he sat on the edge of the bed and applied his handkerchief to the smudge, "that your possession of that necklace is damned dangerous."

"I admit no such thing," Tess replied sternly. "I am surprised at your lack of spirit, sir!" With an oath, Sir Morgan rose and paced with determination toward her portmanteau. "It's not there. I changed the hiding place after our last talk."

"Thinking I would steal into your room in the dead of night and reclaim it?" inquired Sir Morgan. "Unworthy, little one!"

"Thinking," retorted Tess, who was not at all averse to

the notion, "that the culprit would be sure to look there for it, having placed it there himself."

Sir Morgan looked to be on the verge of a veritable frenzy. "So you will concede," he uttered, with severely strained patience, "that the person who placed the diamonds there will not cease in his efforts to regain possession of them. Then you must also concede that you are in grave danger!"

"Pooh!" Tess waved an airy hand. "I don't care for that! It is an admirable opportunity to catch the brute red-handed, and then your lady friend will have no opportunity to point the finger of suspicion at you."

His lady friend, thought Sir Morgan, would be more than a little incensed if her necklace came to light in another woman's boudoir. "Sheer insanity!" he exclaimed.

"Do not think I am unprepared!" Tess delved into the chamber pot that was discreetly hidden beneath her bed. Sir Morgan found himself looking into the muzzle of a deadly looking little gun. "I think I may say without conceit that I am a crack shot, my father having made it a point to instruct me in the use of firearms. Why he did so I cannot imagine, since I'm sure he never thought I would be called upon to protect my virtue! However, it is a useful ability."

"Good God!" was Sir Morgan's only comment.

"I know," agreed Tess sadly. "I exhibit a shocking insensibility. I have often deprecated it! But it is not in me to succumb to vapors, even in the most trying of circumstances." She regarded him anxiously. "Not that the incident today was at all trying—indeed, it was positively felicitous! And I fancy it was meant to merely frighten me, for it was shockingly mismanaged. Had that man wished it, he could easily have contrived that I was crushed by that carriage, but he did not! He obviously does not wish to add murder to his other crimes." She sighed. "I regret only the loss of my cane. It is beyond repair this time, I fear."

Well-acquainted as Sir Morgan was becoming with Tess's erratic processes of thought, these offhand state-

158

ments caused him to sit down, rather abruptly, on the edge of the bed. "I will get you another cane," he said, bemused. "But *felicitous?*"

"Well, yes!" Tess smiled. "It was the strangest thing, but all I could think of in those few moments was my other accident. I remembered it all quite clearly, though I have not done so in years." She reached up and brushed back the lock of dark hair that had fallen onto his brow. "And I recalled at last where we had met before, lion-eyes!"

# Chapter 16

*"Oh,* la vache!" *muttered Delphine* under her breath, as a nervous little housemaid poured a brass can of cold water, then one of hot, into a hip bath. A third can waited to one side. It was not the maid, clumsy as the creature was, who roused Delphine's wrath. She glowered impotently at her mistress.

Tess, ignoring this Friday-face, thanked the housemaid and dismissed her. "I tell you," repeated Delphine, as soon as the girl had gone, "I saw your precious Sir Morgan in whispered conversation with the Duke of Bellamy's valet—and you can bank on it that the pair of them are up to no good!"

"Twaddle!" With approval, Tess regarded the new cane —ebony with a fierce lion's head mounting in silver— which Sir Morgan had sent her by messenger. It was a very handsome article; it was additionally a very cleverly disguised sword-stick.

*"Mon Dieu!"* Delphine exploded with rage. "If it was so innocent, then why did money exchange hands?"

"Did it?" inquired Tess, with a faint spark of interest. "I'll admit Pertwee is marvelously sinister-looking, Daffy, but I doubt Sir Morgan was engaged in anything more nefarious than seeking the secret of Giles's gleaming boots." She looked contemplative. "I wonder what Pertwee does use. Champagne?"

*"Imbecile!"* retorted Delphine, but under her breath.

160

"You will tell me also that I am air-dreaming when I say that your sister is ill, suffering nausea and sleeplessness."

"I'll tell you no such thing," began the countess, but they were interrupted by a knock on the door. The housekeeper stood there. "The Duchess of Bellamy wishes your presence, miss," Mrs. Bibby announced, "in the drawing-room."

"Then I must attend her, must I not?" Tess replied. "You may go, Delphine! I'll have no more need of you tonight." The abigail stiffly inclined her head. She was all out of patience with her mistress, whom she considered to be waltzing gaily down the pathway to ruin without the least regret.

Sapphira had arranged herself with every intention of awing the ramshackle creature who had invaded her house, but Tess walked calmly down the length of the long drawing-room without visible embarrassment and with no indication whatsoever of feeling as though she were entering the presence of royalty. Nor did she curtsy, or bob her head, or show any other sign of respect. "You wished to see me?"

"Hah!" barked Sapphira, immediately determining to keep the ill-bred wench standing. "Where the devil did you come by that cane?"

"Sir Morgan gave it to me." Tess contemplated the item. "Handsome, is it not?"

"It should be!" Sapphira had to admit Morgan knew how to wage a campaign. "Being a family heirloom. I cannot think why he gave it to *you!*"

Tess ventured no explanation, but serenely took a chair. The dowager scowled ferociously; the countess regarded her with unimpaired patience.

"Hah!" Sapphira said again, very successfully concealing a grudging respect. Few people dared square up to her. "What's my son to *you*, girl? You'll do well to forget him!"

"So we're to lay our cards on the table?" queried Tess. "Splendid! I prefer plain speaking, and I see that you agree with me."

Somewhat taken aback, Sapphira surveyed this audacious twit. She was passable, the dowager decided sourly, if one admired blue-green eyes, and finely sculpted features, and dark flyaway brows. She was also definitely unfashionable, in that dark gown, and with that fair hair piled so carelessly atop her head. Not at all in Giles's style, Sapphira mused, and said so. "Don't get notions in your head because he's kind to a cripple, girl! Giles has a way about him with the lower classes, and he can't abide deformity."

"How sad for you!" condoled Tess, with a speaking glance at Sapphira's invalid chair. "He disguises his repugnance very well! I don't think you need let it worry you."

"Tongue-valiant!" The dowager's hands clenched. "I wasn't referring to myself!"

"Oh, weren't you?" Tess raised her brows. "I thought —but obviously I misunderstood! What was it you meant to say?"

Sapphira struggled with her temper, then set off on another tack. "I brought Clio to London for a purpose."

"Yes, to give her a season," enthused Tess. "Upon my soul, you have done the thing most handsomely: balls and routs and tea parties and heaven knows what else! Clio is very grateful, I'm sure."

The dowager duchess was not accustomed to being confronted by commoners who exhibited not the slightest loss of nerve, and she found she did not care for this novelty. "Clio," she announced baldly, "is to marry Giles."

"Oh?" Tess looked interested. "Have you told her so?"

"I have." Sapphira admitted grudgingly that Tess had her wits about her.

"What did she say?" inquired the countess, bright-eyed.

"What's *that* to do with anything?" snapped Sapphira. "Talking don't pay toll! The chit will do her duty by the family, as will my son."

"Forgive me for saying so," begged Tess, "but I fear you may be guilty of counting your chickens before they're hatched. Clio is the most undutiful wretch in existence, and I am not at all certain that her affections have become fixed on the Duke of Bellamy." She frowned. "Nor am I sure I should wish them to be! Didn't I hear someone say he is incapable of resisting any woman who wants him? Or perhaps it was Sir Morgan! Such a man would not do for Clio."

The dowager was struck dumb by this piece of impertinence. *"Not,"* added Tess, "that I don't wish to see Clio form an eligible connection and settle in matrimony, because of course I do!"

To say that Sapphira knew she had met her match would be to stretch credulity to the breaking point; however, she was beginning to understand why Sir Morgan fancied this pert miss. Thought of the inevitable outcome of *that* affair raised her spirits considerably. *"You* wouldn't know, of course," she countered, with a condescending smile, "but persons of quality do not make love matches. Such things are for commoners."

"Ah! That explains it then!" Tess took the snub in good part. "I have seen little indication that the Duke of Bellamy is desirous of fixing his interest with Clio, but I now understand that I must not expect him to wear his heart upon his sleeve. How good it is of you to explain it all to me!" She cocked her pretty head to one side. "Why did you, by the way?"

Sapphira was not prompted to announce that she feared her son was becoming fonder of Tess than was suitable, and consequently said nothing. Tess, not at all quelled by this disapproving silence, launched blithely into an erudite soliloquy that ranged from an advocation of social and political emancipation for the weaker sex to a criticism of the great Wellington's military tactics in the Peninsula, in particular his underestimation of the enemy's obstinacy. "But I am rattling on!" she added, and rose. "You will wish to be alone so that you may arrange the coming nuptials! I wish you every success, though to say the truth I don't see how you are to bring it about! Things seem indeed in a bad way, and you have no doubt set up Clio's back by telling her your plans. She was ever one to act contrariwise!"

The dowager duchess, totally unaccustomed to being led round the mulberry bush, turned a violent shade of red. "Heavens, who would ever have thought we'd have such a comfortable prose together? Certainly not I!" said Tess, and smiled. "Don't despair! You may count on my assistance, if it comes to that." With this generous offer, she exited.

It was not to be expected that the dowager duchess would accept this impudence without demur, and she resorted to her long-established, and very unpleasant, habit of taking out her ill-temper on whoever was unfortunate enough to come within her range. Her children were denied her, all of them being for one reason or another absent from the house, a fortuitous event for which they would have been unanimously grateful, so it was the servants who bore the brunt of her wrath. Since this took the form of issuing contradictory orders and ripping up at everyone who crossed her path, it was little wonder that Bellamy House was soon reduced to a state of chaos.

Into this disorder stepped Sir Morgan, admitted by the second footman, who had been promoted to such duty by the fact that his superiors were otherwise occupied: the butler had locked himself in his pantry, there to partake of a fortifying nip, while the senior footman had hysterics in the kitchen. "Ah?" Sir Morgan took in the situation at a glance. "Kicking up a dust, is she?"

"Yes, sir." Charles's pleasant countenance was wooden. "The young ladies are out, sir, and I believe the Duke of Bellamy has gone to his club."

"I see," replied Sir Morgan, who had already been informed by Giles of these various engagements. "Be about your lady's bidding, Charles—what is it this time?"

"Oysters, sir," said Charles gloomily.

Sir Morgan gave a crack of laughter. "In April? I wish you luck! Go on, man, before she changes her mind and requires your head on a platter instead! I know my way around."

"Very good, sir." Charles departed for the nether regions, wondering if her ladyship would settle for mussels. It was more likely, he thought sourly, that the old battle-axe would throw them in his face.

Thus occupied, the footman did not note that the Wicked Baronet made not for the front drawing-room, but for the stairs that led to the family sleeping quarters. Nor was any other servant more observant, and Sir Morgan made his way down the upper hallway completely unchallenged. At length he gained the chamber he sought, glanced perfunctorily about him, and boldly entered.

The scene that greeted him, though certainly charming, consisting as it did of Lady Tess submerged up to her chin in a soapy hip bath and frowning at a small pamphlet, was certainly not what he had expected. "What the devil are you doing *here*?" he remarked. "Charles said you had gone out."

"Charles was obviously mistaken," responded the countess, glancing up briefly. "Do you think you might shut the door? There is a decided draft."

Sir Morgan obeyed and in the process exhibited himself not the least a gentleman, since he closed himself not out but in, and furthermore locked the door. "This is the most fascinating reading!" claimed Lady Tess, tossing aside the booklet. "Most improper, I suspect, and I don't believe a word of it." She eyed Sir Morgan speculatively as he settled into the delicate chair. "You look remarkably at home in a lady's boudoir. I don't suppose you'd care to turn your head and hand me that towel?"

Sir Morgan looked at the towel, warming in front of the fire. "No. Not until you tell me where the necklace is hidden."

"I rather thought you might feel that way." Tess studied her knees, rising through the fluffy soapsuds like rounded mountaintops. "You came to reclaim it, of course! How disappointing for you to find me here."

"Not precisely a disappointment," commented Sir Morgan, so lost to propriety as to positively relish the sight of a lady bathing by firelight. "Rather, it is a pleasure that I had not anticipated."

"Palaverer!" retorted the countess, with no evidence whatsoever of either annoyance or embarrassment. "Well, I shan't tell you where it's hidden, and you won't find it no matter how you look. Go on and search! You have my permission."

Sir Morgan seemed more inclined to look at Lady Tess

165

than for stolen necklaces. "Think," he suggested, "what would happen were we discovered in such compromising circumstances! You would be sunk quite below reproach."

"So would you," Tess pointed out, displaying admirable *sang-froid*. "You have doubtless had experience in such situations, so I will trust you to see that we are *not* caught."

"You must be," persevered Sir Morgan, "extremely uncomfortable. If you stay in that bath much longer, your skin will shrivel until you look like a prune."

The countless regarded her tormentor, more than a little satanic in the flickering firelight that turned his golden eyes red. "How unchivalrous you are! You are not in the least grateful to me for saving you from charges of theft —not that I expected you to be! However, you might thank me for making a break in your life of uniform dissipation. I'll wager you haven't even thought of the fleshpots for several days!"

"How true." Sir Morgan rose and proceeded to search the room, peering into drawers, poking into the wardrobe, even disassembling the bed. "You might be startled to learn what I *have* been thinking of, little one!"

"I doubt it." Tess propped her arms on the edge of the bath, rested her chin on them, and watched his efforts. "You shan't put me to the blush, you know."

Sir Morgan directed toward her a look that would have made most ladies turn hot with confusion. "You underestimate me! If I wished, I could more than put you to the blush, little one."

"Ah, but we both know you *don't* wish," Tess answered without the slightest hesitation. "I do wish you wouldn't reduce my room to a shambles! I've already told you you won't find the gems." She smiled. "Poor Sir Morgan, to be put to such expedients and shifts! You would not make a very successful housebreaker, I fear."

Sir Morgan was fast losing hold of his temper, a fact that was no whit alleviated by the countess's thorough enjoyment of the situation. "Hell and the devil confound it!" he spat. "You are the most aggravating—and cork-brained —female I have ever met! Will you tell me where you've put that accursed necklace, or must I throttle the information out of you?"

Tess eyed him warily; he looked perfectly capable of carrying out the threat. "No, I won't tell you!" she returned. "And if you don't lower your voice we'll both be in the suds." Sir Morgan's expression indicated that this wasn't an altogether distasteful notion, and she continued hastily. "Furthermore, it is very bad of you to threaten me when I am so totally within your power."

"But I *am* very bad," said Sir Morgan, moving closer, an unholy light in his eye. "Everyone knows that!"

"Oh no, not *bad!*" protested Tess, sliding back down beneath the suds. She wrinkled her nose. "I confess that I'd as lief not be in anyone's power, but if I must be, I prefer it to be yours."

"Generous." Sir Morgan towered over her, looking dangerous indeed.

"Not at all," murmured Tess. "I have already ascertained that I cannot get out of my bath alone, and can hardly summon a servant to help me since the bell-pull is halfway across the room." Meekly, she gazed up at him. "Don't concern yourself! Daffy is not speaking to me, but I daresay someone will turn up eventually."

With an extremely vulgar exclamation, Sir Morgan grabbed the towel, ungently yanked the countess to her feet and wrapped her in it, lifted her out of the tub, then stalked wrathfully across the room. "How kind you are!" said Tess, rather huskily, as she donned a beruffled dressing gown, grasped a hairbrush, and seated herself on the bed. "You may turn around now."

Sir Morgan raised his gaze from the bulbous pincushion that he had been bleakly studying. "Sapphira and I had a most interesting conversation today," Tess remarked as she struggled with the hairbrush. "She means Clio for Giles, did you know? But the Duchess of Bellamy gravely overestimates herself if she thinks Clio will be easily brought to heel."

The Wicked Baronet, who seldom suffered losses, now bore them bravely. With a resigned expression, he took the brush from her hand and attacked the tangles in her long hair. "You are against the match?"

"Not at all." Tess frowned. "But I am not convinced that Clio has a *tendre* for Giles, and I will not have her forced into a marriage that she does not wish."

"A noble sentiment," remarked Sir Morgan, who was not beyond getting back his own, "but what have *you* to say to it?"

"Nothing at all!" parried the countess. "How could I? You are very handy with a hairbrush!"

"Of course!" he responded. "I've had a great deal of practice. Nor is that all I'm handy with! Shall I demonstrate?"

"Do you wish to?" Tess turned to regard him with interest. "I had thought, since you were being so circumspect, that it must be in some way improper to conduct a flirtation in a lady's bedchamber—though I don't see why! It seems to me the most suitable of all places. Have I said something odd?" she added, as he choked.

"Odd!" Sir Morgan studied her. "You don't know chalk from cheese, my girl! If you speak in this manner to all your gentleman acquaintances, you will be left without a shred of reputation in no time."

"Of all the unjust things to say!" Tess retorted indignantly. "As if I should say such things to anyone else, when you are the only rake I know! But what was it you were going to demonstrate? If it was anything like the other lessons I have learned at your hands, I vow I shall enjoy it very well!"

A man of sterner moral fiber would have long past placed himself at a safer distance from his unwitting temptress—would indeed have never set foot within the room. But Sir Morgan was admittedly the most hardened of profligates, and he drew the countess down against his chest. "You would enjoy it!" he agreed. "Were I that lost to reason, Tess. That I am here at all is, to say the least, deuced irregular. I would not see you ruin yourself."

"Could I?" queried the countess, raising herself on an elbow to look down upon his amused face. "It is true that before making your acquaintance I gave little thought to such things—however, I now think I should like to be ruined." Her brow creased. "Not that I am sure *precisely* what it entails."

"I thought not," said Sir Morgan wryly. "Give me the necklace and I shall endeavor to explain."

"Bribery!" With an irritated flounce, Tess sat up. "I am *not* going to give you the necklace, no matter what you tempt me with."

"That is your final word on the matter?" Sir Morgan was grim.

"It is," Tess said gruffly. "It seems we have no more to say to one another, Sir Morgan! You may leave."

The Wicked Baronet, however, was as perverse a creature as ever drew breath, and not one to bow meekly to a lady's requests. He caught Tess's shoulders, shook her, and then kissed her almost brutally.

# Chapter 17

*The King's Theatre in the Haymarket,* home of the Italian opera and ballet, was one of the favorite haunts of the *ton.* This night the Royal Italian Opera House, as it was also known, was so crowded that all five tiers of boxes were filled with royalty and the Quality and the *demi-monde,* and the pit avenues were impassable. Since the rule here was that no one appeared except *en toilette*—even the judges and wits, the squires and beaus and bullies who settled in the pit, and the cits and lower orders who filled the middle gallery—the audience was an assemblage of beauty and magnificence that would not have been inappropriate for a court function, the men decked out in orders and ribbons, the women outblazing each other in the opulence of their jewels and the richness of their dress.

The Dowager Duchess of Bellamy had her own box, purchased on a subscription basis for £2,500 for the season, though she had never been known to set foot within. It was left to the rest of her family to enjoy the benefit of culture so procured, and they did so—this evening at least —without any great appreciation of the treat. Various of the party wore expressions so bleak as to arouse comment from those members of the audience who were more interested in their fellow spectators than in the spectacle, even though Catalini herself was on the stage. Lady Tess, who understood Italian perfectly, gazed rapt upon the highest-paid prima donna in the world.

Tess's interest was not shared by the majority of the audience. Fops and dandies strolled about chattering and showing off the cut of their clothes; spectators in the gallery shouted for silence; pretty courtesans cast knowing eyes about for new admirers; the artists continued their performance, inured to frantic enthusiasm and hideous abuse; while the Quality speculated wildly upon how the Wicked Baronet had been captivated by a Beautiful Unknown. Never, they said, had Sir Morgan showed so marked a preference, for he treated even his favorite flirts with indifference; never had he pursued one woman to the exclusion of all others, for he was known to have a wandering eye; never had they thought he would succumb to a fatal passion, and for a woman who was beautiful but lame. That Sir Morgan's pursuit was serious and his intentions honorable, few took leave to doubt. But would she have him? No one had the slightest notion whether the lady returned his sentiments, though she seemed to enjoy his company well enough. It was a matter of considerable curiosity, and bets were being laid in the clubs.

Tess had no such mixed emotions; she knew perfectly well that Sir Morgan meant to try and charm the necklace away from her, having discovered he could obtain it by no other means. She did not hold it against him that he had lost his temper with her, though his outburst had led her to a certain undertaking of her own. Brief though splendid would be her association with a rake, and Tess meant to enjoy it to the utmost. Soon enough she would return to her country estates, and life would again be dull.

The curtain descended on the artists, posturing before scenic backcloths, and Lady Tess leaned back in her seat. "Very fine!" she said judiciously. "I do admire Novosielsky's horseshoe auditorium, though I cannot see why a chandelier must hang before every box! It dazzles one very offensively, as well as throwing the actors into the shade."

"Very true!" Sir Morgan offered her his arm. "Will you accompany me? I believe your worthy suitor is on the way to pay his compliments."

"Shamus? By all means!" Tess grimaced. "How *nice* it

is not to have to explain why I should find a gentleman so amiable, so upright and honorable, to be so tedious!"

"Isn't it?" Sir Morgan's eyes danced. "I, of course, cannot be expected to value such virtues, being devoid of them myself!"

Tess was not to escape so easily; their departure from the box coincided with the arrival of Cedric, positively staggering in a purple-spotted silk coat and breeches with knots of ribbons at his knees, a waistcoat embroidered with gold and silver, pale lilac stockings, and an immensely high cravat. Rings were on his fingers, which clutched snuffbox, handkerchief, and quizzing glass. The countess took one look at this apparition and—alas!—giggled.

Such a marked lack of appreciation did not sit well with Ceddie, who knew himself to be, despite his finery, at a disadvantage beside Sir Morgan, who wore his evening coat and breeches of deep brown velvet and his Florentine waistcoat with a carelessly elegant air. All the same, Ceddie persevered, paying Lady Tess a very graceful compliment. It did not serve; she bade him play off his cajoleries on Clio, and blithely exited.

Clio, however, was no more appreciative, and practically snapped off his nose. Miffed, Ceddie sought consolation from Drusilla, who proved a much more admiring audience.

Mistress Clio was feeling sadly out of sorts. Her attempt to attract Sir Morgan had met with a bored rebuff, and her efforts to promote a match between Tess and Giles with little more success. She looked sideways at the duke, wondering at her sister's lack of acumen. Giles would be the kindest of husbands, attentive to one's wishes and one's comfort, seldom causing a moment of distress. So what must Tess do but fritter away her chances and encourage the wretched Sir Morgan, who was altogether a different kettle of fish! *His* wife, thought Clio viciously, if ever he saddled himself with one, would never know a moment's peace. If he was not squandering her fortune, he would be dangling after lightskirts. Already the association was having a disastrous effect on Tess's character; she had exhibited not the slightest dismay when Clio revealed that he was informally betrothed to Drusilla. There must be some other way to part them. Clio thought that if only she might concentrate her mind, she would hit on it.

"Your Tess is a remarkable woman," said Giles, handing her a glass of lemonade.

"She is." Clio considered this an uncommonly promising opening. "As I have told you."

"Often." The duke cast an unenthusiastic eye over the visitors crowding into his box. "It is admirable that your companion should move with such assurance in the first ranks of Society. I am forgetting, you have told me she is to the manor born, have you not?"

Clio's fingers tightened on her glass. Were matters to continue in this manner, her nerves would be shattered beyond repair. She greeted Shamus, who was peering around the box with an absurdly disappointed expression, with relief. "You have just missed Tess!" she said brightly. "If you are quick, you may still encounter her. I believe she was especially desirous of speaking with you." Considerably heartened, the curate set out in pursuit.

"Pray enlighten me," begged Giles, "why you should serve the lovely Tess such a backhanded turn. I know as well as you do that she hasn't the least desire to encounter that prosy bore!" Clio said nothing, but stared at her glass. "I see my understanding is deficient," murmured Giles. "It is Morgan, of course. You do not care for him."

"Care for that nefarious hellhound?" cried Clio, forgetting that she had tried to cast out lures to the hellhound not an hour past. "Forgive me! I can't think that acquaintance with him has improved the tone of Tess's mind, but I should not speak so about your friend."

"You may say what you wish to me," the duke replied, unconcerned. "I am not blind to Morgan's defects of character. But you, cousin, *are* blind to one aspect of this thing! I am not in Morgan's confidence, nor do I believe you to be in Tess's; but what if it should come to a match between them? You cannot set your face against him forever."

"I can and shall!" snapped Clio, depressed that Giles

could so calmly discuss her sister's alliance with another man.

"If you do," Giles remarked, with unusual patience, "you will alienate Tess. Do you wish that, Clio?"

"Oh, pray speak no more of it!" Clio looked frantic. "You know he will never marry her."

The duke knew a great deal more than he intended to confide to his young cousin, and her feelings on the subject were already so agitated that he feared another word would cause her to burst into tears. "I understand you are desirous of learning more about Mirian?" he commented idly, and had the pleasure of seeing her stare at him with surprise. "My mother tells me Tess has been asking questions of the housekeeper. Sapphira was a little incensed, but I see no harm in it—in truth, I should like to have some questions answered myself! To that end, I have instigated inquiries regarding Celest."

"Celest?" Clio echoed blankly.

"Celest DuBois, your mother's dearest friend." The Duke of Bellamy's smile was gentle. "If anyone knows the truth of Mirian's flight, it will be Celest."

Clio had far too many things plaguing her to be particularly interested in ancient history, but she recognized that Giles was going to no small trouble on her account, and thought it typical of the man that he should behave so handsomely. She glanced up at him, wondering again at Tess's lack of discrimination. "How good you are!" she murmured somberly.

Meanwhile, Lady Tess was engaged in conversation with her escort as he conducted her past the boxes that ran in a tiered circle from one wing of the theater to the other via the back of the pit. The countess was worried about her sister, and so informed Sir Morgan.

The Wicked Baronet, who had been humbly apologizing for both his hasty temper and his misuse of the countess, as well as expressing his resolution to assist in the return of the pilfered necklace, looked amused. "My promise to be of service to you prompts you to nothing but thoughts of your charge. I am sadly put down." She frowned at him, and he smiled. "No, I am only teasing you. What has Clio done to put you in a fret?"

"Not a fret, precisely," Tess replied, "but she is not at all herself. Clio has never been prone to ill health. Now she is so constantly out of humor that I fear she must be racketing herself to pieces. I cannot think town life suits her! Perhaps it would be best to return home."

"You have a genius for understatement." Sir Morgan deftly guided her through the crowd that thronged the foyer, built by the management in the futile hope that here the beaux might promenade with fewer interruptions to the audience and the artists on the stage. "To be blunt, my love, Clio is looking burnt to the socket. And you must see that it is impossible for you to leave town."

"Your *what*?" inquired Tess, regarding him with interest.

"A phrase of speech! Habit, I fear!" Sir Morgan looked apologetic. "I am accustomed to speaking to all my flirts in that manner."

"Ah!" Tess replied wisely. "It saves you the embarrassment of forgetting their names. Why can't I leave town?"

"How can you even think of leaving me?" Sir Morgan was stricken. "We deal so well together, I had begun to hope—I will not trust myself to say more! It is a great deal too precipitate. Only say that I have not given you a disgust of me!"

"Wretch!" the countess retorted appreciatively. "Don't sham it so! I understand that you mean to stick as close to me as a court plaster until I give you the necklace."

"There is that, too," Sir Morgan murmured thoughtfully. His attention was then claimed by a lady with noble proportions and a shocking *décolletage*. Tess watched with fascination as he deftly parried the woman's rather vulgar remarks with deft compliments.

Though she was unaware of it, Tess herself was the focus of considerable interest. Many were the comments made on Sir Morgan's lady, lovely in an evening gown of blue-green crepe Vandyked around the petticoat, a deep falling border of lace frills and ribbon round the low neck.

Her fair hair was arranged in disheveled curls with a center parting, and a string of extremely valuable gems wound around her slender throat. It was no coincidence that the countess had worn her own diamond necklace. She meant to try and see if the flaunting of such jewels might arouse some particular and suspicious interest. Thus far, it had earned her only a quizzical glance from the Wicked Baronet.

Sir Morgan deftly extricated himself from his accostor and turned ruefully to Tess. She frowned. "I wonder if Clio is upset because she thinks she will be made to marry Giles? I vow I do not understand the chit! From all she has said to me about him, I would have thought she'd like to marry Giles very well. Yet when I asked her if she wished to do so, she answered me with a flood of tears."

Sir Morgan responded only in silence. Wrapped in her own thoughts, the countess accompanied him into the foyer, which was thronged not only with the Quality and well-heeled cits, but with hopeful prostitutes and various riffraff. Tess's makeshift plan was to succeed almost too well.

The man who had followed the countess to the Haymarket, as he followed her everywhere, had not expected such good luck. His gaze lit on the diamonds, and his eyes gleamed. It did not occur to him that this might not be the necklace that he sought. Time was running out; his own life would soon be in jeopardy. It was not difficult for a determined man to make his way through the throng and secure a place near Tess; or, when her attention was diverted by a fat and beplumed elderly lady who demanded Sir Morgan's ear, for him to make a grab for her necklace. Luck deserted the would-be thief at that point; he was grasped by a strong pair of hands and half-throttled before the Bow Street runner who was employed by the management to prevent just such an occurrence appeared to take him away.

Lady Tess watched his departure with a brooding expression, then turned upon Sir Morgan a fulminating glance. *"That,"* she announced, "was extremely poorspirited of you!"

"Oh?" Sir Morgan looked bleak. "You think I arranged the encounter then?"

"I don't know why you must ask me such silly questions," Tess complained. "It is utterly impossible that a man of your character and station in life should be capable of such an abominable proceeding."

"I did not know," said Sir Morgan, mollified, "that you had such a great opinion of my character. How, then, have I earned your censure?"

"And I had thought you a knowing one!" Absently, the countess touched her necklace. "Now that my pursuer has been taken into custody—for it was the same man who accosted me in the park and thrust me under the wheels of the carriage—we will not know who to expect!"

"My apologies!" Sir Morgan was striken with mortification. "I quite see that I am at fault! Do you wish me to have him released?"

"*Would* you?" Tess contemplated him.

"I will do anything you ask of me, little one! Do you not think that, with this villain in jail, these threats to you may cease?"

Tess considered this, not at all pleased to have her adventure end so tamely. With an odd little smile, Sir Morgan watched the various expressions that flitted across her face. "No," she decided, at length. "I do *not* think so. Doubtless there are others involved, and they will not be so easily brought to a standstill. This one was not very clever—a bumbler, in fact! I do not think he could be responsible for the original theft. Nor do I think we should have him released, lest someone smell a rat."

"You never cease to amaze me," remarked Sir Morgan truthfully.

"I have not even thanked you!" Tess was aghast. "It seems that all my life you have been rescuing me."

"I would very much like to continue doing so!" Sir Morgan replied promptly, but to no avail.

"Heigh-ho!" said the countess softly, again touching her gems. "Obviously, that man thought *this* was the necklace he was to reclaim. The poor thing must have been growing

177

desperate! I hope he may not be induced to tell the whole to the magistrates at Bow Street."

"Why not?" inquired Sir Morgan. "Myself, I would be glad to see this thing end."

"If that isn't the height of ingratitude!" Tess regarded him indignantly. "If the man *does* talk he is likely to involve you—although, now that I think of it, he probably does not know of your part in it." Her voice was solemn. "You need not trouble yourself further, if you would rather not. I daresay I can manage well enough on my own."

"Can you?" countered Sir Morgan. "May I remind you that only moments past you were nearly divested of your diamonds? They *are* your diamonds?"

Tess looked bewildered. "Of course they're mine! Don't try to change the subject! I do not wish you to feel *obligated* to me."

"My love, I am not so chivalrous, as you yourself have remarked." Sir Morgan placed her hand on his arm and held it there. "Whatever feelings I may cherish toward you, a sense of duty is not among them."

"Oh," said Tess.

"I was merely thinking," Sir Morgan continued blandly, "that those jewels are rather grand for a poor companion. Lord Lansbury must have been extremely generous to you."

"What makes you think," brightly inquired Tess, "that Lord Lansbury gave them to me?"

"It was one of your countless lovers, I collect? You should know better than to try and fob *me* off with such a Banbury tale, little one! May I recall to you my great experience?"

"Very well." An unaccustomed meekness sat on the countess's face. "It was Lord Lansbury who gave them to me, on my eighteenth birthday. Well, you know how he was! When you took me to him, after that accident, he was as concerned as if I had been one of his own!"

"Precisely," Sir Morgan murmured drily. "And you a penniless orphan!"

"Yes." Tess was rapt. "I have often thought I was very fortunate to be taken in by so kind a gentleman."

"And *I* think," retorted Sir Morgan roughly, "that Lord Lansbury brought up a very reprehensible daughter, Countess!"

"So he did," sighed Tess. "I should not say it, I know, but it is very comforting to know that someone feels as I do about Clio!"

"Vixen!" hissed Sir Morgan, under his breath. But the curate had at last caught up with his quarry, and Tess turned on him a look so brimful of merriment that Shamus completely forgot what he'd meant to say.

# Chapter 18

*Clio knew she looked her best* in a gown of gossamer satin with festooned trimming, bordered with rouleaux of rose-pink satin and slashed sleeves, and a little cap ornamented with rosebuds on her dark curls; and she meant to turn it to good advantage. "Ceddie!" she said, and awarded him a melting glance. "Forgive me for being so out-of-reason cross with you! Pray let us be friends again."

Cedric had little inclination to resume association with a damsel who'd been so unappreciative as to call him a "man-milliner," but he was very much afraid that she'd cut up stiff if he refused, and Ceddie had no wish to engage in a brangle in the middle of Almack's assembly rooms. *Entrée* to this select temple of the *ton* was not easily come by; a shocking amount of intrigue and subterfuge were required to gain footing within these walls; and those unfortunate enough to have never received vouchers to the Wednesday evening subscription balls were regarded as utterly unfashionable. Ceddie couldn't understand why it should be that way, for Almack's consisted of a large bare room with a bad floor, and two or three naked rooms at the side in which were served the most wretched refreshments—lemonade and tea, bread and butter and stale cakes—but he was not one to fly in the face of convention. Almack's was all the crack; *he* would not be the one to announce that it was devilish flat.

"Well?" Clio's patience was wearing thin. She studied Ceddie, who was attired in the knee breeches and striped stockings, blue coat with very long tails, and white waistcoat which were *de rigeur* for an evening spent on these premises. The effect was not as conventional as might be imagined, since Ceddie had also placed a patch at the corner of his mouth, a gold chain and quizzing glass around his neck, and stays around his midriff so that he resembled a pouter pigeon. "Shall we cry friends, Ceddie?"

"If that it what you wish." He looked sulky. "Dash it, Clio, it ain't like you to behave so shabbily."

Mistress Clio had a headache that threatened to crack her skull, and her malaise was heightened by Ceddie's sweet perfume. "I have said I am sorry." She tried for a look of wounded innocence. "Dear Ceddie, I have a great deal on my mind! Poor Tess—but you will not wish to hear of *that!*"

Ceddie wanted very much to hear about the wealthy countess. Under Constant's tutorage—that gentleman had proven as good as his word and had introduced his young friend to every conceivable form of depravity—Ceddie's accounts had gone from bad to worse and were now of the most despondent cast. "Certainly I do!" he responded. "I mean, glad to be of help!"

Clio suspected that Ceddie's notion of assistance was to help himself to her sister's fortune, and she felt as though she walked a tightrope. "It is Sir Morgan," she said, with unaffected gloom. "He has made her an object of great curiosity—her name is being bandied about in the most odious way." She raised huge, damply shining eyes. "Oh, Ceddie, it is the most appalling thing! I don't know what to do!"

"Shocking!" Ceddie's fertile mind worked rapidly. "Tell you what, Clio, we must rescue her from this fix!"

"If only we could," sighed Clio. "The thing is, Ceddie, she doesn't *wish* to be rescued!" Mistress Clio did, however, and from the course of action that she herself had determined upon. If only a more reasonable resolution would present itself—but none had. Clio was left in the unhappy position of being forced to rescue her sister from a rake (Sir Morgan), a fortune hunter (Ceddie), and her own baser self. Further, Tess must be made to see that Clio did not wish to marry Giles, which was a refutation of the truth: Clio did wish to marry him, very much. Idly, she wondered what Giles wished to do. No matter! Her mind was made up. Two of the evils she could dispel, by means of a little resolution. The third, alas, was beyond even her capacities. Clio could only trust to fate.

From long experience with Mistress Clio, Ceddie should have recognized immediately that she was set on cutting a wheedle; but he was engaged in schemes of ransoms and handsome payoffs and failed to heed the warning signs. "Dash it!" he uttered, with honest regret. "There must be something we can do!"

"Oh, Ceddie, you *will* help me?" Clio's pleading glance would have moved the heart of a much harder man. "Have I your word on it?"

"My word?" sputtered Ceddie. "Deuce take it, Clio, why do you need my word?"

"You don't trust me." Clio looked ready to cry.

"It's not that—oh, very well! If it will make you happy, I swear I'll help you!" No sooner were the words out than Ceddie knew he'd made a dreadful mistake.

"Excellent!" Clio was all smiles. "I must tell you, Ceddie, that you and I are going to elope."

Not all of the members of the Bellamy clan graced Almack's that night, although the committee of seven highborn ladies, who ruled there with such absolute authority that they alone had the power of granting vouchers of admission, had denied entrance to no one. The dowager duchess had no taste for such tame pursuits; the duke was engaged in more serious affairs of government; and Lucille, having surprised a housebreaker, remained at Bellamy House where she enlivened her mother's tedium by occasional fainting fits. Constant was present, watching with a careful eye the maturation of his plans; and Drusilla stood just behind the ropes that separated the dancers from the spectators, none other than the Wicked Baronet at her side. This fact afforded Mistress Clio scant comfort; the pair of them did not appear to be on particularly amiable terms.

Drusilla's ill-temper, which showed clearly on her face, resulted from Sir Morgan's obvious indifference to her, as well as from Tess's inexplicable popularity with the lady patronesses, all of whom had deigned to exchange several words with her. That Tess should be admitted here, a distinction greater than being presented at court and more difficult to obtain, was to Drusilla incomprehensible; and that Tess should have become the fashion, which she undeniably had, made Drusilla wish to gnash her teeth in rage. She could not understand why a creature without social graces should be so popular with such discriminating individuals as Lady Cowper and Mr. Brummell and Lord Palmerston, or why Lord Alvanley should be content to spend some twenty minutes in conversation with a female whose hair was coming unpinned.

Sir Morgan looked amused, Drusilla having been so foolish as to make her sentiments known. "You cannot like Tess?" he asked. "Your opinion must be your own, of course; I cannot agree."

"No?" Drusilla shot him a darkling glance. "You have a decided partiality for her, I collect? Gammon, Morgan! I know you a little too well to rise to *that* bait. Lud, it should be apparent to anyone that she's not in your style! No, you care not in the slightest for that simpering creature, and there is no point in trying to persuade me otherwise."

"I can see there is not." Sir Morgan might have been discussing the weather, so disinterested was he. "Therefore, I shall not waste time in telling you that I have a great regard for her." He studied Tess, across the crowded room. "I must, however take exception to 'simpering.' Whatever the lady's faults—and I freely admit that she *does* have faults, Drusilla!—she does not simper. Nor does she act missish, or strike poses, or play insipid little games." His glance flickered over Drusilla. "There is the answer, I fancy, to your earlier question. The lady possesses a refreshing originality."

"In other words," snapped Drusilla, "she's an oddity!" It occurred to her that one did not effect a reconciliation with a gentleman by ripping up at him. "There's no sense in trying to pull the wool over my eyes, Morgan! Sapphira has told me what she asked of you. You are to divert the wench from Giles. How nice that you should have found something to occupy yourself!"

"Isn't it?" Sir Morgan smoothed a flawless sleeve. "I couldn't resist the challenge—and I fancy I've done tolerably well."

"Mr. Facing-both-ways!" hissed Drusilla, driven wild with jealousy by the suggestion that the Wicked Baronet's deft addresses were not falling on deaf ears.

"Pray moderate your manner!" begged Sir Morgan. "I would not wish word of this to reach the lady, lest all my efforts go for naught." His smile seemed positively evil. "It will not be long now, I think! But I must leave you now, Drusilla. You will accept my regrets?"

"Why?"

"To rescue my Tess from her prosy curate." Again that disquieting little smile. "It will make her even more grateful to me."

This was only logical; Drusilla tapped his arm with her fan. "I vow you are the most impudent devil that ever existed!" she said, with a meaningful glance. "You will understand if I do not wish you success?"

Sir Morgan gravely inclined his head. "Perfectly." Drusilla watched him disappear into the crowd. Even Constant's barbed comments could not move her now; she knew Tess's ultimate discomfort—nay, fall from grace!— to be only a matter of time.

In regard to discomfort, however, it was doubtful that the countess could endure a greater degree than was currently her lot. The worthy Shamus had listened patiently to her discourse on Wellington's reconnaissance of the situation at Badajoz, during which he narrowly avoided capture by the enemy; and the marvelous recuperative power of the French army which, inspired by Napoleon's wrath, sought to recoup the loss of Alameida; and when she paused for breath launched into a dissertation of his own. From a discussion of the countess's various attributes, all of which admirably qualified her for the role of curate's wife, Shamus launched into a candid confession of his own sentiments regarding her, and voiced an earnest request that Lady Tess should allow him to shoulder her burdens and become her partner for life.

"Good God!" said Tess, to whom this nicely phrased proposal sounded very much like an invitation to enter a prison cell. "What can you be thinking of, Shamus, to make me an offer at *Almack's?*"

"I have always deprecated," replied the curate in his weighty manner, "this tendency toward levity. I cannot think it quite the thing. But I flatter myself that, when you allow yourself to be guided by me, we will deal together very well."

"You flatter yourself, indeed!" The countess's suitor was not a little startled by her vicious tone. "So I am to be made into a pattern card of respectability?"

"That is not the way I would phrase it," Shamus replied judiciously, "though it is true, my dear Lady Tess, that your conduct since you have come to London has been a trifle reckless. You will forgive me, I know, if I say that your association with a gentleman of poor reputation is a subject that has gained some observation in the world. In all conscience, I must go so far as to say that he is to blame for your notoriety, which I can only consider shockingly reprehensible! He is precisely the sort of man to encourage you in every sort of excess, doing you a great disservice thereby."

"Sir Morgan is not quite so depraved as you paint him," replied Tess, amused in spite of her anger. "Were he the villain you think him, he would hardly be admitted here."

"I am saddened that you should defend him," Shamus said sternly. "And I am very surprised to see Sir Morgan at Almack's. I had thought the lady patronesses would have been more particular; it is surely their duty to protect the impressionable young ladies who so gracefully adorn these premises."

"You refine too much on the matter, Shamus!" Tess was growing rapidly bored. "Sir Morgan has excellent *ton,* and no interest whatsoever in impressionable young ladies." She smiled. "To tell truth, I suspect he is welcome here simply because he enlivens the tedium of the lady patronesses! Lady Jersey as much as told me so."

"Then I can only consider them foolish." The countess sighed and the curate leaned closer to her. "You are quick to defend the man, Lady Tess! Surely *you* cannot be so deceived in his character!"

"Well, no," admitted Tess, "I don't believe I am. But you must not listen to *me*, Shamus! I am the favorite of the moment and therefore quite prejudiced."

Shamus was stricken all aheap by this patent wrongheadedness. "Lady Tess!" Firmly he grasped her hand. "I beg—no, I insist—that you must not follow so disastrous a course! You know that to be your husband has long been an ambition with me! I assure you that your happiness must always be my first aim. All that you say convinces me that we must be married immediately."

"Have you taken to brandy?" inquired the countess, bright of eye. "Since you insist on making me a declaration while I am telling you I nourish a—a passion!—for another, I can only conclude that you must be a trifle castaway!"

"I will forgive you those words," the curate replied pompously. "You obviously are not aware of what you say. I cannot think that even *you*, Lady Tess, would prefer a rake to a man of honor."

"Sir Morgan is very much relished by those who know him well!" announced the countess, forcibly extracting her hand from his grip. "Myself among them. My patience is exhausted, Shamus! I have told you countless times that I will *not* marry you! If you persist in plaguing me with your infernal prose, you will not only make a Jack-pudding of yourself, I shall box your ears!"

This plain speaking pierced the curate's armor; he fell

back a step. Even then he might have argued, but he saw Sir Morgan approaching through the crowd, as did Lady Tess, whose face brightened with an effect almost magical. "I see that further conversation on this subject is at the moment impossible," Shamus said with barely repressed anger. "I hope you might not have to repent of your choice."

"Thank you, I won't!" The countess did not even turn to see him walk wrathfully away.

"Tell me what has roused your displeasure!" invited Sir Morgan, as Tess unclenched her fists. "I shall set it right immediately."

"I fear," Tess said ruefully, "that I have behaved badly. Shamus has the most unhappy knack of sending me straight into the boughs."

"It is your own fault," Sir Morgan replied, "for encouraging him to dangle after you. Why ever did you?"

"What a beast you are!" The countess nodded graciously to a gentleman of her acquaintance. "I'm sure I never encouraged Shamus to think I would marry him— truly, I'm sure I did the opposite!"

"You relieve me! I had wondered if you nourished a fondness for the clergy, in which case you and I should never suit. Well, think!" he added, in response to her reproachful look. "It would be deuced disappointing if you were to start moralizing over me once the knot was tied."

"Moonshine!" Tess wore an indignant expression. "So far am I from sermonizing that I told Shamus I preferred a rake to a fool. He will probably never speak to me again, and it is no more than I deserve."

"Now that *is* a great pity!" responded Sir Morgan, and smiled at her surprise. "I had counted on the worthy curate, with his stultifying virtues, to send you straight into the arms of sin."

But the countess was not attending him, watching instead the approach of Cedric. "The devil!" she said. "Sir Morgan, I *must* speak with you privately. I have reached a decision and it is only fair that I tell you of it. Oh, curse Ceddie for an addle-plot!"

Sir Morgan glanced at that young man, who had a most determined look in his eye, and silently agreed. "A decision, little one?" he inquired. "This sounds ominous! That I am at your service, you already know."

"I suppose it would be ruinous," mused Tess, "if I gave the others the slip—but I know not else how to do it!"

"No," agreed Sir Morgan, fascinated. "I do not think I wish to risk invading your bedchamber again, though not for the reason you might think. What, then, do you suggest?"

"*I*," Tess pointed out, "am not the one with experience in assignations! I had thought you might hit on something."

"I have!" Sir Morgan replied promptly. "Vauxhall!"

"Vauxhall?" Tess could not think what the pleasure gardens had to do with her present dilemma.

"My dear," said Sir Morgan pensively, "you have a great deal yet to learn about intrigue. If one is to risk one's reputation in a clandestine rendezvous, one might as well derive some amusement from the encounter."

Tess thought she would enjoy any encounter with Sir Morgan save the last, and was sorry the flirtation must end. "As you wish," she replied unenthusiastically, and cursed herself for feeling regret over a step that she had always known to be inevitable. Sir Morgan wished the diamonds; very well, she would give them to him, and then she would remove herself and her obviously unhappy sister from Town. Perhaps in the country Clio might regain her spirits; Tess would not, but she could be miserable anywhere. "I will leave the details to you."

Sir Morgan possessed a great deal of acumen, and it was clear to him that Tess did not relish the rendezvous. "Have I displeased you?" he asked quietly. "You seem to be quite out of charity with me."

"Oh, no, not that!" Tess raised startled eyes to his. "Please, I cannot tell you now, but I will explain everything!"

"It would distress me beyond description to make you unhappy," said Sir Morgan, with a frown. It was unpleasantly clear to him that his ladylove was behaving in a remarkably skitter-witted fashion, a fact which, though it caused him unease, roused in him no dismay since he already knew her to be enchantingly cockle-brained. Behind him, Ceddie cleared his throat, and Tess's expression changed to anxiety. "I will inform you," Sir Morgan murmured, "of the details."

# Chapter 19

*"Nonsense!" said Clio,* without a great deal of conviction. Drusilla and Constant exchanged a glance.

"Are you taking your powders?" Drusilla made a fine show of concern. "You are looking very pale, Clio!"

This was the grossest of understatements. Clio was as pallid as any lady who had ever resorted to leeches to reduce her color and then fainted away gracefully in company. "I am," she replied, raising a hand to her brow. "It hardly signifies. What are you telling me about my mother? I cannot credit it!"

"You are prodigiously like her," observed Drusilla craftily. "My dear, these nervous agitations will not do. Try and control yourself!"

"Monstrous!" cried Clio, pacing up and down the room. "I refuse to believe a word of it."

"My dear Clio," interrupted Constant, deeming it time he took a hand, "surely you do not mean to accuse Drusilla of falsehood! It would be shockingly impertinent of you. Believe me, we have only your best interests in mind."

To believe this clanker Mistress Clio would have had to have been a veritable ninnyhammer, which she definitely was not. She knew that something lay behind this seeming solicitude. "I don't see," she said abruptly, "why you should be telling me this *now!*"

Again they looked at each other. Constant frowned and Drusilla's expression changed to benevolent concern.

"Pray don't fly into a passion," she begged. "You must see that we had no choice. You are on the verge of contracting an alliance, and it would be hardly fair were your prospective husband not told how things stand." She smiled with exquisite understanding. "Odd humors, queer starts, a lack of stability—he would suspect all too soon, my dear!"

Her face as white as her muslin walking dress, Clio sank down onto a chair. "It isn't true!" she repeated again. "We would have seen some sign."

"Do you accuse us of telling you untruths?" Constant inquired indignantly. "I am shocked, but it is no more than I expected. You must not argue with your elders, Clio, it shows an unbecoming want of conduct." He sighed heavily. "I fear, dear sister, that our suspicions have been proven correct."

Drusilla shot him an admonishing glance, which he pretended not to see. Constant was expanding his small role into an entire melodrama, and she had no appreciation of his histrionic abilities. "But Clio is little more than a schoolgirl!" he added hastily. "We can hardly be surprised if she reacts childishly. Though I admit it is a grave solecism to refer to a lady's age!"

In Constant's case, thought Drusilla grimly, it was a solecism to have ever been born. "Dear Clio," she remarked, "you must see that we are motivated solely by concern for you. You should not wish to give your husband a disgust of you, as must surely be the case when he learns that your mind is overheated, that your emotions lack restraint."

Clio considered that she was exhibiting remarkable restraint. To their mingled regret, so did Constant and Drusilla. "My mother married," Clio protested, "without any ill effect. I never saw any indication of a disordered intellect! You must be mistaken."

"Oh, no!" With a great deal of effort, Constant crossed his knees. "You must concede that we know a great deal more about the matter! No doubt your mother learned to disguise her malady but, to be blunt, there is no question she passed it on to you." His pudgy features wore a look of pious sympathy. "Would you pass it on to *your* children in turn? Inflict upon your husband the pain that your poor father must have suffered? Think on it, child!"

Clio stared obediently at her hands, wondering what hypothetical husband they had in mind. Perhaps Drusilla thought she would marry Giles, as Sapphira wished, and wanted to spare her brother pain. If so, her concern was commendable, though misplaced. Since Clio could not very well explain her plans for the evening, which would make her quite ineligible to marry anyone, consisting as they did of an intention to be found in Sir Morgan's lodgings and a subsequent elopement with Cedric, she remained silent. She would be ruined, Clio thought nobly, but in the process she would give Tess a disgust of both gentlemen. With those two thus removed, the countess could only turn to Giles.

Though Drusilla watched the girl with every indication of compassion, her thoughts were far away, to be precise at a certain écarté table covered with a black velvet cloth embroidered with gold, where a fortunate lady might carry off £50 at a single stroke. Drusilla had not been so fortunate, and she saw that she would have to apply to her mother for rescue. Sapphira would in any case be irate, and read her erring daughter a terrible scold; but could Clio in the meantime be shown obstinate and uncooperative, Sapphira might yet show her daughters some sign of respect. And, thought Drusilla, who knew well how to worm her way into a young man's confidences, could Clio be shown to be so foolhardy as to slip the leash and ruin her reputation by disappearing with that young man prior to marriage, Sapphira would quite rightly wash her hands of the chit.

"Perhaps we have been too severe," she said kindly. "No one but the family knows of Mirian's unhappy malady. Perhaps, were you to take care to exhibit no unbecoming violence of feeling, your husband would not suspect." She looked thoughtful. "It must be a young man; an older, more experienced one would be sure to guess the truth."

Clio did not look cheered, though this accorded well

with her own plans. "The family?" she echoed. "Giles also knows?"

"Giles better than anyone!" replied Drusilla. "It is why he refused to go along with *Maman*'s plans for the pair of you. I see that I must tell you all, Clio. It was because of your mother's illness that Giles did not marry her, and it is because of *that* that Mirian ran away."

This should have been the master stroke, a girl of Clio's temperament not being expected to view with complacency the man who had cast off her mother, and Drusilla waited eagerly for her reaction. Clio, however, was not so easily led. "I don't believe a word of it," she said stubbornly. "The allegation that my mother was a lunatic is insupportable."

Drusilla's lips pursed. She had not settled on this course of action without considerable thought, for once she removed Clio from the field, Giles's eye was likely to settle once more on Tess. But Sapphira would never permit *that* match to take place, and if Giles defied her would cut him out of her will, an action to be greatly desired. And, thought Drusilla smugly, Sir Morgan would be free to resume his pursuit of herself.

Constant guessed at the motives which drove Drusilla and found them highly diverting, but he too wished fervently to alienate Sapphira from Clio. "Not precisely a lunatic," he amended, before Drusilla could give voice to unwise speech, "but definitely queer in the attic." Clio looked confused and he further explained: "Windmills in the head, my dear! Touched in the upper works."

"Alas," mourned Drusilla, with a quelling glance at her brother-in-law, "it is all too true. You should know it yourself, Clio! When Mirian met your father, was she not living retired, with a female in attendance?" From Clio's expression, she knew that she had scored a hit. "A keeper, of course," she added, before Clio had time to reflect that Mirian, being in flight from her family, could hardly live otherwise. "If you doubt *me*, Clio, you have only to ask Giles!"

It is highly unlikely that Clio would have done so, having discovered that conversation with that gentleman was injurious to her peace of mind, had she not encountered him in the hallway during her flight from the drawing-room, and had not he taken one look at her face and thrust her without preamble into his study. "Drink!" he commanded, thrusting a glass of brandy into her hand. Clio obeyed, and choked. "Now, tell me what's troubling you."

"I cannot—do not ask me—it is much too dreadful to discuss!" replied Clio disjointedly.

"Surely," said the duke, watching her with a frown, "you cannot still be worried about Morgan and Tess? If so, your concern is excessive, cousin. He will do her no harm."

"No harm!" Clio was relieved to seize upon a distraction, and annoyed that Giles should accept the situation when she knew perfectly well that he was not indifferent to Tess. On reflection, she determined that the duke was too much a gentleman to interfere. "*Your* concern, Your Grace, is not excessive enough! He will abuse her and abandon her, after running through her fortune, and you tell me not to fear? I wonder at you, sir!"

The duke might have expressed surprise that a female in Tess's supposed situation should possess a fortune, but he was not so callous as to tease a damsel who was obviously in the grip of a fit of melancholia. "My name," he remarked, "is Giles. I would appreciate it if you would call me by it."

But Clio displayed little reaction to this mark of favor; she feared she'd said too much. "You must not think Tess has formed a lasting attachment!" she cried, clutching his arm. "It is no such thing! Sir Morgan has swept her off her feet, but she will return to her senses and realize where her heart truly lies."

"Excuse me," begged the duke, a look of puzzlement on his handsome countenance. "Do you mean to tell me that your Tess is enamored of her curate?"

"Shamus? Gracious, no!" Clio paused, wondering how to best deal with this delicate situation. "I haven't seen the slightest indication that they should suit."

"You relieve me," responded Giles. "Neither had I." He looked down at her face, so pale and drawn that only the huge blue eyes seemed alive. "I wasn't born yesterday, cousin. I do not think that it is the—I mean, Tess—who has overset you so dreadfully."

"No," said Clio, giving in to a momentary weakness. Drusilla, after all, had said that she should ask Giles. "I have just learned the truth about my mother. It is only natural, I think, that it should cause me some distress."

"Oh?" The duke's brows lowered forbiddingly. "Who has been telling you tales?"

"It hardly matters." Clio averted her gaze. "Someone should have informed me sooner. Surely I should know of something that must affect my entire life! Not that I do not understand why the family should wish to wrap it up in clean linen!" she added quickly, lest he think she presumed to criticize his actions. "I understand perfectly."

"I am glad," replied Giles, "since I do not." Not ungently, he forced her to look at him. "My dear cousin, I would not care if my dirty linen were washed in public, if I *had* dirty linen, which I do not!"

"How like you to put a good face on it!" Clio sniffled. "I know, Your Grace, that my mother was a lunatic."

Since Giles had spent several years in close proximity with Mirian and had seen no indication of lunacy, his surprise was by no degree small. He tried his utmost to disabuse Clio of the notion that had taken such firm root in her feverish little head, but to no avail; the comment that Mirian had suffered nothing more severe than hey-go-mad humors only inspired Clio to hang round his neck in tears.

"No, no!" she sobbed, releasing him at last. "Do not try to console me, it is a great deal better that I should know!" Shyly she looked up at him. "You must not think I condemn your actions, Your Grace! It is perfectly reasonable that you should not wish to ally yourself with a woman of such unstable character. I think it Mirian who behaved badly, to take your change of heart in such bad part as to run away."

Giles had endured, at the best, a trying day; and it was not the least brightened by this interview. But he gave no indication of minding that Clio had sadly creased the sleeve of his jacket, and wept all over his waistcoat, and now exhibited beyond all doubt her belief that he, the highest of sticklers, had behaved like a curst rum touch. "I perfectly see why she did it," Clio continued somberly. "To realize that you, for whom she nourished a warm regard, should think her mad—I too would probably have fled."

"I trust you won't," said the duke with near savagery. She looked puzzled. "Take French leave! There is no need for it, Clio."

"Oh, no!" cried Clio, at her most innocent. "Why should I? The situation is quite different."

Giles had endured long experience with the females of his family, all of whom were inclined to the telling of tara-diddles, and he easily read the signs. He also recognized the futility of pressing the issue. "I wish you would tell me who is responsible for this farrago of nonsense."

"Oh, let us speak no more of it!" Clio brushed the tears off her cheeks. "It is kind of you to shield me, and I would have expected no less of you." She smiled, rather wistfully. "I think that Tess is very fortunate, cousin!"

"Do you?" Giles gallantly offered his handkerchief. "I do not understand you, Clio! Only moments past you were lamenting her probable fate at Morgan's hands."

"You need not pretend with *me*!" reproved Clio. "I know the whole—have known from the start! I only hope you may forgive Tess her foolishness concerning your friend. It stems not from any vicissitude of character, but from inexperience."

"Forgive her?" Giles looked all at sea. "Who on earth am I, Clio, to condemn your—ah!—Tess's conduct?"

"I have told you," Clio responded severely, "that you need not pretend! I fear Tess's preference for Sir Morgan may have wounded your pride, but I assure you things are not as they seem. She will discover that she is far from indifferent to you, Your Grace, once she has looked into her own heart."

The duke's reaction to this information beggars all description. "The deuce!" he ejaculated, studying Clio with distinct astonishment.

"I know I should not have spoken of it," said that damsel, crumpling his handkerchief into a sodden wad, "but I thought you should know how things stand with her. All is not yet lost! I have matters well in hand."

This ominous announcement was not wasted on the Duke of Bellamy, but he had more immediate problems with which to deal. "I see I must confess," he replied, in tones that were not quite steady. "Hoist with my own petard! And well-served by it." Clio frowned. "My dear," he added, "you have completely mistaken the case! I must count myself honored that you should think I would be eligible for Tess—since you obviously think Morgan is not! —but, believe me, I nourish no warmer feelings than liking and a certain admiration for Tess, nor does she for me."

Of course he would say so, mused Clio, stricken anew by the honorable nature of the man. If only her earlier schemes had worked! But fate had been consistently against her, most memorably on the occasion when, hearing Tess and Giles in the library, she had locked the door, only to discover on opening it an hour later, in the presence of witnesses, that Sir Morgan had also been present and that they had pleasantly passed the time in playing three-handed whist. "I am glad to hear that her shocking behavior hasn't turned you against her."

Giles feared his words were falling on deaf ears, but he persevered. "I am fond of Tess," he said carefully. "She is as lovely as she is silly, and I'm sure she'll lead Morgan a merry dance, and that he'll adore every moment of it." Clio looked at him with brimming compassion, and the duke stifled a sigh. "Were *I* to marry her, however," he continued with a touch of acerbity, "she would drive me to murder her in an extremely short period of time! My interest in Tess was prompted only by a most ignoble curiosity. I wished to discover what sort of female had roused Morgan to admiration. Believe me, Clio, they will deal together admirably!"

Clio was not deceived. She walked to the doorway and turned, her eyes once more damp with tears. "You need not fear," she confided. "I give you my word that Tess will not marry Sir Morgan."

The Duke of Bellamy was not one to tilt at windmills, and so he let her go. Once she had ample time in which to attain the privacy of her room, he opened the door and demanded of a housemaid that his valet be sent to him immediately, in tones so viciously unlike himself that the maid gasped.

On noiseless feet, Pertwee glided into the room. He was an impeccable little man whose sinister air derived from the fact that his pale eyes were set much too close together in his ferretlike countenance.

The duke had thrown himself down into a chair, a brandy decanter on the table at his elbow, and an expression of the utmost ferocity on his face. "Pertwee!" he thundered. "Something deuced odd is going on in this house."

"Yes, Your Grace," agreed the valet, who was very much in his master's confidence. "If I may venture to say so, Your Grace, there are various unwholesome rumors concerning the young lady. They are preposterous, as I have been so bold as to point out, but persons of the lower orders are inclined to believe anything."

The Duke of Bellamy lifted his brandy glass, but he did not drink. "At whose door are those rumors to be set? Never mind! I can guess."

"Yes, Your Grace," replied Pertwee.

"All the same," and now Giles did drink, "I shall want proof."

"Very good, Your Grace," agreed Pertwee.

"And the other?" demanded the duke, rising abruptly and striding toward a heavily laden bookshelf.

"All is in good order, Your Grace." It was obvious from Pertwee's demeanor that he did not approve. "The note has been delivered to the lady. I fancy, Your Grace, that she was pleased to receive it."

"I imagine," retorted the duke, removing a volume

from the shelf, "that she was! What a *contretemps* this is, Pertwee."

"Exactly so, Your Grace," replied the valet primly.

"You know what has to be done." The duke opened the volume and removed from it a pair of dueling pistols, one of which he extended to his manservant. "Here! You may need this."

"If I may say so," responded the valet who, though villainous of appearance and stout of soul, was not particularly fond of firearms and not at all happy about the extra duties that his master and Sir Morgan had imposed on him, "I devoutly trust not, Your Grace!"

"Where is your spirit of adventure, Pertwee?" Giles touched the remaining pistol. "Made by Manton, no less! Were I not afraid she would shoot Morgan with it, I would give this to the countess! Perhaps I am being foolish, and no attempt will be made."

Pertwee had no such hope. "I conjecture, Your Grace, that the villains grow desperate."

"The villains," responded the duke drily, "are not alone in that. If ever I saw such an addlepated pair!" He frowned. "There is one additional thing, Pertwee."

"Yes, Your Grace?" inquired the valet unenthusiastically.

"Yes, Pertwee!" The Duke of Bellamy smiled. "You will be well rewarded, I promise. Mrs. Bibby has in her possession a key to every room in Bellamy House, I believe?"

"Yes, Your Grace."

"Good." Giles displayed not the least regard for his valet's patent apprehension. "You will discover among them the key to Miss Clio's room."

"I will, Your Grace?" Though devoted to his master, Pertwee was not at all eager to add theft to the endeavors undertaken in the duke's behalf.

"You will." The Duke of Bellamy's tone brooked no argument. "Once you have appropriated that key, with no one the wiser, you will lock Miss Clio in her room. Then you will give the key to me."

It was not often that Pertwee ventured to contradict his master, but he did so now. "When the young lady discovers that her door is locked, Your Grace, she will raise a terrible uproar."

"So she will." Blandly, Giles pushed up the lid of his snuffbox with his left thumb, *à la* Brummell, removed a pinch of snuff, and closed the box with his index finger. "It can hardly signify, since the household already thinks she's at least half-mad."

# Chapter 20

*The Duke of Bellamy's highhanded action* had consequences that even he could not have foreseen. Clio, locked in her chamber, was prevented not only from involving Sir Morgan and Cedric in what would doubtless have been one of the most shocking scandals of the decade; she was also prevented from relaying to Tess her knowledge about Mirian, and from getting word to Ceddie that the elopement had been forestalled.

Thus Cedric waited, growing more and more ill-tempered as the appointed hour came and went and Clio did not appear. It was not affection for that damsel that kept him so long outside Bellamy House, hidden in the shadows, but the fact that he was in dire financial straits, having been called upon to meet a bill of £1,000 to which he'd unwisely signed his name. To give Cedric all due credit, he had no intention of going through with the elopement, despite Drusilla's pointed hints that such an action would prove to his benefit. Ceddie might have been castigated by those who loved him little as a slow-top, but he saw that such a course would bring down upon him grave censure. Clio's fortune was too small to tempt him and Drusilla, despite her vague promises, hadn't a farthing to call her own. Furthermore, the squire was like to cut up so stiff at his son's elopement that he would refuse to ever again hear Ceddie's name.

Cedric had not yet despaired; in the person of Lady

Tess he had a last hope of recovery. *She* was wealthy enough to pay off all his debts without feeling the slightest strain, and Ceddie saw a way in which she could be persuaded to do that very thing. He would return Clio to her sister with her reputation intact, taking her nowhere more exceptionable than to his aunt in Grosvenor Square. If Clio flew into the boughs, no matter; Lady Tess would be all the more grateful that he and his aunt could keep still tongues in their heads. Where on earth *was* Clio? wondered Ceddie, shifting positions uncomfortably.

And then a woman stole stealthily out of Bellamy House. Ceddie's hopes rose only to be dashed again; the woman walked with the aid of a cane. Lady Tess! he thought incredulously. Had she learned of the elopement? Was she coming to confront him? The countess passed by him unaware, and Ceddie's curiosity grew. Another figure slipped out of the house, this one a man, for all the world as if he followed her.

A carriage stood near one corner of the square. Ceddie had paid this vehicle little heed, other than to think that it was an oddly antiquated sort of thing to find at a fashionable address; but now he watched with some surprise as Lady Tess made straight for it. Her follower appeared to be equally startled; he called out her name in some distress. The countess glanced over her shoulder and hastened her pace, reached the carriage, and scrambled inside. The man raced after her, and actually had a hand on the carriage door, when the coachman, with a heavy cudgel, struck him down. The carriage rattled away. Without a moment's hesitation, and with nary a thought for the body which lay senseless in the street, Ceddie set out in cautious pursuit.

Nor did Tess spare a thought for poor Pertwee, which is not surprising, since she'd no idea he'd been stricken down in her service; indeed, she had not even remarked his identity. If anything, she assumed her follower had been one of the diamond thieves, foiled in making another attempt to regain the gems. This was not precisely logical of the countess, but she was not in a very sensible frame of mind. Tess was surprised that she should view the coming confrontation with such dismay, for she had always known that the day would dawn when she must bid the Wicked Baronet a final *adieu,* and disappointed that he was not waiting for her in the coach. It did not occur to Tess that a mistake had been made; in his note, Sir Morgan had told her that his carriage would be waiting for her at that place and time; she could only assume that he was far more familiar with the protocol of assignations than was she. The carriage seemed a little shabby to belong to a man who was allegedly a top sawyer with four-in-hand, but it seemed reasonable that he should make an attempt at anonymity.

She glanced out the carriage window. Bright moonlight lent pale stone houses a ghostly majesty, softened the contours of the elegant restraints through whose windows she saw soft velvet cushions, red and gold rooms. Tess only half-noticed them, paying little attention even to the lively oyster houses and the wide footpaths of the Haymarket. She was engaged in reviewing the progress of her acquaintance with a rake.

How much time she passed in this melancholy pursuit, Tess did not know; but it suddenly occurred to her that it was taking an uncommonly long time to reach Vauxhall. Again she peered out the window, her senses alert. There was no sign of arches and pillars hung with colored lamps and garlands of flowers, no exotic Turkish minarets, no Arabian columned ways. There was only open countryside. Tess called to the coachman, pounded with her cane on the carriage roof, to no avail. The carriage picked up more speed, and she feared they would be overturned. With an unhappy foreboding, the countess affected certain adjustments to her person, took firm hold of the cane, and settled back to wait.

It seemed that the journey lasted an eternity, more than ample time for Tess to reflect upon Sir Morgan's perfidy. How easy she had made it for him! She had played right into his hands, delivering herself alone and unprotected to the enemy. The countess did not delude herself that someone else might be responsible for her dilemma; Sir Morgan had made the plans himself. The Wicked Baronet indeed! she thought bitterly, and took little consolation from the fact that he had inadvertently cooked his own goose. She had set out on this expedition with every intention of giving him the diamonds, but he had shown himself devious and untrustworthy, and she had changed her mind. Had he lied to her all along? Was he set on reclaiming the diamonds for a one-time inamorata, or had Sir Morgan himself stolen them? Tess supposed she would eventually find out. One thing was certain: the necklace was hidden safely away, and Sir Morgan would not set hands on it without doing her bodily harm. Tess wished she'd thought to bring her gun along. Dare he manhandle her? Foolish question! There was obviously very little that the Wicked Baronet would not dare.

In this manner the journey was accomplished, the old carriage rattling through the moonlit countryside, and the countess wracking her brain for an avenue of escape. When at last the coach jolted to a stop, Lady Tess was in a towering rage.

"What, if I may inquire," she demanded in her iciest tones when the carriage door was yanked open, "is the meaning of this outrage?" She had expected no answer, and none was given; but the countess made such a good accounting of herself that it took six burly men to subdue her, none of whom were spared contact with the cane.

Tess recognized her surroundings immediately, though this time she was not privileged to view the inn's taproom or the huge fireplace, or conducted to the little bedchamber at the rear. Instead she was bundled around the back of the building by the stables, down a narrow flight of stairs, and into a small, filthy room. The door slammed; Tess was alone. She repaired as best she could the damage done during the scuffle, though there was little she could do without the aid of mirror, brush, and comb. At least they had left her a candle and her cane. She moved to inspect the dusty bottles that lined the walls.

The countess was not long left in solitude. Rough voices

sounded outside the door and a venerable ancient, rheumy of eye and overpowering of stench, stepped into the room. Tess, who had expected to confront Sir Morgan, stared. So did the ancient, who had *not* expected to find the prisoner perched upon a shelf and sampling a bottle of Old Constantia. With one wary eye fixed on her cane, he straddled the room's sole wooden chair.

"Well, my fine lady!" he exclaimed, with ominous joviality. "I reckon you know why you're here. Just hand over the sparklers and we'll get along right famous, and no harm done."

"I see you are under the delusion," retorted Lady Tess, "that I am a cabbage-head. You dare not let me go lest I immediately acquaint the authorities with the nature of this place." She contemplated the bottle. "Smuggled, I conjecture. Whoever would have thought that I, the Countess of Lansbury, would consort with free-traders and thieves?" Her thoughtful gaze moved to the old man. "I suppose you are aware of the consequences that will fall upon you when my body is found? One does not go blithely murdering gentlewomen without fear of reprisals, my man! Are the rewards so great that you will risk your neck for them? Not that the lot of you wouldn't be the better of a good hanging!"

The ancient regarded her mournfully. His sight might be less than it once was, but he'd no more than clapped his eyes on this delicately nurtured lady than he knew she'd be a rare handful. "Nay!" he replied. "I don't aim to get my neck cricked. I'm only wishful of getting my dabbers onto those sparklers, and then you'll be free as a bird."

The countess was not so easily deceived. "A pretty scoundrel *you* are!" said she, with curling lip. "I suppose now you will tell me that I have only to promise to say nothing and you will set me free! After I return the diamonds to you, of course."

"Aye," the ancient replied hopefully. "Give me your word that you'll keep dubber mum'd."

"Preposterous!" announced Tess. "You dare not take

the chance of releasing me, lest I go straight to Bow Street."

The old man blanched at this mention of those august representatives of the law, known more commonly to his ilk as "hornies" and other terms less repeatable. "Give me the necklace!" he growled. "Happen you'd best deal with me, lady, than the gentlemen upstairs. *They'd* as soon cut out your gizzard as look at you!"

Sir Morgan, reflected Tess, was decidedly a man not to be trusted. That he should callously place her in such a dire predicament weighed heavily on her heart. None of this, however, showed on her face. "Surely," she responded sternly, "you cannot think I have them with me!" The ancient gaped at her. "Really," said Tess, "this thing has been handled as badly as possible from beginning to end! You have set about solving this business in entirely the wrong way. Your first error was to place the necklace in my portmanteau, and your second was to try and use me as a cat's-paw. Why did you, by the way?"

Somehow, thought the old man, this inquisition had gotten sadly out of hand. So authoritative was the countess that her words would have caused even the bravest, which he was not, to quail. "There was a Runner come after the sparklers," he replied humbly. "He wouldn't bother *you*. We knew where you was going, your woman having said so, and we reckoned it'd be easy enough to pinch the sparklers from you with no one the wiser."

"How incredibly stupid!" declared Tess, and proceeded to read her captor a stern lecture on the evils of lawlessness, and the appalling consequences thereof.

"Begod!" spat the ancient, left all of a muck of sweat by the suggestion that he himself would dangle from the nubbing cheat. "Stop this gabble and tell me where the sparklers are hid!" He leered. "Or it'll go the worse for you, my pretty one!"

"I daresay it'll go the worse for me anyway," replied Tess, with a shrug. "You might bear in mind that you will never find the necklace without my help." She eyed him. "You might save yourself, if you let me go."

"Nay, that won't wash!" The old man spat on the dirt floor. He had, Tess noted, remarkably few teeth, which perhaps partially accounted for his eccentricities of speech.

"Even," she offered handsomely, "if I promise *not* to go to Bow Street? Think, man! Do you *wish* to hang?"

The ancient definitely did not, nor did he wish to come afoul of the cutthroat gang above-stairs. "You vow not to snitch on us?" he inquired slyly.

"I do," asserted Tess. "You need have no fear that I will not keep my word." She paused as he ruminated. "You can trust me."

"No more than pigs can fly!" snapped the old man and rose menacingly.

"I must remind you," said Tess, with a great deal more courage than she felt, "that it is to your benefit to keep me alive. Only *I* know where the necklace is."

"Aye, and dead men tell no tales," responded the ancient in a most chilling manner. He jerked his head toward the ceiling. "You'll talk right enough before *they*'re through with you! Happen it'd be easier on you if you'd told me." He cackled as she blanched. "Think on it, lady! I'll give you some time. Happen I'll come again; happen *they* will." And then—" He grimaced evilly.

Tess watched in gloomy silence as he walked to the door. Things couldn't be in a worse case, she thought. She was incorrect in that assumption, as the ancient quickly proved. He turned to peer malignantly at her. "It's a brave lass you are!" he announced and shook his head. "It's mortal afraid *I*'d be to stay here. Rats, you know! Poisonous little beasts! They'll get in your pretty hair and nibble at your toes." With a last cackle, he went out the door. Tess heard a key turn in the lock.

She also heard, in the thick silence, ominous rustlings that proved she truly did share her little cellar with various members of the rodent family. The countess was not at all fond of such creatures. She drew her feet up beneath her and gloomily contemplated the candle, which was burning low. When it went out, the room would be dark as the pit.

Despite her brave words, Tess was aware that her situation was extremely perilous. She could hardly hope to escape so many determined ruffians, though she supposed she might temporarily delay her fate by breaking bottles over their heads as they entered her cell, a feat made all the more difficult by the dim light. She was not fleet of foot; she could hardly hope to outrun them. And, due to her folly in entrusting herself to Sir Morgan, she could hardly hope for rescue. If only she'd told someone where she'd planned to go! That would have availed little, she realized, since her destination was supposed to have been Vauxhall.

Disillusioned as she was, Tess had to concede that the Wicked Baronet was an extremely clever man. He would not get away with it, of course; both Clio and Delphine would raise a terrible outcry when her disappearance was discovered, and neither would fail to point the finger of suspicion at him. Doubtless he would have a ready explanation, Tess thought queasily, and would profess himself all undone when her lifeless body came to light. Perhaps it was as well. Despite his vicious ill-treatment of herself, she found she did not wish him to hang. Rather, she would prefer to dole out punishment herself, not that the opportunity would be granted her. Tess knew full well that she was slated for death. The villains might be spared the trouble, she reflected grimly; she would certainly be driven mad when the candle burned its last and the rats came.

As it happened, darkness had not yet descended when she heard a shuffling at the door, though the candle was definitely guttering. She leapt to her feet, cursing as she grasped the cane. Fool! she thought, to be spending her last moments pondering the character of a man who could in one moment embrace her passionately and in the next condemn her to a particularly nasty end. And a fool himself to have provided her with a sword-stick. She drew the rapier and positioned herself by the door. The noble Lansburys always fought to the end.

It was not much of a struggle; the brigand had obviously been unprepared for resistance and was further hampered by the lack of light, Tess having thoughtfully placed the dying candle as far away as possible. She withdrew her sword from the man's side and stood looking down at him with an expression not of triumph but of dawning dismay. That familiar slender figure was not clad in the rough attire of her captors. Hastily she grasped the candle and brought it closer. "Good God!" she gasped, as the light fell on his waxen face. "Ceddie!"

# Chapter 21

*Bellamy House was in an uproar,* Delphine having, in a conciliatory mood, gone to make her peace with her mistress only to find Tess's room ransacked and the countess gone. A quick inspection of the remainder of the house further revealed that Tess was not on the premises, and that no one had seen her depart. One other person was unaccounted for: the Duke of Bellamy's personal servant. Since Daffy could hardly think that Lady Tess had gone out accompanied by that very superior valet, she very much suspected that mischief was afoot.

Delphine had been laboring under a strong sense of misusage ever since their arrival at Bellamy House, and an even stronger conviction that her mistress would land in the briars; and the information that the countess had disappeared set the seal to her distress. Vividly recalling the mishaps that had plagued her mistress, Delphine feared that Lady Tess had again come to grief.

As was clearly necessary, Delphine raised the alarm. However, she was herself in a state of no small perturbation, and consequently took her unhappy news not to one of the people who might have dealt competently with the emergency, such as the Duchess of Bellamy or the duke, but to Lucille, who responded with such strong hysterics that the entire household was set on its ear.

They were all crowded in the front drawing-room, in various stages of undress, the dowager in a huge nightcap that made her look like a bad-tempered chef, and Constant in a violently crimson dressing gown with a tasseled Turkish cap upon his head. Lucille was stretched out on the sofa, while Delphine waved burnt feathers under her nose; Drusilla wandered up and down the room, totally unconcerned with anything but how this development might benefit herself; and Clio, released from her room by no less than the duke himself, stood by the doorway with one arm around a sleepy Evelyn.

"Well-a-day!" pronounced Sapphira, who didn't seem the least bit upset that one of her daughters was stretched out in a dead faint, while the other was looking remarkably like a tart in an extremely revealing robe. "What's missing, besides that abominable wench?"

"Very little," Giles replied quickly, forestalling indignant comment from both Clio and Delphine. "Some odd pieces of silver and porcelain, but nothing of particular value. I do not know what may have been taken from Tess's room."

"No need to call in Bow Street then." Sapphira shot a look at Clio. "Tess probably took them herself, and we'd hardly want Clio's companion hauled before the magistrates. Good riddance to bad rubbish! I always knew that one was no better than she should be."

"How dare you say that about Tess!" cried Clio, clutching Evelyn so tightly that he winced. "She may be hurt, or worse! Lying somewhere in the streets, struck down!"

"If that one's lying somewhere," offered Drusilla idly, "it's by choice. And I can imagine with whom!"

"That rankles, does it?" inquired her mother, with interest. "I thought it might. Chuckle-head!"

Fortunately for family relations, Lucille returned to her senses and, with Delphine's assistance, managed to sit up. *"Maman!"* she moaned. "We've been robbed! That man who was skulking about the house—I told you how it would be!"

Sapphira greeted this observation with the bad temper for which she was celebrated, in one breath chastising her daughter for air-dreaming, in the next accusing her of arranging the entire thing for the sole purpose of creating a scene.

"Oh, do hush, *Maman!*" interrupted the duke. "This is a serious business. You may badger my sister some other time." He helped Lucille to her feet. "Come! You will be happier in your room."

Lucille thought she'd be happier somewhere far distant from Bellamy House, but she allowed Delphine to take her arm. Clio watched their departure soberly. She, too, recalled the mishaps that had plagued Tess. There seemed to be an uncommon number of them, she thought in retrospect, and aimed at some purpose she didn't know. She said so.

"I dislike your manners, miss!" snapped Sapphira, still smarting from her son's highhandedness. "Don't speak till you're spoken to!"

"Put a damper on it, *Maman!*" advised Giles, watching Clio with a frown. "My cousin has a point."

"There was the man who invaded her room at the inn and then the highwaymen." Clio was touched by his defense. "And that carriage accident, when Tess so narrowly avoided injury."

"And the man in the park," offered Evelyn helpfully, then clapped a hand over his mouth. "Crickey! I promised not to tell." The cat was out of the bag; the duke fixed his son with a stern eye and demanded to be told the whole. Unhappily, Evelyn obeyed.

*"And,"* concluded Clio triumphantly, "the man who accosted her at the theatre! Please, Your Grace, call in Bow Street! Send out a search party! It is obvious that Tess is the object of some plot!"

"Pooh." Drusilla yawned. "The anxiety you are in has deranged your ideas, cousin!" She glanced at her mother to make sure Sapphira's attention had not strayed. "I'm sure it isn't wonderful, considering that you were set on an elopement tonight! A pity this has happened to overset your plans."

"An *elopement!*" The dowager turned a hideous mottled red. "What the devil is this?"

"Perhaps," mused Drusilla, "the young man ran off with Tess instead."

This had not occurred to Clio who, it must be confessed, had accepted her imprisonment with resignation and no small relief. A person could only do so much, no matter how great her devotion to another and her desire for a happy ending, and Clio had exhausted her resourcefulness. Therefore, she had raised no outcry, lest someone appear to release her. As a result, she was guilt-stricken. It was not beyond the limits of credulity that Ceddie should have kidnapped Tess. What he would do with her, Clio dared not think.

"Cousin Clio!" With fascination, Evelyn regarded her ashen face. "Are you going to have the vapors? Shall I fetch Aunt Lucille's hartshorn?"

"No," Clio replied with resolution. "I shan't swoon." There was nothing she could do now but make a clean breast of things. No matter what it might cost Clio personally, Tess must be found.

But the duke forestalled her, and not inadvertently. "There was no elopement planned," he said calmly, flicking open his snuffbox. "Drusilla is, as usual, stirring up coals. Do not distress yourself, Clio! I have already sent word to Bow Street."

Sapphira greeted this intelligence with a terrible explosion of wrath, announcing herself cursedly provoked at the fuss made over a female who was no better than a lightskirt, and blaming Clio for the remarkable occurrences that had taken place since her arrival at Bellamy House. "What a fix!" said Drusilla, happy to see the deterioration of the relationship between her mother and Clio, and not reluctant to worsen matters. "Neither *Maman* nor Morgan will thank you, Giles!"

Clio frowned, wondering what the Wicked Baronet had to do with this shocking state of affairs. Drusilla was quick to enlighten her. "You have your wish, *Maman!*" she continued brightly. "Tess's disappearance will give rise to just the sort of scandal-broth that you wished. How clever of you to leave it to Morgan to bring the thing about!"

Total pandemonium might have resulted from this provocative remark—Clio had opened her mouth in absolute fury and the dowager had risen half out of her chair—but hasty footsteps sounded in the hallway. The door flew open; Sir Morgan, looking like the fiend incarnate, stalked into the room. "Oh, Morgan!" cried Drusilla, the only one to have not temporarily lost the use of her tongue. "Is the thing done already? We must congratulate you!"

Sir Morgan did not immediately answer, being engaged in holding off Clio, who had launched herself at him, raking her fingernails down his face and plummeting her fists against his chest. "What the deuce?" he inquired, not unreasonably, as he caught her wrists.

"What have you done with Tess?" wailed Clio, tears running down her cheeks. "How could you? You are odious! This is unforgivable! Oh, poor Tess!" And then she lapsed into total incoherency.

"Here!" Sir Morgan delivered Clio up to the duke, who didn't appear at all unwilling to have her weep all over his waistcoat once again. "What the devil is this all about?" He glanced quickly around the room. "Tess isn't here?"

"No." Giles suddenly looked very serious. "I conclude that your, er, plans went astray?"

"I was delayed." Sir Morgan scowled. "No matter—I see now it was deliberate. What has happened here?" Briefly Giles explained. "Pertwee is also among the missing," he concluded.

"Good." Sir Morgan appeared unaccountably relieved. "All may not yet be lost."

"I've sent for a Runner," added the duke.

Drusilla had no interest in this cryptic conversation. "Only fancy!" she said. "Has Tess, then, run away like Mirian did? How odd of her! It will bring her under the gravest censure, of course." Clio sobbed.

"Draggletailed twit!" remarked the dowager, though whether she referred to her daughter or Mirian or Tess, she did not explain. "I knew it would come to this. And without your help, Morgan! You certainly botched the affair."

This brought from Clio renewed wailing and protest. "You—you *seducer!*" she cried, regarding Sir Morgan venomously from the safety of the duke's arms. "How could you so deceive my poor Tess, and at a nasty old woman's whim?"

214

From the dowager's direction came a choking noise, and from Constant an unwise titter. "I don't know where you get those idiotic notions!" remarked Sir Morgan to Clio. "But I see I must disabuse you of them, if Tess is ever to have any peace. She has never stood in the least danger from me."

"Bah!" snorted Sapphira. "I wonder you will be forever trying to humbug us all." But she reckoned without her son.

"I have," announced the duke, in so quelling a manner that even his mother fell silent, "heard quite enough of this nonsense! You will moderate your behavior, *Maman,* or you will be sent from the room." The dowager's mouth dropped open. "Furthermore, on the morrow the lot of you will begin to prepare for removal to the house in Marylebone. I will no longer tolerate this internal mischief-making and meddling."

"Giles!" Sapphira's eyes bulged, fishlike. "You cannot mean to turn us out!"

"I mean," replied the Duke of Bellamy sternly, "to do precisely that. I cannot comprehend how you could scheme at the ruin of a guest in this house. Can't you see what the outcome of such a thing would be? You would have brought down scandal on all of us, most of all yourself."

"Fiddlesticks!" The dowager was severely shaken, but still game. "You are making a great deal of fuss over the wench. Who is she, that you should be so concerned?"

"I do not need," Giles said icily, "to explain my actions to you."

"Where the devil is that curst Runner?" growled Sir Morgan.

"Dear Giles!" With a saintly demeanor, Drusilla knelt and drew Evelyn into her arms. "You cannot mean to leave your son without a woman's tender care!"

The Duke of Bellamy glanced at his son, who looked as though he greatly looked forward to that happy state of affairs. His arm tightened around Clio. "I don't."

"I think you're foxed!" announced Sapphira, drawing herself up to deliver a tirade on thankless children and serpents' teeth. Drusilla prudently withdrew to a window seat, effectively divorcing herself from the scene.

Alas, the dowager duchess was interrupted by a further commotion in the hall. The door opened; the butler announced, in shaken tones, the advent of the long-awaited Runner. With him was Pertwee.

"Hell and the devil confound it!" ejaculated Sir Morgan, staring at the valet's bandaged brow and stupefied air.

Pertwee unhappily eyed the Wicked Baronet, and wondered if the duke would stand idly by while his valet was strangled on the spot. "I am very much afraid, Your Grace," he said to Giles, "that I have failed in my mission. The circumstances were not what we had anticipated, Your Grace, and I was overpowered."

"That he was!" confirmed the Runner, a dapper little individual with a chubby countenance and the beginning of a paunch. "We found him wandering in the streets, right mizzy-mazed. Aye, and that's why I wasn't there aforetimes, him not recalling his address."

The others might gaze upon this individual with varying degrees of fascination, but Sir Morgan was not so easily distracted, nor was he unacquainted with this particular denizen of Bow Street. "Tess!" he interrupted, fixing Pertwee with a steely eye.

"There was a coach waiting and she was in it before I could stop her, sir!" Pertwee gulped. "Indeed, I tried my best! I even called out! And I had my hand on the door itself when I was bludgeoned."

"What kind of a coach?" growled Sir Morgan.

"Very shabby, sir!" Pertwee exhibited disdain. "Not at all the rig of a gentleman."

Why this information should please Sir Morgan, Clio had no idea, but it undoubtedly did. "Where are you going?" she cried, as he strode to the door.

"To find Tess! I think I may know where she is." He looked at the Runner and jerked his head. "Come along, man, I have need of you."

"But what will you do?" Clio insisted, not inclined, despite Giles's assurances, to trust the Wicked Baronet.

"After I find her?" Sir Morgan's swarthy features were very, very grim. "Probably wring her neck!"

"Never fear, missy!" said the Runner, as Clio gasped. "We'll fix it up all right and tight!" He set off at a trot after Sir Morgan, who was already halfway down the hall.

"Hush, darling!" soothed the duke; Clio had once more dissolved in tears. "I assure you everything possible will be done."

"Humph!" The dowager regarded this touching scene with a kindly eye. "You will apologize for your earlier rudeness, Giles!"

The Duke of Bellamy was not of a yielding nature, even when the lady of his choice was clasped very willingly in his arms. He turned on his fond family a face as cold as a marble statue. "Tomorrow," he repeated. "All of you." His icy eye moved around the room, resting on Drusilla, who was half-hidden in her window seat, moving to Constant, who dropped like an abandoned puppet against the sofa. "Oh, no!" groaned the duke. "Where the deuce is *Evelyn?*"

# Chapter 22

*"I must say,"* said Ceddie, clutching his ribs, "that it's a damned poor way to repay your rescuer!"

"Balderdash!" replied Lady Tess absently, from behind him. "It's the merest scratch. For which you may thank the dim light and those ridiculous corsets that you wear! Else I would have had you right through the heart."

Cedric was not of a robust constitution, despite his sporting tastes, and this callous attitude made him feel distinctly lightheaded. He was extremely annoyed by the countess's thankless attitude toward himself, and highly indignant at the treatment he'd received at her hands. Nor was Ceddie at all grateful for the fact that she had revived him by pouring an entire bottle of smuggled brandy over his head, or that she had torn her fine petticoats to bind his wound; and he was rendered hideously uncomfortable by the fact that she held him at sword point.

"Move!" commanded Tess, and Ceddie felt the rapier's price between his shoulder blades. He moved.

Unbeknownst to Ceddie, Tess was not having an easy time of it. Though the full moon rendered the countryside clear as noonday the ground was rough and uneven. Tess clutched the rapier in one hand, its casing under the opposite arm, and used a stout stick as a cane. Her stride was not steady; her shoes were not designed for tramping down country lanes. Nor had she shaken the depression attendant upon the realization that Sir Morgan had callously abandoned her to a decidedly unpleasant fate. The Wicked Baronet, she thought somberly. How could she have been so deceived in the character of the man? She had thought him reckless, but no worse. It was not pleasant to discover herself a fool.

It was the dead of night and her captors were presumably abed, having decided to let the rats' company induce in her a more cooperative frame of mind. They might well have done so, Tess mused, if not for Ceddie's impromptu performance. She supposed she should be grateful to him for it, no matter how base his motives. What those motives were, she could not begin to guess, but that they were disgraceful there wasn't the least doubt. Tess hoped that the ruffians were not early risers, and that no one would come to check on her in the middle of the night. Ceddie's halting progress would get them no great distance from the cobbled courtyard by daybreak. She nudged him again, rather viciously.

"I've been wounded!" Ceddie protested indignantly. "Dash it, Lady Tess, you're dealing with a sick man! God only knows how much blood I've lost."

"*I* know!" snapped the unfeeling countess. "At the most, ten drops! It would serve you right if I left you here for the others to find. I doubt they'd thank you for upsetting their plans."

"If that don't beat all!" Poor Ceddie considered himself grossly abused. "I come to pull your coals out of the fire, and you accuse me of being hand-in-glove with your kidnappers. I tell you what it is, Lady Tess. You're paperskulled!"

"*Not* so paperskulled," reproved the countess, "that I don't think it's very odd that *you* should appear! Nor do I believe your Banbury tale that you just happened to be in Berkeley Square when the carriage took me up."

Ceddie did not consider it a propitious moment to explain that he'd meant to elope with Clio; he lapsed into sullen silence, thinking that he'd have been far wiser to apply to his irascible sire for financial assistance. Much as Ceddie hated to give his head to the blunt-tongued squire for washing, he could not imagine that his father would prove less reasonable than Tess, who had stabbed her savior, nigh immersed him in brandy, threatened him in the most harrowing manner, and now held a sword at his back. To think he'd considered marrying her! Ceddie shuddered. He wasn't totally convinced that she would not leave him for the inn's bloodthirsty inhabitants to find.

Tess's state of mind might have been more coherent than her prisoner's, but it was hardly more cheerful. She had little hope of a clean escape, the stench of brandy that emanated from Ceddie's bedraggled person was overpowering even in the night air, and furthermore her feet were wet. "Where the devil is your horse?" she hissed. "Don't tell me again that you've misplaced it, Ceddie, because even you can't be *that* harebrained!"

"Well, I did," retorted Ceddie sulkily. "I left the brute around here somewhere." An exasperated sound came from behind him, and he dared to turn. "Dash it, Lady Tess, it's dark! I can't be expected to think of everything!"

"Very true!" Tess promptly agreed. "I *didn't* expect it of you." The countess herself was looking a little the worse for wear: her gown was torn and filthy, her already tangled hair had curled riotously in the damp air, and there was a large smudge of dirt on her nose. She sighed. "We might as well rest for a moment—in which you will once more try and explain!"

Ceddie did try, without marked success, as was clearly demonstrated by Lady Tess's sword, pointed unwaveringly at his throat. "Yes, yes!" she interrupted impatiently. "You told me all this before, and I still don't believe a word of it. We shall skirt the issue of *why* you were in Berkeley Square, since you don't seem inclined to admit the truth, and since I think I may guess!" The rapier's tip moved fractionally closer and Ceddie gulped. "Why did you follow me?" inquired Tess.

"Thought you might be in danger!" croaked Ceddie. "Didn't like the appearance of things at all!"

"Moonshine! You thought I was off to keep an assignation, and thought you might use it to blackmail me."

220

"Were you?" inquired Ceddie, briefly forgetting his perilous situation. "Dashed if I'd of thought it of *you!*" The rapier inched forward. "No harm in it," he added hastily, "if you *were* off to meet a gentleman! If you *had* met him, but you didn't! Came here instead and if it weren't for *me* you'd still be locked up in that curst cellar!"

The countess made a strangled noise that sounded remarkably like "empty-headed fool," but the sword came no closer, and Ceddie was encouraged to continue. "Thing is," he confided, putting his cards on the table while still he could, "I'm in queer street! You know, under the hatches! Thought if I saved you, you might return the favor!"

"Ah!" exclaimed Lady Tess. "You wish me to redeem your vowels. That sounds very much like you, Ceddie." He waited hopefully. "However, I am not totally convinced. This affair of the necklace has been so badly mismanaged that I am almost positive that you had a hand in it."

"Necklace?" Ceddie wondered if the countess's imprisonment had deranged her mind.

"We have wasted enough time!" Tess wielded the saber in a careless manner that made her captive's blood—what remained of it—turn to water. "Onward, Ceddie! I strongly advise you to think very hard on where you left that damned horse."

"Very well!" snapped Ceddie. "I warn you I'm feeling deuced queer. It will be your own fault if I swoon dead away."

The countess displayed no sympathy for his debilitated condition. Instead she looked pointedly at the tree against which he leaned, which looked remarkably like a gibbet. "I wonder," she mused, "if that's where the highwaymen were hanged?" Ceddie cast a wild-eyed glance at the tree, and broke into a trot.

Thus they progressed through the night, though neither of them had the faintest notion of what direction they traveled or where the path might lead them, with Ceddie cursing the misguided knight-errantry that had prompted him to follow Tess, and the countess enlivening the journey with gruesome speculations on what might be their fate if they were caught. Consequently it was with no small relief that Ceddie heard an unmistakable whicker. "My horse!" he cried thankfully. "You see, I didn't lie to you, Lady Tess!"

"Correction, bantling!" came a deep voice from among the trees. Ceddie's hair stood on end. "Not your horse but mine, though yours will be rounded up soon enough." Sir Morgan stepped forward, his swarthy face more satanic than ever in the bright moonlight. "I give you joy, Countess! May I say I'm damned glad to see you, little one?"

"You may *not!*" snarled Lady Tess. "Don't seek to disarm me! I had thought Ceddie too much a slow-top to be the leader of a gang of cutthroats, but now I realize that *you* are the ringleader, Sir Morgan, and that Ceddie is in league with you." She brandished the sword-stick. "Well, you shan't have me without a fight, and so I warn you! I fancy I could skewer Ceddie in a trice."

A lesser man might have been taken aback by such vehemence, but Sir Morgan was not entirely unaccustomed to indignant ladies who hurled insults, like crockery, at his head. "No, love, I knew *that!*" he said, and advanced.

Lady Tess's words had not gone unheeded by Ceddie, and he immediately understood that Sir Morgan was responsible for their predicament. He might yet, he thought, collect a reward, if not from the countess, then from a grateful government, for so great a brigand as Sir Morgan must surely have a price on his head. With that idea in mind, he wrenched the sword-stick from Tess's relaxed fingers. "Advance another step," he cried, "and I'll have your life!"

No coward, Sir Morgan did not pause. "Ass!" gasped Tess as Ceddie lunged, and brought down her heavy stick on his sword arm.

Ceddie was no novice in the art of fencing; had not the countess deflected his aim, Sir Morgan would have been speedily dispatched. "*Now* look what you've done, you

222

idiot!" wailed Tess, as the Wicked Baronet crumpled to the ground. "I shall never forgive you!"

Ceddie might have had experience with the *épée*, but he had never before seriously wounded a man. He looked at his victim, covered with what seemed a vast amount of blood, and swooned.

Lady Tess paid not the slightest heed; she was on her knees beside Sir Morgan making further depredations on her petticoats so that she might staunch the blood that flowed so freely from his wound, and, it must be confessed, weeping. "Oh, you wretched man!" she sobbed. "You may have your damned diamonds and I will consider myself fortunate to be rid of both you and them!" Sir Morgan looked positively corpselike, or so she thought, though her vision was unquestionably blurred by tears. "Don't you dare die, you beast!" she added, with fine feminine logic. "I have a great deal to say to you!"

"And I to you, my love!" Sir Morgan opened eyes that held a distinct twinkle and spoke in a voice that betrayed not the slightest tremor of pain. "No, don't fly into a passion! It's only a flesh wound."

It was highly possible that the countess, realizing herself most ignobly deceived, might have finished the work Ceddie had begun, had not just then a fourth person appeared leading three horses. "Hallo, Aunt Tess!" said Evelyn cheerfully. "What have you done to Sir Morgan?"

"Evelyn!" Tess's voice was weak. "What are *you* doing here?"

The young viscount grinned. "I followed Sir Morgan from Bellamy House! He had to bring me along because he hadn't time to take me back." His sparkling glance fell on Ceddie. "What's the matter with him?"

"He fainted." With undiminished strength, Sir Morgan pulled Tess to her feet.

"Paltry fellow!" decreed Evelyn.

"You exhibited a great deal of compassion," murmured Sir Morgan to his captive, "for a man whom you believe responsible for your misfortunes. May I hope that you hold a kindness for me, little one?"

223

"No." The countess was prey to a great number of conflicting emotions. Had not the Wicked Baronet retained a firm grip on her arm, she would have stalked majestically away. As it was, Tess contented herself with scowling murderously at him. "How could any woman nourish a fondness for a man who had her locked in a cellar? I wish only the privilege of seeing you hang."

"Cripes!" Evelyn was wide-eyed. "A cellar?"

"With rats!" Recalling her grievous mistreatment, Lady Tess looked mulish. "What now, Sir Morgan? I suppose you'll drag me back to the inn so that your cohorts may finish the thing!"

"I rather thought," Sir Morgan replied apologetically, "that we'd retire to my home, which lies nearby, though after all this excitement you will probably find it devilish flat." She blinked, bewildered, and he smiled. "I was on my way there the night we met at the inn, having stopped in only for a chat with our old groom—he taught me to ride, you see, though he's now long retired from such work."

"Ah!" said Tess. "An ancient individual lacking a great many teeth and badly in need of a bath?" Sir Morgan's startled expression was confirmation enough. "I fancy I may have made his acquaintance! It was he who told me what I might expect from rats, the kindly old gentleman."

"Poor old Carruthers," lamented Sir Morgan. "I have often said that he would come to a bad end."

It occurred to Lady Tess that she stood in great danger of feeling quite in charity with the fiendish author of her misfortunes. "Why did you change your mind?" she inquired rebelliously. "It would've saved us a great deal of trouble if you'd simply gone home!"

"You intrigued me," said Sir Morgan.

"Aunt Tess!" interrupted Evelyn, who'd followed this exchange with interest, despite its various incomprehensible points. Ceddie stirred and moaned. "Are you thinking Sir Morgan is in league with the robbers? Truly he is not! He told me everything on the way. He has taken every measure for your safety. Just think, he set Pertwee to following you!" The boy's tone was awed—whether from admiration for Sir Morgan's cleverness or for his boldness in utilizing the superior valet could not be determined.

"The devil!" muttered Tess.

"What happened?" asked Ceddie, weakly rising to his knees. Memory returned, and with it a fresh onslaught of squeamishness. "Confound it, Lady Tess! I think you've broken my arm." The countess paid not the least attention to this accusation, being engaged in staring at the Wicked Baronet with an appalled expression that Ceddie perfectly understood. He could not, however, at all understand why she should allow herself to be embraced by the brigand. Ceddie concluded that the various deprecations made on his person had affected his eyesight.

"Don't fret, little one!" Sir Morgan released Tess and looked fondly down upon her stricken face. "I promise I don't hold it against you that you should have thought me capable of such villainy! Rather, I consider it an indication of your superior intellect, though I promise I should never lock you in a rat-infested cellar, no matter how greatly you provoked me!" He smiled his crooked grin. "Just think what a tale we may relate to our spellbound grandchildren!"

"It seems to me," Evelyn stated critically, "a queer time to be making a declaration! Are we waiting for the men from Bow Street?"

"Pernicious brat!" said Sir Morgan.

"Bow Street!" ejaculated Ceddie, and sank back on the ground. It took several moments' discussion to convince him that the authorities were coming not to arrest him for wounding a man but to aid the Runner already watching the inn in rounding up its occupants; and several more moments to convince the countess, belatedly recalled to Sir Morgan's condition, that he was not like to expire on the spot, having in truth suffered only a flesh wound. At last they were all mounted, Ceddie alternately complaining that he felt feverish and chilled, and announcing that Sir Morgan may have diddled Lady Tess but *he* knew they were being led straight back into the dragon's lair, there doubtless to be subjected to hideous tortures, if not worse; to which Evelyn, leading Cedric's mare, replied that it wasn't surprising Ceddie should nourish such crack-brained ideas, since from the smell he must've consumed enough brandy to float a battleship. Tess, mounted sideways on Sir Morgan's horse and held in place by his sound arm, was silent, her gaze fixed on the Wicked Baronet's dark face with an expression of acute anxiety.

# Chapter 23

*The dowager duchess sailed* into her son's study with all the majesty of a disabled battleship. In her wake trailed her daughters and her unhappy son-in-law. Constant was feeling decidedly bilious, a fact which he unhesitantly laid at Clio's door. They had gone along smoothly enough before *she* arrived at Bellamy House to set them all at odds. He cast the girl a look of acute dislike and sank, panting, into a chair.

Clio did not see that venomous glance but the duke did, and his countenance grew even more stern. "Lucille," he said, not unkindly, "you need not stay."

Lucille looked at him, then at Clio, who was pale as a ghost with great dark shadows under her eyes, then at the two strangers who watched them with such ill-concealed curiosity. "I think I must," she responded, dropping her gaze to her hands.

Sapphira snorted and sat down. "Well?" she demanded. "What's so important that you must call us here?" Giles received a malevolent glare. "You're getting mighty big for your breeches, boy!"

The duke ignored this unkind, and unjustified, slur and waited with grim patience for the various members of his family to settle themselves. Drusilla looked at the strangers, and he thought he saw her blanch. "First of all," he announced, when they were all silent, "you will be pleased to learn that both Evelyn and Tess are safe." His cool glance moved to Clio, whose exhausted face revealed mingled relief and apprehension. "I am in momentary expectation of more news. But we will discuss that later. It is for an entirely different reason that I have called you here."

"What?" demanded Drusilla, inspired by the happy news to rather viciously crush the fabric of her skirt. "We are very busy with our packing, Giles—as you should know."

"This will take but a few moments." The duke had to admit that, whatever her imperfections, Drusilla wasn't one to turn craven and flee. "You will recall that Clio's mother had a very dear friend by the name of Celest Dubois." A contemplative expression on his handsome face, the Duke of Bellamy moved to the fireplace. "I wonder why we did not think to apply to Celest when Mirian disappeared?"

Lucille's composure had been restored by long immersions in a portable Turkish bath designed to steam impurities from the system. "*Maman* forbade it," she offered. "She said Celest was a giddy gadabout and we weren't to encourage her pretensions."

The dowager duchess, who had belatedly recognized one of the silent strangers, a plump lady with a mischievous countenance and prematurely white hair, had the grace to look embarrassed. "Wet-goose!" she snapped at her elder daughter. "I'm sure I made no such remark." Her irate gaze moved to Giles. "Devil take you, make an end! What is all this about?"

"I wonder," mused the duke, with a plaintive air, "if I might be a changeling? I sincerely trust I haven't the least resemblance to any of you. But we waste time! Doctor Martin, Celest, let me make you known to my family."

Even Clio roused from her stupor to stare at her mother's girlhood friend as, ignoring the others, Celest moved quickly to her side. What precisely the woman said, Clio could not later recall, but her kindness was so overwhelming that Clio was hard put not to weep again. Celest sat down beside her, gently patting her hand.

So moving a scene touched no other heartstrings. The dowager's bosom swelled as she realized she dare not order the detested Celest—daughter of a wealthy merchant and consequently unfit to mingle with the blue-blooded Bellamys, a fact pointed out to the rebellious Mirian time and again—from the house. Drusilla's reaction was no less perturbed, though she tried to hide behind a mask of perfect indifference.

"What do you hope to accomplish?" growled Sapphira, glaring at the doctor, who in turn regarded Clio thoughtfully. "Giles! Why have you brought these people here?"

"I grew curious," explained the duke, "about Mirian's reasons for leaving us." Celest glanced briefly at him. "My failure to ask questions at the time was reprehensible, and so I confess. But Tess was mighty concerned with having the truth, and I began to wonder at it, particularly in view of the fact that Mirian had told her husband and her daughter nothing of us."

"What a rowdy-do!" interrupted Drusilla, growing noticeably fidgety. "I'm sure it's not to be wondered at, the way she crept out of here like a thief in the night!"

"Quiet!" roared the dowager, and Drusilla subsided. "Go on, Giles."

"It seemed apparent," continued the duke, "that Mirian's silence was prompted by a wish to forget unhappy memories. Since her years with us were *not* unhappy as I recall, I was in a puzzle to account for her inexplicable behavior." He looked at Clio, who was watching him wide-eyed. "Then Tess recalled Celest to me. I thought if anyone knew the truth, she would." He flickered open his snuffbox. "I was proved correct."

"Naturally!" snapped Sapphira, with well-concealed pride. She scowled at Celest, who still held Clio's hand. "Let's have it!" To the dowager's annoyance, Celest looked inquiringly at Giles. He nodded.

"Mirian came to me," the woman said, in tones as kindly as her appearance, "straight from this house. She was with me several days while we decided what she was to do. I was at first in favor of her returning here, but when no effort seemed to be made to find her, I began to believe that she would be much happier away from this family. And so she was." Celest's angry face softened as her eyes rested on Clio. "Your mother doted on you, child! Oh yes, we maintained a correspondence. I feel as though I already know both you and Tess."

Mention of her sister caused Clio's spirits to again sink; her fears had grown so wildly that they could not be set at rest by the simple statement that Tess was safe. Where was Tess? she wondered. And Sir Morgan? The countess would be safe nowhere in that wicked man's vicinity.

"We did not meet," Celest continued, rather sadly, "after Mirian wed Lord Lansbury. She wished no reminder of her old life, or so I now believe. It is perfectly understandable. Mirian was treated abominably."

Sapphira could not let this slur pass unchallenged. "Poppycock!" she snorted. Both Drusilla and Lucille were silent. Giles watched his doting family as keenly as if they were criminals and he a peace officer determined to prevent their escape.

"Not at all," Celest replied calmly. "I do you the honor of assuming you were unaware of the tales Mirian was told. It was very cleverly done! I believed it myself until the duke enlighted me."

"*What* tales?" demanded the dowager, her eyes moving without hesitation to her daughters, twin pictures of guilt.

"I didn't know!" gasped Lucille, wringing her hands. "I vow I didn't! I thought it was the truth."

"You refine too much on it!" Drusilla shot her sister a vicious look and simultaneously attempted to achieve the air of one with a conscience unburdened by past duplicities. "It was all a jest—we did not mean that Mirian should take it seriously!" At the sound of that plural pronoun, Lucille moaned. Drusilla glared at her. "It was a much your idea as mine, sister!" she snapped. "Don't think I'll take the blame for you *this* time! You were jealous of Mirian's standing with *Maman*, and all too eager to engage in a little trickery."

"No!" wailed Lucille.

"Yes, I think," interrupted Celest. "The both of you played equal parts in the tale Mirian told me."

"Nothing," roared Sapphira, hands clenched like claws

230

on the arms of her chair, "could be more provoking than this missishness! Speak without roundaboutation, if you please!"

"I believe I had best explain," offered Celest. Lucille looked frantically about the room, but Giles stood near the doorway, and Drusilla's hand held her clamped in her seat. "Not this time!" Drusilla hissed. "You're in this up to your neck, so don't bother to pretend and faint, or offer us megrims!"

"If you will, Mrs. Martin," interrupted Giles. "Tell it to them as you told it to me."

"As you wish." Celest's voice held praise. "I know that it cannot be other than painful for you! To make a long story short, Mirian was told that she was the result of a liaison between her mother and the previous Duke of Bellamy, brought up in Bellamy House on sufferance after her mother's death." The dowager, stunned by the notion that her husband had played her false, gaped. "*That* was the part of the tale that I found hardest to believe," Celest added. "It didn't suit my notions of the duchess's character that she should behave so handsomely to one of the old duke's byblows—but Mirian did believe it, and I allowed her to convince me."

"I don't understand," protested Clio, frowning as she tried to make sense of the tale. "Are you saying my mother was illegitimate?"

"Mirian's birth was as impeccable as my own," replied Giles, in tones so haughty that several of his auditors fervently wished themselves anywhere but in his presence. "The slight made on her parentage was merely my sisters' invention."

"But why?" Clio was greatly befuddled. "Surely she didn't run away because of *that?*"

"She did," Celest admitted. "You have forgotten the most odious aspect of the tale, Clio. Had Mirian in truth been the old duke's daughter—and she believed herself to be—she would have been the current duke's half-sister, and she fancied herself in love with him." Celest smiled. "She was not, of course, any more than he was with her, both being entirely too young for any form of permanent

231

relationship—but with the very notion of incest, the damage was done."

"Incest!" repeated Constant, for the first time taking an interest in the conversation. "What a shocking thing!"

"So it would have been," agreed Celest, "had there been a word of truth in it, which there was not. May I say, Duchess, that I consider your daughters to have behaved with the greatest impropriety? They were responsible for Mirian's flight, having between them cooked up that atrocious tale."

Sapphira closed her mouth, which had fallen open. She said nothing, having not yet recovered the use of her tongue, but the glance she awarded her daughters left little doubt that an unpleasant interview awaited them. "I feel faint!" moaned Lucille. "I think I must go to my room."

"You'll go nowhere," the duke asserted, "until we've reached the bottom of this thing."

Clio was shocked by the tale she'd just heard and by the unpalatable reminder that Giles had thought himself in love with her mother, whom she so closely resembled. She scarcely realized when Celest's husband seated himself on her other side. Clio answered his quiet questions without hesitation, so stunned that she did not question his curiosity about her frame of mind, or the precision with which he gauged her despondency and listlessness. Nor did the others pay particular attention to the inquisition save Celest, who was long-acquainted with her spouse's brusque ways. The doctor was an irascible individual, careless of manner and dress; he was also the best medical practitioner in all of London. Celest herself had a shrewd eye; she wasn't the least surprised when he finished his interrogation and shot her a fulminating glance. "Complexion powders be damned!" he barked. "This girl is being drugged."

This announcement brought Giles across the room with an oath that made even the dauntless Drusilla quail. "You won't lay that at my door!" she said hastily. "Apply to Constant!"

That gentleman was roused from reverie by his brother-in-law's ungentle hands, which grasped Constant's lapels and half-lifted him from his chair. "What?" he gasped, terror-stricken by Giles's obviously violent intent.

"Complexion powders," Drusilla explained succinctly, roused to animation by the possibility of seeing mayhem enacted before her eyes.

Constant turned pale as death. "No harm done!" he stammered. "They were only to make the girl moody and vaporish. We couldn't have Sapphira changing her will!"

"My will—" the dowager began ominously, but the doctor cut her short. "No harm!" he repeated incredulously, then cast an exasperated look at Giles. "It's fortunate the girl had the good sense not to take those powders regularly! From what I can determine they're strong enough to put a horse to sleep permanently!" Constant made a choking noise, occasioned by the duke's strangling grip on his neck. "No need to go throttling him, Your Grace!" added the doctor. "We can't have *you* standing your trial!"

Constant, released, sank plump into his chair and applied a handkerchief to his pallid brow. "You ought to be grateful to me!" he protested. "Those powders were a great deal safer than what Drusilla wanted me to give the girl!"

"And what was that?" Giles turned his chilling glance on Drusilla. That lady promptly took a page from her sister's book, and swooned.

Clio, understandably, couldn't have cared less if the entire Bellamy clan—with one notable exception—expired on the spot. "Please tell me the truth," she pleaded of Celest, during the ensuing *mêlée*. "Drusilla told me my mother was of unstable temperament—that there was lunacy in my family."

"Poppycock!" bellowed Sapphira, who'd overheard the remark. "There's no more truth in that than in any of Drusilla's other tales. Your parents both came of noble lines, and neither had the slightest taint of lunacy. Mirian was as sane as I."

This, since the dowager was looking both belligerent and wild-eyed, was not precisely reassuring. "It's true," soothed Celest. "You would do well to forget everything Drusilla has told you. She is a very vicious woman, entirely accustomed to having her own way." They glanced at the prone figure. Taking advantage of the momentary preoccupation, Constant slipped unnoticed from the room.

"It's not true, then," Clio asked with little hope, "that Drusilla is to marry Sir Morgan?" Giles might have said those nuptials would never come to pass, but Drusilla had strenuously claimed the opposite.

"Certainly not!" Sapphira snapped. "I would hope Morgan has more sense!" Clio looked confused, and the dowager sighed. "I know I've encouraged you to think he is the grossest libertine, and little wonder you did not question me, since Morgan is hardly one to explain himself! However, Giles will tell you that Morgan is engaged in working with him to improve social conditions among the lower orders. Morgan makes the investigations, consequently earning for himself a reputation for enjoying low life—which he probably does!—and Giles labors to have reform enacted." Her expression was irate. "Fools, the pair of them!"

The doctor, who bent over Drusilla, rose when she exhibited reluctant signs of life. "We can do no more here!" he announced.

"You must come to visit," Celest said to Clio, giving her hand a final pat. "Bring your Tess."

"You'll be well enough!" The doctor's shrewd eyes rested on Clio's face. "I'll have a tonic sent around. Mind you take every drop of it!" He bowed to the duke. "I trust I need not assure you that we will neither mention a word of this!" With his wife in tow, he made an abrupt exit, muttering all the time about madmen and villains and the inexplicable behavior of the aristocracy.

The Duke of Bellamy, who was looking far from his usual composed self, drew Clio into the hallway and closed the door just as the dowager launched forth on a tirade concerning vipers clasped to her maternal bosom and snakes in the grass who thought to feather their nests. "My dear," he said somberly, "I cannot tell you how

234

deeply I regret that you should have been so mistreated in my house."

"Pray don't regard it!" Clio replied hastily. The revelations of the past hour had left her totally overset. "Tell me instead about Tess! You said both she and Evelyn were safe—how?"

"They are." The duke, she thought, looked almost boyish with his hair disarranged and his immaculate attire so disheveled that his rumpled cravat had slid around under his left ear. "I do not know the whole of it, but your swain is with them."

"My swain?" repeated Clio, reaching up to straighten the crumpled neckcloth. Giles caught her hands. "Cedric," said he. "I hope you will forgive me for meddling in your elopement, but I feared you would do something foolish. I was not convinced that you wished to marry him, you see."

It did not occur to Clio to question how the duke had gotten wind of her plans. She stared at his cravat.

"Did you?" the duke persisted, "wish to marry him? If so, I'm sure your sister may be brought to agree—though I would think you could aim much higher, cousin."

Clio had no notion where this conversation was leading, or how Giles knew of her relationship to Tess, but she didn't wish him to labor under a needless burden of guilt. "I don't care above half for Ceddie," she admitted frankly. "It was for Tess's sake—oh, I don't know how to explain!"

The duke gave her no chance to try. "If Cedric has not engaged your heart," he murmured, "then perhaps there is hope for me."

"Oh, no!" Clio tried to disengage her hands. "I mean—my mother! You must not let yourself be deceived by my resemblance to her!"

"I thought that was it!" Giles drew her closer, despite her protests. "Clio, I am not the least deceived, nor do I cherish you because you bear a faint resemblance to Mirian! I was little more than a lad then and she was older than I. My fondness for your mother was hardly of a variety that would lead me, remembering her, to ask you to marry me!" She blinked and looked up at him. Giles smiled. "The truth, Clio, is that I have tumbled head over heels in love with a smart saucy girl with fine eyes and dark hair and the manners of a wild schoolboy!"

"Giles!" Clio's head was spinning; she felt as if she could die from sheer happiness. At that most unpropitious of moments, the study door flew open, and Sapphira stalked into the hall. "Constant is gone!" she announced, ignoring the fact that her son had clasped young Clio in an ardent embrace. "What the devil do you mean to do about it, Giles?"

"I? Nothing," replied the duke, with marked irritation. He looked down at Clio, who stirred in his arms.

"Nothing!" repeated Sapphira in stark disbelief.

"I would prefer," Giles said impatiently, "to avoid a scandal. Constant is doubtless already on his way out of London; let him go! He won't dare show his face here again."

His words reminded Clio of her sister, who was also presumably absent from the city. "Please?" she asked shyly. "Tell me where Tess is?"

The duke was not immune to that pleading glance. "Tess and Evelyn," he replied in bemused tones, "are safe in Morgan's keeping. You need not worry about them."

He might have known that his assurances were for naught. "Sir Morgan!" gasped Clio, convinced that her sister was at that very moment being ravished by the Wicked Baronet. Sapphira wore a similar expression of dismay, though for entirely different reasons, as she speedily made clear.

"I am not at all pleased," the dowager duchess stated with laudable restraint, "about the things that have been going on under my nose. I can do nothing about *that,* but I can and will see that Morgan doesn't fall prey to a greedy adventuress!" She glared at her son. "Giles, have the carriage brought around!"

The Duke of Bellamy was not the least inclined to explain to his ill-tempered parent Tess's true identity, or to Clio Morgan's noble heart, nor did he at all wish to set off on a fool's errand; but one glance at Clio's worried face was sufficient to inform him that she would have little time for romance until her sister's safety was assured. "Very well, but in the morning!" said the sorely tried duke. "First, I have some far more pressing business to conclude."

# Chapter 24

*Sir Morgan's country home* was a sprawling house of warm red brick with thick walls, a high-pitched tile roof, and countless additions in various disparate styles of architecture, among them Gothic doorways and mullioned windows, a sixteenth-century octagonal tower, and Tudor gables. Surrounding the mansion were extensive gardens containing apple trees and lilac bushes, oaks and elms and beeches, terraces and angled walks and whimsically clipped yew hedges, enclosed by high brick walls covered with climbing plants. Lady Tess thought she had never seen a lovelier home, or one that was more comfortable.

She stood at the window of Sir Morgan's bedchamber and gazed down on the south terrace, where Evelyn introduced a reluctant Ceddie to Sir Morgan's menagerie of pets, which included gold and silver pheasants, pigeons, a poodle and a parrot and a greyhound, as well as a well-stocked aviary and two great vicious-looking mastiffs that served as guard dogs. With only the smallest of sighs, the countess turned to study Sir Morgan, sprawled in what appeared the soundest of sleeps across the huge and canopied ancestral bed. The end of her adventuring had come, and Tess was feeling decidedly flat. It was only exhaustion, she firmly told herself; she had spent the night jealously guarding Sir Morgan's rest, despite the doctor's assurances that his wound was nothing to signify. What did that old fool know? she asked silently. But it was true that Sir Morgan had seemed in the best spirits, even catching her and kissing her as she hurried from one room to another, and was now resting easily enough. She curled up in a large armchair near the fireplace and closed her eyes.

In point of fact, Sir Morgan had slept little more than the countess, having passed the night plotting dastardly schemes for her downfall. He did not expect to accomplish this feat without a certain amount of difficulty, but Sir Morgan had a gambler's temperament, an equable disposition, and a cool nerve. He also possessed a certain ruthlessness.

Through half-closed eyes, he watched the countess settle in her chair. She looked the merest girl in his housekeeper's best gray dress, which was considerably large for her slight figure, with her silvery curls in riotous disarray. Sir Morgan did not care for the exhausted shadows around her lovely eyes. Time, he decided somberly, to end this charade. And then he thought, inconsequentially, that even in sleep she retained that look of faint surprise.

Lady Tess, however, was deep not in sleep but in despondency. Forced at last to admit to herself that she had grown entirely too fond of the Wicked Baronet, she could not escape the conclusion that such emotion was the greatest folly. He might like her well enough—she could not doubt he did—but she was not the sort of female for whom any man might hold warmer feelings. She was a crippled bluestocking, a dowdy and unfashionable spinster fit only to tend her garden and read her books. Sir Morgan had courted her with an eye to the diamond necklace; he would forget her as soon as their paths diverged; and to dream of a connection of a more particular nature was sheer madness. She opened her eyes to find him regarding her rather lazily.

"You're awake," she said, and silently cursed her sudden awkwardness. Above the waist, Sir Morgan wore only a bandage on his shoulder, and the effect of this blatantly displayed masculinity was heady indeed.

"So I am," agreed Sir Morgan. "Come here!"

"What is it?" cried Tess, hurrying to his side. She could not quench the fear that he was mortally injured, a fear confirmed by his irritable demand that he be nursed by no one but herself. "Are you in pain?"

"I am, and none but you can ease it." Sir Morgan grasped her wrist and pulled her down on the bed. "You have much to answer for, Countess! I fear you've dealt me a killing blow."

"I?" Tess frowned as she touched his brow. "You don't *feel* feverish. Perhaps I should send for the doctor so that you may be bled."

Sir Morgan refrained from stating his doubt that the good doctor would be willing to undertake the measures necessary to cool his overheated blood. He propped himself up on his sound elbow and clasped the countess's hand between his own. "We must talk. Why the devil did you cut such a rig in London, Lady Tess?"

She looked down at their hands, his skin so dark in contrast with her own. "It seemed the easiest thing. I did not want to go to town, but feared Clio would fall into a scrape if allowed to set out alone." Her smile was rueful. "Instead *I* fell into a scrape, and Clio behaved remarkably well. I only hope she does not mean to have Ceddie, though from what he says it does not sound like they will make a match."

"They won't," Sir Morgan replied promptly, his golden eyes fixed unwaveringly on her face. "Giles and your sister will suit very well—as you would know, had you paid the least attention! The pair of them positively reek of April and May."

"I am not the most observant of chaperones, it seems!" Tess sighed. "As to the other—how long have you known?"

"Who you are? From the beginning! You will recall that I had met you as a child? I am not so easily bamboozled, little one! But surely you are not so shy of appearing in Society that you must try and pretend to be a servant."

"Not *shy*, precisely." The countess frowned. "I have no taste for such meaningless pleasures and senseless conventions, and I knew I could not but appear a figure of fun."

Sir Morgan was aware of the effort it had cost her to

240

make that admission and therefore refrained from remarking that it was positively bird-witted. "You *did* enjoy it," he pointed out gently. "You will enjoy it even more once Clio is off your hands."

"Stuff and nonsense!" retorted Tess, looking even more surprised. "You cannot think I mean to return to London? No one knew who I was! Once the truth comes out, as I am sure it must, everyone will say I behaved outrageously." She shook her head. "I will return home."

"You must, of course." Sir Morgan's hands tightened on hers. "I trust you will not stay long there—unless, that is, you have decided to marry your stuffy curate!" Her indignation was reassuring. "My love, everyone knew you were the Countess of Lansbury, even Giles—though not, I admit, the rest of his family. We thought it best they were kept in the dark, both Sapphira and Drusilla having infinite capacities for mischief."

*"Knew?"* asked Tess, greatly startled. "How?"

"I told Giles about you myself, after the incident at the inn." Sir Morgan's golden eyes twinkled. "He knew who you were immediately he saw you; not many ladies answer your description, little one!" She looked very much as though she'd like to know what that description was, and he promptly obliged. "A beautiful, stubborn, untidy female with clouds of silver hair, flyaway eyebrows, and lashes so thick that they make her lovely blue-green eyes look smudged." Judiciously, he studied her. "A tall lady, delicately fashioned but nonetheless most pleasing to behold, with elegant features, a long and slender neck, lovely skin; a woman made to be caressed, yet as unaware of her passionate nature as of her loveliness."

"A woman," interrupted the countess, pleased in spite of herself by all the flummery, "who limps!"

"Giles in turn told Brummell," continued Sir Morgan, undaunted by this untimely reminder of her infirmity. "We thought it best. The Beau has a strong bent toward sardonic humor, and while I knew he would never keep such a good tale to himself, he could be trusted to divulge it with discretion. No matter how charming a mere companion might be, my love, she would never be admitted to Almack's."

"But *why*?" cried Tess, her delicate cheeks flushed. "Lord, what people must have thought of me!"

"They thought you charming," said Sir Morgan, "if a trifle eccentric. You were a novel change from the countless encroaching mushrooms who ape the nobility!" He chuckled. "You could hardly hope to keep your identity secret! You are of exceedingly high lineage, you succeeded to your title through an act of Parliament, and your godmother is no less than the Duchess of York. *She* has been exceedingly diverted by your progress, Brummell having kept her informed, and demands that you be brought to Oaklands so she may see the beautiful bluestocking for herself."

"Oh, dear." Tess looked mortified. "I see I have been excessively foolish. *You* had to tell Giles to inform Mr. Brummell. Why?"

Sir Morgan knew it behooved him to speak carefully. "I had my reputation to consider!" he protested. "Had I been thought to dally with a servant, my countenance would have suffered grievously!"

"Ah yes! The diamonds, of course." Lady Tess's chagrin deepened. "What a ninny I have been! I fear I made a great deal of trouble for you."

"You did," agreed Sir Morgan. "I cannot bring myself to regret a moment of it. Where *are* the diamonds, incidentally? Still at Bellamy House?"

"No. I was bringing them to you." Tess fumbled with her bodice. "Before that, they were hidden beneath a loose floorboard in my room."

Sir Morgan stared at the gems that glittered in her hand. "Sweet Jesus!" said he. "You've had them with you all the time?"

"I have." Tess grinned. "Wouldn't the thieves be furious to know they actually had the diamonds within their grasp? Fortunately, they did not think to search me." Sir Morgan swore. "*Why* did you suggest that expedition to

Vauxhall?" she asked quickly. "Logic tells me you had an ulterior motive."

"I did." The Wicked Baronet looked as if he held no high opinion of the countess's abilities in the art of reasoning. "Suffice it to say that I intended to flush our culprits into the open and be rid of them."

"And they outwitted you. What a sobering reflection! Had you only told *me* of your plans, I would have been better equipped to deal with the situation. A pistol, I have learned, is an admirable instrument with which to even out unequal odds!" Sir Morgan made an explosive noise and Tess exhibited concern. "Don't excite yourself, you are not well! I was in no danger, truly." Her gaze returned to the necklace. "What are we to do with it now?"

Sir Morgan was growing rapidly bored with all concerning that item; he took it from her and tossed it carelessly onto a table. "Paste," he explained kindly. "Bianca sold the original long ago. She did not want the truth known for obvious reasons, chief among them that her creditors would raise a fearful racket if they suspected her pockets were to let. Hence my involvement. I was to find the necklace and restore it to her before Bow Street could discover the truth." The countess was speechless, her dark brows raised and her lips slightly parted, and he ruthlessly pressed his advantage. "I do not scruple to tell you, my love, that you have been an infernal nuisance, forever thinking I was after that accursed necklace when I was, in fact, in pursuit of something else."

"Oh?" Tess looked bewildered. "I'm sorry for it! What did I misunderstand?"

"My intentions, fair fatality!" Sir Morgan tugged on her hand, deftly toppling her over sideways. "Never have I been treated in such a cavalier fashion! I swear it is a marvel I have not sunk into a decline, the way you have held me at arm's length."

"Poppycock!" retorted Tess, in a voice that was not precisely steady. She stared up at him. "I have done no such thing. But there is no longer any need for you to be talking such skimble-skamble stuff, or to pretend and make me the object of your *amours*." She looked, he thought, rather wistful. "The world may never know the reason that you quit me, for you can hardly explain that you had no other view but that of retrieving the necklace; but no one will be the least surprised that you grew tired of such a dowdy female."

"Tiresome creature!" whispered Sir Morgan, into her ear. "Consider what the world would say if they knew you had passed the night in my bedchamber, leaving me only to retire to your own country estates, never to be seen in Society again! I would be thought the greatest beast in nature. No, Tess, you could not be cruel to that degree."

The countess took a firm grip on her traitorous emotions. "You must have a fever, Sir Morgan: you are delirious! What on earth can it matter if I *am* compromised—and it is a farrago of nonsense, for none but ourselves know I'm here!"

"I would be a model of decorum," offered Sir Morgan, burying his fingers in her hair. "I will forswear all others, even abandon my visits to the fleshpots!"

Lady Tess was not of a prudent turn of mind, and certainly not of sufficient strength of will to resist one last improper exchange with the Wicked Baronet. "You absurd man!" she said, and chuckled. "As if I would ask of you such a thing. You should be bored within a sennight without your, er, debaucheries."

"That settles it!" exclaimed Sir Morgan, unmanned by so reasonable an attitude. "You *must* marry me! Never had I thought to find a female so understanding of my little foibles." He gazed down on her perplexed face. "Don't, I beg you, accuse me of taking a distempered freak, or offer me further absurdities! I am making you an honorable proposal of marriage and if I am making a sad botch of it, it is because I have never before done so—or wished to do so!—in all of my life."

"You," retorted Tess, trying ineffectually to free herself, "are talking fustian! Pray do so no more! I know perfectly well that you do not wish to marry me."

"But I do," replied Sir Morgan, with a queer little frown. "If it is not repugnant to your feelings, little one."

"Repugnant!" gasped Tess, on the verge of a temper tantrum. It was perfectly obvious that Sir Morgan was taking advantage of her natural concern for a wounded man to resume his flirtation. That she did not have the slightest concern for Ceddie, who was similarly wounded, did not occur to her. "I am," Sir Morgan added callously, "offering you a love match."

Tess could not believe that such good fortune could be hers, or that Sir Morgan was not merely suffering a brainstorm. She broke into incoherent speech, which was liberally spiced with such handsome phrases as "truly sensible of the honor" and "very much obliged," but which to Sir Morgan's acute disappointment did not include the words that he wanted to hear. "I see I must coerce you," he interrupted rudely, and kissed her with an enthusiasm that left her trembling and weak-kneed.

"Morgan!" gasped Tess. "You *do* mean it!" And then she returned the embrace with so much ardor that a less jaded gentleman would have been shocked by her lack of restraint.

Thus engaged, Sir Morgan and the countess were completely oblivious to the frantic barking of the mastiffs outside. Their preoccupation, however, did not survive the explosion of a pistol close at hand. Tess shrieked and later swore her blood turned to water; and Sir Morgan swore viciously.

"Sir Morgan!" cried Evelyn, bursting into the room and then stopping dead in his tracks. "What are you doing to Aunt Tess?"

"Reviving her," replied Sir Morgan promptly, while the countess blushed bright red. "Only fancy, she fainted dead away!"

Evelyn knew a clanker when he heard one, and Tess was entirely too rosy-cheeked for a lady recovering from a swoon, but he had no time to puzzle over the crotchets of adults, being big with news. "Ceddie just shot a man! Isn't it the most *famous* thing? And I thought him a shabby sort of fellow!" He frowned. "Though he did sort of spoil the whole thing by being sick in the drawing-room."

"Do you think," inquired Sir Morgan, casting a severe

look at the countess, who had succumbed to a choking fit, "that we might be told the identity of his victim? I shouldn't wish to lose one of my servants in such a way, though I do understand that it was a brilliant manner in which to enliven your tedium."

Unabashed, Evelyn giggled. "As if I'd let Ceddie shoot one of your people! It was a fellow from the inn—he escaped the Bow Street men. Which reminds me, there's a Runner downstairs."

"There would be," said Sir Morgan bitterly, leaning across Tess's shaking body to grasp the necklace. "Here, give this to him, with my compliments."

"But poor Bianca!" protested the countess, brushing her sleeve across her damp eyes. "And her creditors!"

"I have forsworn my other ladyloves, remember?" Sir Morgan tossed the necklace to Evelyn, who caught it neatly. "This is an admirable way to be rid of at least one of them: Bianca will certainly never speak to me again." He scowled at Evelyn, who was staring at the necklace with eyes as big as saucers. "Begone, brat! And see to it that we're not disturbed."

"Sometime," murmured the countess, sounding short of breath, "you must tell me about your vast number of conquests, and how it is you escaped so many snares."

"Gladly," replied Sir Morgan, with his crooked smile. "It will take a lifetime, my love! They were legion."

"Ah, yes." Tess basked in the warmth of his regard. "How sorry they would be to learn that you wish *me* to profit solely from your great experience!"

It was apparent to Evelyn that the scene about to be enacted would not be at all suitable to his young eyes. He cleared his throat, which availed nothing. "Sir Morgan!" he shouted. "I'm afraid I can't do that. My father would listen to me, probably, but I don't think I could persuade Aunt Drusilla, or *Grandmère*, to stay away."

*"What?"* demanded Sir Morgan. Evelyn prudently stepped backward.

"Clio, too," he added apologetically, "but now I must call her 'Mother,' did you know? She and my father were married by special license this morning." Sir Morgan looked thunderous and he gulped. "They're here, didn't I say? The coach just pulled up outside. *Grandmère* is mad as toads, and calling Aunt Tess all kinds of names." On that ominous note, he scampered out the door.

# Chapter 25

*It was late afternoon* when the Duke of Bellamy's elegant carriage arrived at Sir Morgan's country house. The journey had not been a particularly pleasant one, the travelers being thoroughly out of charity with one another, except the duke and his new duchess, so engrossed in each other that they were deaf to the vituperative comments that passed between Sapphira and Drusilla, unaware of the silent disapproval radiating from Delphine, and unmoved by the dowager duchess's bitter diatribe on lovebirds who billed and cooed in the most revolting manner while Rome burned around them, and chicks who were so bird-witted as to shove their strongest well-wisher out of the nest.

Drusilla was first out of the carriage, racing in a most ungenteel manner to the front door, there to collide with the dapper little Runner who had a wounded ruffian in tow. This seedy individual was a trifle foxed, due to the brandy he'd consumed while a bullet was dug out of his thigh; and Drusilla bore a marked resemblance to the buxom country lass with whom he often shared such rustic trysting places as cow byres and haylofts. Consequently, he greeted her with tearful reproaches and maudlin profanity. The Runner was not one to neglect his duty; despite Drusilla's indignant protests, he arrested her on the spot.

"My daughter?" repeated the dowager duchess, when applied to. "Never saw the hussy before!" She glowered at her speechless daughter. "How dare you claim a connection, girl? Take her away!"

The resultant altercation promised to be of no short duration. Clio slipped past the combatants and through the front door. "Clio!" cried Evelyn, running into the hallway and grabbing her hand. "You must come and congratulate Ceddie, for he is the hero of the day!"

There was nothing Clio wanted less than to lay eyes on Cedric, but Evelyn was pulling her down the hallway and into the drawing-room. The sight that greeted her there briefly drove all other considerations from her mind. "Heavens!" ejaculated the new duchess.

Signs of unmistakable conflict littered the lovely room. Furniture was overturned, fine porcelain figurines lay shattered on the floor. Clio looked hastily away from a pool of fresh blood. "Ceddie!" she gasped.

"He'll be right as rain," offered Evelyn cheerfully. The young viscount thrived on excitement. "Ceddie is very brave, for all that the sight of blood makes him cast up his accounts. Just think, Clio, he captured a dangerous criminal! One that escaped even Bow Street's net!"

Clio could not imagine anyone less heroic-looking than Ceddie, sprawled upon the sofa, his immaculate raiment in a shocking condition, his face as white as once had been his rumpled cravat. She said so.

"If that ain't the height of ingratitude!" Ceddie replied indignantly, removing his arm from his eyes. "You should thank me for rescuing your sister from a gang of bloodthirsty ruffians! It would have gone damned hard with Tess if I hadn't shown up, and she will tell you so."

"No, she won't!" interrupted Evelyn. "She'll tell you that Sir Morgan and I rescued the pair of you! Why you had to go and stab Sir Morgan is more than *I* can understand—though it's perfectly clear why Aunt Tess skewered *you!*"

"She didn't!" moaned Clio.

"Oh, yes, she did!" Gingerly, Ceddie touched his ribs. He was feeling rather sulky, having been virtually ignored by all save Evelyn, who had an appalling tendency to dwell upon such queasy-making topics as tortures and hangings and gore. "Devilish thankless female! I should have let that scoundrel murder her."

"Murder Tess?" Clio stared. "You're all about in your head, Ceddie!"

"No, I ain't!" Ceddie sat up carefully. "That Runner's told us the queerest tale. Your sister's been racketing about with a stolen diamond necklace, and if that ain't the outside of enough, I don't know what is!" His gaze fell upon the pool of blood and he sank back weakly, distracting his flip-flopping stomach with recollections of the Runner's praise for his quick thinking, and the man's delicate hints of shared rewards.

Clio had digested this shocking information with no small dismay. "Where *is* Tess?" she asked.

Evelyn made a face. "Cuddling with Sir Morgan," he replied with marked disapproval, "in his bedchamber. He doesn't wish to be disturbed."

"I'll wager he doesn't, the blackguard!" shrieked Clio. Convinced that the countess was indeed being ravished, she rushed into the hallway. Since the Duke of Bellamy awaited her there, and since Giles took that admirable opportunity to whisper a few fond words to his blushing bride, with the result that she so far forgot her mission of rescue that she replied in kind, it was some few moments before they ascended the stair.

All the duke's assurances could not convince his duchess that their unwilling host was not a monster of depravity, and she was further overset by the scandalous sight that greeted her when she threw open the bedroom door. "So!" Clio stared at her sister, who sat crosslegged on Sir Morgan's bed, with the Wicked Baronet's head in her lap, feeding him grapes from a fruit basket while he regaled her with details of his past love-life. "Tess, have you lost your mind?"

"Hallo, Clio!" The countess calmly selected an apple. "Or I should say, Your Grace! I make you my compliments, child. There is no need to wish you happy: you will be."

"Yes, I have married Giles." Clio glared at Sir Morgan, who appropriated the apple and took a bite of it. "You will come and live with us, Tess! We shall put around some tale to explain your presence here, for it cannot go unremarked. Drusilla will spread it about, you may be sure!" Tess looked sublimely unconvinced, and Clio wrung her hands. "You must listen to reason!"

"My dear Duchess," interjected Sir Morgan, settling himself more comfortably, an act which necessitated that his pillow should sprawl in a most reprehensible manner upon the bed, "you must not request my Tess to behave sensibly. It is a great deal too much to ask of her."

"*Your* Tess!" shrieked Clio. "Never, you evil man!"

"Don't tease yourself, child," soothed the countess, reclaiming the apple. "Sir Morgan's intentions are entirely honorable." She smiled at the duke, who was watching his bride with a sottish expression. "Let us drink to your happiness! Giles, there is brandy on that sideboard."

No whit disgruntled to be addressed as if he were a lowly footman, the duke filled four glasses and handed them around. "To your long life and continuing felicity!" declared the countess and disposed of her brandy in one swallow. "Now," she added, setting down her glass, "I fancy some explanations are in order! Morgan, tell Clio about the necklace."

Sir Morgan did so. Sapphire eyes huge in her pale face, Clio sank down abruptly on a velvet-covered ottoman. "The man downstairs," concluded the countess, before her sister could speak, "was the last of the lot, and the necklace has been turned over to Bow Street. The danger is over. I vow I shall miss it!"

"I, too, must confess," said Giles. "Clio let it be known, Morgan, that you were romantically involved with Drusilla." He looked contrite. "I fear Drusilla's conduct bore her out. I further fear that I also dropped a hint or two."

"You *what?*" roared the Wicked Baronet, sitting up abruptly. Clio quickly averted her gaze from his undraped torso. "Damn you, Giles!"

"I know. I should have denied the tale." The duke smiled sheepishly. "It was for Tess's sake that I refrained; I did not wish her to be caught unawares by your legendary charm." Warily, he eyed Sir Morgan's irate countenance. "Consider," he begged, "all the unfortunate females whom you have heartlessly cast aside."

"That's torn it!" groaned Sir Morgan, and sank back against the pillows.

"Have you?" inquired the countess with interest. "Cast those poor creatures off? I suppose they bored you, so it's entirely their own fault." Neatly she disposed of the remainder of the apple, then looked up at the Duke of Bellamy. He was regarding her with utter fascination. "It doesn't signify, Giles! I wasn't for an instant taken in. Where *is* Drusilla, by the by? Evelyn told us she had accompanied you."

"Drusilla," replied the duke wryly, "is on her way to Bow Street, having been mistaken by the Runner for an accomplice to the robbers. *Maman* has decreed that a few hours in Newgate are just what my sister needs to take the wind out of her sails." He looked fondly upon Clio. "My entire family may go to the devil in a handbasket for all I care. I will not allow my wife to be plagued by any one of them."

Happily for Clio's sensibilities, which were greatly pulled by these remarks, the dowager duchess, leaning heavily on Delphine's arm, sailed at last into the room. Her dark gaze went unerringly to the bed. Tess sat transfixed, clutching the apple core. "Baggage!" pronounced the dowager. "Bachelor's fare! The merest straw damsel to boot, not even fit to be called a demi-rep!"

Naturally neither Clio nor Delphine could accept such hideous insults without protest. The battle was quickly joined, with such strife that the countess winced and covered her ears, and with such loudly voiced recriminations that Evelyn came running to observe the fray. "Cripes!" said he, and cast an anxious eye at Sir Morgan. "I told them you didn't wish to be disturbed, honestly I did!"

"Quiet!" roared Sir Morgan, with such violence that even the dowager duchess paused mid-speech. "I'll have you know, Sapphira, that the lady of whom you are speaking in such unattractive terms is to be my wife! Nor do I intend to sit here quietly and allow you to further abuse her."

"Oh, Tess!" sobbed Clio, as the dowager gaped. "How *can* you?" Delphine surveyed her mistress through narrowed eyes. So the Wicked Baronet's intentions were of the most honorable? *"Ma foi!"* said she.

"I don't recall," Tess interjected serenely, "that I said I would." She smiled kindly at her sister. "You would have been quite taken with Sir Morgan's manner, child! He expressed himself with the greatest propriety."

Sapphira's temper, which at its best was unbenign, had been greatly frayed by her laborious ascent of the staircase. She leaned even more heavily on Delphine's arm, scowling ferociously, and nicely throttled by her own rage.

"Tess, you must not!" Clio hastened across the room and grasped her sister's hand, determined to make one last attempt to save Tess from a terrible fate. "A man of his reputation—he cannot but betray you, again and again!"

"He has said he will not," retorted Tess, ignoring Sir Morgan's stifled oath. "Besides, Clio, even were he extremely unfaithful, he would be irrepressibly funny about it."

"You cannot mean that!" Clio was rapidly coming to consider her sister a raving lunatic. "Tess, the man is a rakehell!"

"I rather think I do mean it," Tess replied thoughtfully. "Yes, I know my sense of humor is reprehensible, but there it is! And," she frowned, "I very much think I would rather be married to Morgan, with all his potential peccadilloes, than to any other man in the world."

"Oh, Tess!" wailed Clio. Delphine looked increasingly contemplative. "Hussy!" snapped the dowager duchess. "My darling!" Sir Morgan breathed.

"I have not," interrupted the countess, "said I *would* marry him. Indeed, I think I should not." She disentangled herself from Clio and turned a somber countenance to Sir Morgan. "After all these years of unfettered bachelorhood, you can hardly wish to saddle yourself not only with a wife, but with one who is lame."

The Wicked Baronet was so greatly moved by this wistful little speech that he pushed Clio off the bed and took her place. "Why don't you just say straight out that you're in love with her?" complained Evelyn from the doorway. "It would be much more simple."

Thus reminded of his audience, Sir Morgan cast an enraged glance around the room. "Out, the lot of you! You are making mincemeat of the only honest proposal of marriage I have ever wished to make."

"More fool you!" snorted the dowager.

"Do you?" breathed Tess, oblivious to all but Sir Morgan's voice and the hand that rested on her arm. "Truly wish to marry me?"

"Sweet Christ!" uttered Sir Morgan wrathfully. "What do you think I've been trying to tell you these past weeks?" He rose with agility from his sickbed to personally usher out the gawking spectators and behind them slammed the door.

"Oh, Morgan!" the countess said baldly. "I do love you."

Thus Lady Terpsichore Mildmay wed Sir Morgan Rhodes on a bright summer morning in St. George's, Hanover Square. The *haut ton* was in attendance and Mr. Brummel served as the groom's best man. So blissful was the union that Mr. Brummel was used to remark in later years, to those visitors who sought him out in Calais after his disgrace, that his sole claim to heavenly favor was the arrangement of the match. Perhaps the Beau exaggerated his small part in the affair, but this much is fact: they lived happily ever after, Tess and her Wicked Baronet.

# Historical Romance

*Sparkling novels of love and conquest against the colorful background of historical England. Here are books you will savor word by word, page by spellbinding page.*

| | | | |
|---|---|---|---|
| ☐ AFTER THE STORM—Williams | 23928-4 | $1.75 |
| ☐ ALTHEA—Robins | 23268-9 | $1.50 |
| ☐ AMETHYST LOVE—Danton | 23400-2 | $1.50 |
| ☐ AN AFFAIR OF THE HEART<br>Smith | 23092-9 | $1.50 |
| ☐ AUNT SOPHIE'S DIAMONDS<br>Smith | 23378-2 | $1.50 |
| ☐ A BANBURY TALE—MacKeever | 23174-7 | $1.50 |
| ☐ CLARISSA—Arnett | 22893-2 | $1.50 |
| ☐ DEVIL'S BRIDE—Edwards | 23176-3 | $1.50 |
| ☐ ESCAPADE—Smith | 23232-8 | $1.50 |
| ☐ A FAMILY AFFAIR—Mellow | 22967-X | $1.50 |
| ☐ THE FORTUNE SEEKER<br>Greenlea | 23301-4 | $1.50 |
| ☐ THE FINE AND HANDSOME<br>CAPTAIN—Lynch | 23269-7 | $1.50 |
| ☐ FIRE OPALS—Danton | 23984-5 | $1.75 |
| ☐ THE FORTUNATE MARRIAGE<br>Trevor | 23137-2 | $1.50 |
| ☐ THE GLASS PALACE—Gibbs | 23063-5 | $1.50 |
| ☐ GRANBOROUGH'S FILLY<br>Blanshard | 23210-7 | $1.50 |
| ☐ HARRIET—Mellows | 23209-3 | $1.50 |
| ☐ HORATIA—Gibbs | 23175-5 | $1.50 |